ADVANCE PRAISE

Talionic Night in Portland: A Love Story plunges the reader into a domestic noir fever dream. Theresa Griffin Kennedy takes us down the less-celebrated paths of Portland through the eyes of a woman at a crossroads. At times hot, at times darkly somber, *Talionic Night in Portland: A Love Story* explores untamable desire and the complex nature of passion.

– **Suzy Vitello**
author of *The Moment Before*

Talionic Night in Portland: A Love Story, by Theresa Griffin Kennedy is a raucous, steamy romp through the lesser known underbelly of hip Portland, Oregon. Fasten your seatbelts readers. You're in for a deliciously raw ride.
– **Liz Scott,**
author of *This Never Happened.*

A revenge story, *Talionic Night in Portland: A Love Story,* is the bizarre tale of two emotionally stunted adult survivors of childhood sexual abuse. Yes it's grim, it's dirty, it's unpleasant, but there's more here. Daisy and Tab are two deeply troubled characters who manage to use their outside beauty to mask the swirling mess inside. Their facades are perfect, their sex life sublime, but things are still so very wrong. Kennedy has a real affection for her two broken characters, and a quirky and humorous way of presenting these folks as confident, smart, and adult-like as they try urgently to understand themselves, each other, and the world. Not for the faint of heart - raunchy sex abounds here - but it serves as the language the two speak to each other. There is the slightest, most delicate chance for redemption here, and Kennedy is all in for this ride into, and out of, the desperate Portland Talionic Night.

—**Dianah Hughley,**
Powell's City of Books

ISBN: 978-0-578-70458-6

First Edition: 2021

This novel is a work of fiction. Names, incidents, and various locales are the product of the author's imagination. All characters appearing within this work are fictitious. Any resemblance to actual persons, living or dead, or to any events depicted in the stories is purely and entirely coincidental.

Published by:
Oregon Greystone Press
Phone # (503) 465-8407
tkdupay@gmail.com
https://sites.google.com/site/oregongreystonepress

Interior layout by:
Kyle Chicoine
kylechicoine@gmail.com
https://kylechicoine.com

Cover Illustration by:
Jim Agpalza
https://jimagpalza.com

Trigger Warning:
graphic sexual content

TALIONIC NIGHT IN PORTLAND:

A LOVE STORY

Theresa Griffin Kennedy

OREGON GREYSTONE PRESS
PORTLAND, OREGON

Talionic Night in Portland: A Love Story

I dedicate this book, which is my first novel, to the memory of Kenneth "Rowdy" Rhys Mechals who lived from 1965 to 2020. In this novel, the character Tab is based on Rowdy. He got his nickname from his mother Christine, due to his calm and reserved demeanor. The nickname was meant as an affectionate joke, because Rowdy was anything *but* rowdy. Rowdy was born in June of 1965 and passed away in January 2020 of a suspected drug overdose. The persona of Tab is an idealization of course, but is still based on Rowdy's general character and his exceptionally sweet, tender demeanor. Rowdy was a grade ahead of me, and attended Chapman Elementary with me, and Lincoln High School, graduating from Lincoln in 1984. He lived in Portland most of his life and was known and loved for his gentle, vague and unassuming character. Rowdy stood six feet two inches. He had canary yellow hair and beautiful golden brown eyes—just like the character Tab. Rowdy was incredibly handsome and surprisingly humble about how attractive he was. In the end, he struggled with depression and substance abuse, but he was an extremely important part of my young life and someone I will *never* forget. Rowdy taught me how to love and be loved in return as a young girl who was prone to feeling scared. I tried to locate Rowdy for several years but probably didn't try hard enough. Those who could tell me where he was chose not to, and those chances to reconnect slipped through my fingers. I only wish I could have gotten to him in time, before loneliness, depression and the bottomless sadness consumed him. Rest in peace Rowdy and forgive me for not calling you back in 1988. I should have but again, I was scared and now it's too late. You will never, ever be forgotten and I carry your face, and your voice and your eyes in my mind and in my heart forever.

Theresa Griffin Kennedy

V

Talionic Night in Portland: A Love Story

At some point in life the world's beauty becomes enough. You don't need to photograph, paint or even remember it. It is enough.

–Toni Morrison,
author of *Tar Baby*

In nature, nothing is perfect and everything is perfect. Trees can be contorted, bent in weird ways and they're still beautiful.

– Alice Walker,
author of *The Color Purple*

We are all in the gutter, but some of us are looking at the stars.

– Oscar Wilde,
author of *The Picture of Dorian Grey*

Talionic Night in Portland: A Love Story

Preface

When writing a preface it is customary for writers to explain, often in flowery, heartfelt and searing language how the process of writing a book is nothing less than agonizing hard work and even sheer torture. Often writers proclaim that writing a novel sometimes makes them miserable, depressed, or anxious to the point that they pull their hair out, get drunk or even use anxiety medication. I wish I could go along with this popular romantic misconception, but I can't. I cannot promote the stereotype of the artist suffering for his or her art because that would be misleading to the public and to each individual reader of my work.

There was no part of writing *Talionic Night in Portland: A Love Story* that I didn't entirely enjoy. The process of writing the book you hold in your hands was fun, amusing and sometimes even mildly hysterical. There were other times when the prose transformed, becoming darkly disturbing and even melancholy, but I was never once angry, or cursing the Oregon sky because the writing of it was not fluid or entirely natural to me. For almost two years, I allowed the organic process of writing this story to stew and cool, so that new and unexpected depths could arise and the story could take off in strange and unusual directions I would not have anticipated. I trusted myself enough as a writer (who has written consistently for over thirty five years) and I trusted the universe enough to allow that part of the craft of writing to happen organically, and without interference from me.

Though the writing of this book was *not* torturous in any way, it was a journey of sorts, but always a journey that I was up to, and that I absolutely loved. While it did take me a while to know in what direction the book would go, I was never worried it would not reach its final destination as my first novel. I never felt *I* was leading the book, but rather that the book was leading *me*. I was the simple recorder of the narrative that came to me, seemingly from out of the ether.

I knew I wanted to incorporate ribald humor within the content, (or at least attempt to do so) but I also knew I wanted to shock a bit, too. Why? Because through surprise, we are challenged and transformative learning is often the end result, *and* because surprise is entertaining and fun. Despite the initial lightheartedness of some of the content, I knew the book needed to have a deeper import—some kind of significance regarding real life. It took me several months for the theme of the book to become clear. The message, if there is one, in this comic romp is simple; that sexual trauma happens to the best of us, but it does *not* have to define us, nor rob us of happiness in our lives. We can be like the trees with bent branches, deformed, yet still beautiful. We can be like the many that exist in the gutter but are still looking at the stars.

Understanding the impulses that accompany the survival of sexual trauma can help us understand deviant behavior and even criminal impulse, and it is for *this* reason that you should read this book. This short novel should resonate with readers, and perhaps some part of Daisy or Tab, or Torch, Blaze or Gayle will come alive for you. Perhaps you'll see yourself in this odd assortment of characters, as they struggle to maintain the façade of sanity that the modern world seems to require. That façade often means denying impulses we don't readily understand, and may never understand, realizing that despite it all, we may never succeed in gaining mastery over the traumatic experiences that shape us.

So, if you want a deeper understanding of what it means to be human, if you want a guided tour into a Portland you could never have imagined, but does in fact exist, then you should probably read *Talionic Night in Portland: A Love Story*. Whatever happens, you will definitely realize that nowhere have you read such an odd and unusual story, where the weirdness of Portland is so categorically and unapologetically celebrated.

Author's Note

*D*espite the sometimes humorous nature of this first novel, some raunchy sexual content, along with the occasional dark passage, this book provides a fairly realistic view into the real consequences of sexual abuse and exploitation. Premature sexual experience can transform a life, and often not for the better, but nearly always permanently. Despite this grim reality, we can still claim our place in the world, strive for happiness amidst the ghosts and demons of our past and live our lives without apologizing to anyone.

CHAPTER ONE

Beating a Steady Tattoo

*Y*OU CAN'T RECALL THE EXACT day or time of your last visit because once again, it's a blur in your mind. The details blend in with other visits until one recollection becomes as shadowy and malleable as the next—becomes a filmy dream with the scent of rotting apples lurking somewhere in the periphery, and an open window with drifting muslin curtains you seem to remember having made by hand.

Exhaustion and need beat a steady tattoo, an annoying Congo drum rhythm within your brain. The only thing that does ring clear in your consciousness is the name, *Tab*. His name, his face, his willingness to accommodate, coupled with what appears to be a deceptively pleasing blank mental state, and the fact that he can either take you or leave you—these are the things you don't easily forget.

Your knuckles hurt from knocking, so now you're slamming the side of your balled up fist on the wood door which rattles dangerously in its frame. You hope the neighbors can't hear as you beat on the door. It's late, after midnight again, and recently, (you can't recall when) one of the neighbors complained about the noise. She stood outside the door as you lay on the living room floor and joined at the hip. She began yelling profanities through the thin wood. She was sick of listening to you two going at it all the time. You were a couple of "disgusting animals" in her estimation and she was going to call the police if you didn't keep it down from now on. You smile vaguely at the memory while your fist continues to pound the door. You recall how you both started coming simultaneously within only seconds of her banging on the door, how the startling intrusion made the pleasure even more thrilling, forbidden and intense.

Tab finally answers the door. He's barefoot and dressed only in his usual jean overalls, which are faded and light blue. They are impeccably clean, but the left strap is unbuckled and hangs down revealing a peach colored nipple. Once again you marvel at his unlikely Farmer Brown body, the welcome reality of his even jaw, the good teeth, and the wheat colored skin. You notice he's got two or three potato chip crumbs stuck to his lower lip. The tiny fragments seem to sparkle in the dim light, a salty tease you wouldn't mind tasting. He motions

1

you in. You're still focused on his mouth, though the potato chip crumbs do nothing to diminish Tab's natural, easy charm.

You step into the foyer briskly, and toss your new Tumi briefcase to the side. You bought it earlier that afternoon, wasting $400 of your hard earned money on something you don't really need. The buyer's remorse you experienced was immediate, but since Helen has one, you have to have one, too. It sails to the right in one single movement, landing flush and upright against a new gallon can of white Miller paint.

Tab licks the potato chip crumbs from his mouth with lazy sensuality and smiles that dumb dazzling smile of his, filled with the paternal understanding that tells you he's glad to see you. You feel the caress of his breath on your neck as he leans in, closes the door quietly behind you, and turns the deadbolt. He's been hard at work on another restoration job, sanding some part of yet another antique desk, vanity, or captain's chair. Minute wood particles cling to his thick wrists and the abundant golden hairs on his forearms. Santana's *Oye Como Va* drifts in quietly from the Ghetto Blaster in the kitchen.

"Hold on, baby," he says thickly. "I gotta get this stuff off me, first."

He makes a big production blowing the wood dust from his hands and forearms, smacking his flesh and energetically skimming if off. You can see he's showered and is clean, shining and ready for trouble. He looks you right in the eyes, and starts smacking his lips loudly in a comical gesture, making the obscene exaggerated noises of a person eating. Your scalp heats up, and your cheeks get hot as you stand watching him. Your face is expressionless, your eyes darkly annoyed.

He opens his arms in a semi-circle, magnanimously, like a king, and waits, deadpan. You walk to him purposefully; your heels click on the hard wood floor. Your expression changes suddenly though, because you've waited all day for this moment. You lose all the air in your sail as you look up at him with the defeated sad-sack stare of the chronic addict hoping to score some dope. He smiles down at you. He *knows* he has the junk you need. You hop up, 'the poor mouth' still on your face, and he catches you under the buttocks, hoists you up easily, holding you firmly with well-developed arms as you wrap your legs around his waist, clinging like a monkey. You lay your head on his shoulder, a tired child, grateful, as you breathe in the scent of Ivory Soap and Old Spice.

"Looks like baby's ready to roll, huh?"

"I'm here, right?"

"Okay, sassy, then let's get down to it."

"I wanna take a soapy bath, first."

"Whatever you want, baby."

Tab pulls the red velvet Scrunchie from your hair, and tosses it to the floor. Your hair falls down your back in glossy ringlets just as your mouths meet, teeth clicking briefly. Your tongues come together, bathing in a sea of warm toothpaste kisses. You taste the faint and alluring hint of the cheap Monarch vodka he likes to swill after invariably falling off the wagon every few months. The booze means Tab has had a few drinks—probably because he's fought with either his wife Ruby or his longtime girlfriend, Verona, neither of whom he lives with. It will mean he's worked up, and the sex will be extra special—the tortured, mildly angry fuck that only Tab can give you; the kind of fuck that leaves you breathless, satiated and grateful in that happy way that sometimes makes you giggle like a fool.

You wonder how it happened. You can't quite figure out how you ended up with a country bumpkin named after the mediocre beefcake Hollywood actor, Tab Hunter. Though Tab's legal name is Tab Hunter Blaine, still you're at a loss to explain how it happened. You're a 37-year-old professional, a writer and assignment editor working for a TV station. And Tab? Well, Tab is a 52-year-old sometime Lothario with a heart of gold and a laminated certification card as a grade school custodian. He's from Cottage Grove, originally, and in his eighteen years here, he still refers to Portland as "The Big City."

You've learned that Tab is proud of being a high school graduate—because he almost didn't make it—if not for the neighbor lady who encouraged him back in Cottage Grove. Her name was Blanche Breckenridge, and she lived just five blocks from his house. He still mentions her from time to time with the dreamy fondness that makes you secretly resentful. She was a divorced, childless woman in her early forties, a former beauty queen, and Bette Paige look-a-like with teased auburn hair, when she took Tab under her wing.

Along with introducing Tab to the pleasures of imaginative sexual intercourse at the ripe-old-age of only fourteen, she also encouraged him to stay in school, and to read what he enjoyed reading. When she died of a massive heart attack while making chicken noodle soup, landing on her back smack dab in the middle of the kitchen floor, legs splayed and her eyes bugged out, the soup spoon still gripped firmly in her hand, Tab was only nineteen and still her regular lover.

He was inconsolable for days, holing up in his bedroom and refusing to eat. When he attended Blanche's funeral a week later, he sobbed loudly, intermittently hysterical, hanging his head, his arms limp in his lap, saying he had nothing left to live for. At one point, the funeral director asked him to retreat to a private mourning room. The two middle-aged female assistants were all over him, instead. They looked like twins as they sat next to him on either side, massaging his shoulders, toying with their teased blue-black curls, and stroking his (in need of a trim) canary yellow hair. They offered him sips of hot cocoa, hot buttered rum, and tissues to wipe his eyes with. They called him "baby" and "sugar pie" and stuffed their calling cards into his jacket pockets, telling him to call if he ever needed anything. And they meant anything. The rum made Tab drunk and even more unreasonable, and the cocoa collected in the corners of his mouth. "I want Blanche! I want my Blanche!" he sobbed as they fussed over him.

As you get to know Tab, you realize his life is segregated into two parts, "Before I knew Blanche..." and "After Blanche died..." You realize Tab's intense loyalty to the memory of Blanche is mostly couched in the somewhat incestuous bond they shared. He lost his mother when he was ten, from lung cancer, and was raised by his father, whom he adored and his stepmother, with whom he did not bond. Blanche, also an unrepentant smoker, became a parental figure of sorts, a teacher, and in a way, a mother, too.

The positive impact she had on his life is undeniable, but sometimes you wonder if sex at fourteen was actually good for Tab. You have expressed this to him numerous times but he explains that it's different for boys. "They want to get off, baby," he has said more than once. But you wonder about that, particularly when he gets anxious and teary-eyed over mundane matters that most people wouldn't think twice about.

You also know, as much as you hate to admit it, that if not for Blanche, Tab's life probably would have been very different, and not in a good way. He stayed in school mostly to please Blanche, and she'd been there when he walked down the aisle in the school auditorium in Cottage Grove to collect his diploma. She sat proudly dressed in her cheap red satin gown, purchased mail order and straight from Fredrick's of Hollywood. She clapped and blew kisses. In her hand she clutched a thick envelope packed with $250 in ten dollar bills—her gift to Tab if he stayed in school.

His father Ed, a high school dropout and welder by trade, watched his son collect his diploma and his fat payoff with tears in his eyes—and a fervent gratitude to Blanche. They stood together after the refreshments were served— apple juice, Oreo cookies and Saltine Crackers with Cheese Whiz. They agreed emphatically that what Tab needed was continued discipline and a strong hand to curb his dreamy, vague personality which could lead to all sorts of potential trouble down the road. Ed was so grateful to Blanche that she'd gotten involved in Tab's life, that he couldn't stop thanking her for helping his son: "Like a good Aunt would!" he stated with passionate conviction. His voice continued to break with emotion as Blanche smiled understandingly, her hand on his shoulder and a 'you betcha' smile on her pretty painted face.

The entire neighborhood was grateful to Blanche. She had made a huge difference in the life of a boy many considered slow but sweet. None knew of course that while Tab was mowing Blanche's lawn, watering her flowers in front and tending to her vegetable garden in back, washing her car, and delivering groceries for those five long years, he was also enjoying heartfelt private lessons with Blanche in her all-black bedroom, replete with requisite velvet paintings,

4

Lava Lamps, lit scented candles and massage oil. No one knew Blanche was tutoring Tab in the fine art of bedroom pleasures that would color the rest of his life. And no one seemed to want to know either.

When Blanche claimed to have sprained an ankle, soon after Tab graduated from high school, and asked Ed if he wouldn't mind if Tab spent the weekend with her, (to make sure she didn't fall and hurt herself and to wash the breakfast and dinner dishes) Ed agreed on the spot, no questions asked. The three days Tab spent in Blanche's dark house, with the draperies pulled shut, was a daze of lubricated sex, wandering Blanche's house naked, French kissing in the kitchen, anal sex in the laundry room, dildos, leather belts, and long nights of vodka swilling, porn videos and endless sex-play. Tab felt he had died and gone to heaven—or at least pussy heaven.

Yes, in a very real way, Blanche saved Tab's life. Despite knowing this, a part of you still wishes you could meet her and say: "You know, Blanche… its Blanche, right? Well, Tab and I are fucking now, so can you just kindly step aside? Bitch!" Your feelings toward Blanche, a dead chain-smoking former beauty queen who didn't get past the eighth grade continue to mystify you. You feel nothing but pity and revulsion for Ruby and Verona, both of whom you've seen in photographic and literal form, and with whom you are abjectly terrified. But why be jealous of a dead woman? Is the memory of an attractive woman, now dead, more of a threat than an actual breathing woman still alive and in the real world? Probably, you suspect, as men are always more in love with the memory of a woman, or the image of a woman, rather than the real woman as she actually is. And Tab you discover is no different in this respect.

And yet despite his limitations, Tab is not without complexity or charm. He enjoys reading Greek mythology, and has exactly 329 books on mythology in his apartment, carefully catalogued and arranged in nice blonde cedar bookshelves he made himself. His work as a grade school custodian is of course unfulfilling. He complains bitterly when the kids think he's the janitor, and each time this happens he gives a detailed report, including names, dates, and time of day, what was said, and how it was said. Invariably, Tab perceives these slights as intentional acts of cruelty meant to break his spirit and induce suicidal ideation as he stares forlornly into his mug of warm milk at night, brooding over the injustice of it all.

Tab is also obsessed with the Rodin sculpture, *The Thinker* but more on that later.

Most importantly to you, he's your new secret lover of only seven months. The secrecy part needs to stay that way. His wife, Ruby, and girlfriend, Verona, are certifiably nuts, not to mention the fact that you can't yet visualize introducing Tab to your college educated friends and snooty colleagues with their tiresome airs and aristocratic pretentions. There would be too many questions, too many awkward attempts at explaining all the funny circumstances and odd realities of Tab's life, and his unusual esoteric interests, which includes a nearly savant knowledge of complex Greek mythology, Buddhism and death rites.

You imagine him at one of their get-togethers, dressed in his old Levi jeans, and light blue IZOD Alligator shirt. He would proudly announce to the person sitting next to him that he decided to "dress up" for the occasion and that's why he's wearing his "good clothes." He'd sit with a cocktail in hand, smiling serenely at the gathered vultures networking and gossiping, and planning to hook up later. They'd know as soon as he opened his mouth that he was blue-collar, working class all the way. They'd look at him, smirk and ask each other if he was a local fancy man, noticing his good looks and wondering out loud about an older man like that. Weren't *all* good-looking simpleton men like Tab also Gigolos? The thought of Tab meeting your friends makes you feel anxious and protective. You'll put it off, forever if you have to, or at least indefinitely, if only to spare him and you the ordeal—but mostly him.

Along with working as a school custodian, Tab earns extra money on the side by doing maintenance work for local area apartment homes on the weekend. He does this to pay the child support for the two children he never sees, spirited away to Furnace Creek, California by his vindictive first wife ten years ago. His son and daughter, Jack and Jill, barely know him and sometimes he cries about it. On more than one occasion you've stood next to him as he stood over the kitchen sink, his palms flat on the counter, his head down, and the tears falling into the clean basin one by one as you silently stroked his hard back, realizing that all too often words are simply useless.

His side job doing maintenance is in fact the result of how you met. He had knocked on your apartment door one winter afternoon tasked with the mission of replacing your toilet seat, and spraying for bugs. The toilet seat had mysteriously discolored sometime after you moved in. Its fetid appearance made you fear microscopic parasites and other diabolical microbes intent on your slow agonizing destruction through MRSA. That you ended up fucking him on the bathroom floor was testimony only to your desperation as a newly divorced woman, and his humble prowess as the vague, well-meaning ladies man who never intentionally means to hurt anyone. But it's too late to slow things down. Tab has the medicine you need, and you won't be quitting him anytime soon. Tab's face, body, and voice are what you think about upon arising in the morning and the last thing you think about at night, before slipping into bed. Tab, with his improper grammar, his habit of saying "what not" and "It don't matter to me, baby doll" is what you need, what you want.

So, that at the end of yet another fruitless day spent writing, and submitting, while cheating on your duties as assignment editor for the TV station, it is Tab you must have. It is Tab, barefoot, mouth encrusted with salty potato chips; Tab in his overalls; Tab with no boxers on underneath; Tab, lazily explaining some extant concept of mythology you'll never quite grasp. It is Tab, willing to listen, willing to please, grateful that unlike Ruby and Verona, you never complain about the future, or a commitment, or marriage, or God forbid, ever giving him anymore kids. Yes, it is Tab.

****

You're late again. It's hard to be on time when you hate her guts as passionately as you do. Everything about Gayle repulses you, from her 300 pound frame, to her face covered in half an inch of pastel *Mary Kay* cosmetics. She laments constantly about how there aren't any good men left anymore, but you know that's not it—it's just that no decent man would want to be with her. And her mood swings are the worst part. She's up, she's down, she's your friend, or she's salivating onto her chin, wild-eyed, as she breathes hatred in your face because you edited out a sound bite that was either factually suspect or superfluous.

And then of course she loves to tell you and your coworkers Helen and Tiffy, and the young interns, about her daughter's suicide attempts. She named her daughter *Mary Jennifer,* after the doomed daughter who killed herself at age twenty one—daughter of the famous Hollywood actress Jennifer Jones, and the ruthless fleshy director David O. Selznick. They had both abandoned their previous spouses and various children to be gloriously unified in mutual sin. Their union inevitably turned from perverse lusty attraction to indifference, to quiet hatred, and then to disgust and ultimately silence, at which time their daughter threw herself off a skyscraper onto the concrete below.

Everything about Gayle makes you want to flee, or vomit, or both. But the suicide stories really are the worst; they literally make the hair on the back of your neck stand up, and your stomach turn sour. She tells the stories and laughs, then explains she's laughing "to keep from crying." Of course, you think to yourself; of course. Gayle's daughter has attempted suicide no less than five times. With each incident the girl seems to get closer to her goal. You have it in your mind to find her one day and warn her about her mother—to plead with the girl to save herself and run far away, as far away as humanly possible. You recall Gayle's recent self-indulgent office soliloquy:

"The last time she called me she told me to stop givin' her advice, or she'd start hurtin' herself again. She said her doctor told her to cut me off but she still felt sorry for me, and was hopin' I'd finally accept some blame in how she turned out. Well, I told her: "I had NOTHIN' to do with you gettin' involved with drugs in high school." I told her: "I worked all those years so you could go to a private school and wear designer jeans." Was it my fault some baseball coach

molested her when she was a twelve-year-old kid with pimples?!"

You sat with Helen and Tiffy, aghast. You said nothing, looking down, waiting for the moment to end. Gayle, clueless as always, interpreted the collective silence as acquiescence and sympathy, and reason enough for her to go on.

"Yeah! That's what I say. Hell no, was I at fault!" Gayle concluded viciously.

You realize you're beginning to hate Gayle in an unhealthy way. You imagine stuffing her bedroom curtain rod's full of raw Mackerel, because of course you *have* been to her awful maniacally pink home. Or dousing her plush living room carpet with Nasturtium seeds, water and Miracle Grow while she's out of town on yet another vacation. But more than anything, you start fantasizing about committing criminal mischief with spray paint, sulfuric acid, and pancake batter in her second office, the one with the million dollar view, where she practically lives in the heart of downtown Portland.

You're starting to worry about your mental health. You've never hated someone before to this extent and now you're beginning to *like* it. You're reminded of the day you took over an hour for lunch just to spite her. Knowing she'd panic if she thought you weren't monitoring the young reporters, you had snickered to yourself, smugly satisfied. That was one of your many duties, staying on top of the young reporters—reminding them to introduce themselves after the camera's start rolling while out in the field, and making sure they had enough cover stick to hide all their adult acne represented only a small fraction of your endless duties babysitting the kids.

After having lunch, while you were downtown, walking toward a bench outside of *Ross Dress for Less*, you passed a dangerous looking old drunk. He stumbled near you, smirked, and then bellowed to no one in particular: *"The more evil ya git—the more ya ENJOY it!"* Your eyes fluttered, and you looked down, passing him quickly, but knowing you'd be thinking about his words for the rest of the day, if not the rest of the month. You remembered how crazed his face looked, and how you had thought of demonic possession, wondering if perhaps you should run the other way. But in the end, you just looked at the ground, ignored the man and sat demurely on the bench as he shuffled pathetically down the street toward Burnside.

You begin to think Gail is becoming worse though, given her malignant narcissism, and her deliberate passive aggressiveness. She seems to enjoy tormenting her poor daughter who is already in analysis and on multiple psychotropic meds for depression and bipolar disorder.

You think back to the Technicolor nightmare you had only a few days ago which left you terrified and in a state of unwelcome Blood Simple. In the dream you had walked into Gayle's home, decorated as it was like Jayne Mansfield's Pink Palace. You found her lying obese, sweaty and covered in make-up in a bubble bath while loudly complaining into a cell phone about a fast food order. On a small marble table near the tub you saw a huge coffee table cookbook, entitled "Let's Eat SIN!"

You walk over, grab her cell phone and hurl it against the wall where it shatters, each fragment magically transforming into a white diamond the size of an unshelled walnut. You laugh manically, throwing your head back, your eyes wild as you bellow: "The time is NOW Gayle! The time is NOW!" Gayle puts her hands to her mouth, terrified and shakes her head from side to side. A scream rises up in her throat as she begs: "No, oh God, please! No! No! Noooooooooo!" You grab the book and start pulling the pages out, balling them up and forcing Gayle to swallow them whole. On each page the name of her daughter, is typed over and over in capital letters: MARY JENNIFER. MARY JENNIFER. MARY JENNIFER.

You force the pages down Gayle's throat as she begs for mercy, gagging, dry heaving, struggling to breathe. The sharp edges of the thick paper tear at her esophagus, and she begins weeping and choking on the blood, telling you she didn't mean to destroy her daughter's life—it just happened that way. Pretty soon she's gagging and then asphyxiating, her throat clogged with balled up paper and coagulating blood. Then she's dead. You've done the world a favor. You've killed Gayle. But when you awake with a start, your heart sinks to learn it was only a dream; Gayle is not dead, it was just a dream, or a nightmare, or wishful thinking on your part. Yes, you're starting to worry about your mental health. It's not normal hating your boss like this… is it?

****

Tiffy and Helen have been out doing another Rip-N-Read, this one on a Portland conman asking for donations from local area churches to pay his rent, but using the money for his gambling and drug habit, instead. Gayle can't understand that its 2005, and the newspapers and TV stations are now cooperating, instead of planning each other's demise. Gayle is still stuck in 1981 when the Rip-N-Read in both camps was standard and accepted procedure. Now, the newspapers and magazines are going belly up. They're sinking and doing things they'd never considered before—promoting the TV stations, by linking TV stories to their own written articles on their internet websites. Gayle can't quite grasp that technology is changing the world. She's still lost in warrior mode, kill or be killed, winner takes all, stomp the enemy, step on his throat and laugh.

But the fantasy is still there, swirling in your mind's eye—her office, innocent and unsuspecting, and so very pink, awaiting destruction, with you as the force fate has chosen to mete out the mayhem. In your mind, the office is waiting—for the breaking and entering you fantasize about committing. You realize now that you really are planning it and in one form or another, it's going to happen. You're beginning to wonder if it's destiny that you carry it out on some dark Portland night when the street lamps flicker weakly, and the security guards decide to nap.

What will happen if you're allowed to wander in, a blue faced phantom with bulging eyes, ill intent, and a big black bag full of toxic substances and pancake batter? And why would you obsess like this? You're not the kind of person to do something illegal... are you? You're known as the competent, quietly assertive professional who is staid, reserved and for the most part, boringly conventional.

What is it about this year that has closed off something in your mind, in your heart? You wonder if perhaps it's because you're pushing forty, or if it's the divorce—that bastard! But of course, you know what it is. It's all of those things, but it's also because of living in Portland. This closed off city, nothing more complex than a small town, where so many live under the conviction that you have to be a snob to be successful, while pretending to be a generous liberal who cares about the losers of the world who can't seem to help themselves. The class system is alive and well in P-town. You've lived here your whole life and you know how hard it is to penetrate the various non-inclusive realms. Unless you have connections or the luck and looks of a voluptuous blonde film star, it's difficult to get very far.

You recall the book reading with the "famous" author. You'd been friends on Facebook and had even messaged each other after she lamented that her writing group was minus one of its writers. She made it seem as if she was looking for another writer for the group. When you sent her a private message and asked to join, she explained that there just wasn't room—even though they'd just lost one member. Apparently, you weren't good enough to be part of the group, or perhaps it was only because you weren't *published* yet, but either way, she said no.

When she unexpectedly came to the reading of another writer sometime later, you felt now you had your chance to actually meet her. But somehow you knew she would end up snubbing you. You'd heard the rumors before about how arrogant she'd become since her one bestselling book—how she wasn't nice anymore. As she stood next to the much younger author at the reading, posing for photos, you waited politely for her to have a free moment. It was after she walked to the front counter of the bookstore that you approached and touched her left arm lightly. She turned to look at you and you smiled and said: "Hello Farah! It's so nice to meet you. I just wanted to thank you for letting me use that quote." The look on her face was not surprised. She knew what you were referring to, and indeed she knew who you were. The quote of course had been discussed already via Facebook several months before. She had agreed to let you use it, a couple of sentences from one of her books, as the epigraph to your book. Needless to say you ended up tossing it.

The money shot was the look on her face when after you thanked her, she looked at you serenely and asked: "What's your name?" She had made her point and like a ten-year-old, she was proud of herself. Though some people would have been angered by such a blatant and deliberate snub, you were actually thrilled by it. It confirmed her mediocrity, not so much as a writer or author, she was relatively talented, and had been supremely lucky, but rather it confirmed her natural inclination toward envy, pettiness and competitiveness with other women.

Your response was to gaze at her with equal serenity as you told her only your first name. In return, she smiled her freezing superior smile, and said nothing further. "Well, anyway, it was really nice to meet you!" you murmured lightly. She continued smiling benevolently like the Queen of England and then turned her back on you. Just like that. She dismissed you without another word, but it was not unexpected—her snubbing. It was what you always *knew* would happen and in a literal way, her behavior pleased you. It demonstrated she really was as insecure and comically imperious as you had heard through the grapevine from all the other writers in town. The "famous" author was more of the same of what Portland had to offer. The transplants who come to Portland—do well, but are generally inclined to jump into the swimming pool and act like the water belongs to them and no one else—treating lifetime residents like the help. It was to be expected and one of the reasons you sometimes fantasized about leaving, moving elsewhere, where you could start fresh and perhaps no one would know you. But where could you go if you left Portland? Where could you go that wouldn't feel like Siberia?

You've also thought that perhaps more than your belief that everyone is against you because you're a lifer, it's just as simple as having a really bad name. The name your parents burdened you with is: *Daisy Rose Butterfield*. You can't remember how many times people have openly laughed when they picked up your resume for a reporter job, or even as a waitress when you worked summers in college. The amused faces, the occasional: "Is that really your name?" or worse yet: "Were you named after a romance novel heroine?" The jokes, you've heard them all. The Daisy Buchanan references, the Princess Daisy jokes, the "What's your favorite flower?" with the requisite: "The daisy, or the rose?"

You've sent manuscripts to the various small-town publishing houses in the hopes maybe one day your short stories or novel would be published, but they couldn't seem to get past the hilarity of your name. One woman editor, gazing at you with a refined contemptuous patience explained: "I think my assistant looked over your manuscript, and unfortunately… this press doesn't publish…

romance novels." When you kindly explained that you don't write romance novels, but rather fiction dealing with real life, in other words literature, she looked confused, her eyebrows knitting together daintily. It was then you realized she hadn't seen your manuscript, nor had her assistant ever laid eyes on your manuscript, which had simply been tossed unread into the slush pile.

Portland is a town known for its unspoken class system, if only because of the simple geography of the city. Back near the turn of the century, with the verdant hills looming high to the west of town, it was the west hills that became the inevitable location the well-heeled decided they ought to live and procreate. If they were going to live in "stump town" with all its wonderful natural resources and scenic vistas, one might as well high-tail it to the hills so they could look down on everyone else. There, the decent folks could rest easy above the drunkenness, the chaos and the murdered floaters drifting peacefully along the polluted Willamette River. There, they could avoid the prostitutes, the venereal disease, the tear stained cheeks of the abandoned women and the local riffraff on the water front, as they caroused in taverns and filthy disease infested brothels.

You realize that though Portland is now thought of as a cosmopolitan city—and it's certainly not as dangerous as it once was—in other ways the Rose City hasn't changed much. The exclusivity of Portland's business scene and political scene are just as impenetrable as its art scene, and literary scene. This is why you can't get published. That and the fact that most of the movers and shakers in those arena's are not natives but out-of-state professionals with secrets to guard of their own, blindingly white capped teeth, and chips on their collective shoulders. The kind of people who enjoy suffering fools, particularly Portland lifers like you—realizing with their kind of rapt observational powers that *you* know far more than *they* ever will about the city you all call home.

You know all of Portland's nooks and crannies, its ghosts, its unspoken past and the silent shame of all those people who came before. People can see it in the calm reserve of your eyes, in your easy acceptance of the judgment of others. Knowing they resent you for it, knowing they wish they had your history, knowing that you know so many people they don't have a clue about, you can only feel a kind of detached pity for them.

You realize that your success may simply come down to changing your name, your bio, perhaps a dye job or maybe some minor facial reconstructive surgery. But you're willing to at least change your name. What were your parents thinking when they burdened you with it, anyway? A new name might be just the ticket. How about Daisy Stone? Or Daisy Steel, or Daisy Blackthorn, or maybe just D. Blackburn, with any gender indicator conveniently wiped out? Yes, a new name might be just what you need, in this town of wandering ghosts.

CHAPTER TWO

A Girl Named Daisy Rose

*T*HE HOUSE PHONE RINGS AS you sit at the breakfast table, instantly remembering it's been almost twenty four hours since Tab called. You stare at the phone as it rings insistently. You're bone tired, and just want to go to bed and get some sleep, but it keeps ringing.

Lately, Tab has been on a kick about phone sex, and wondering why you're not into it, mildly indignant even. He's explained that since Verona's done it, even within the last few months, then naturally you should, too. You tried to tell him it's too dangerous, that you're a professional, reminding Tab that *that* means you graduated from college and are part of a respectable profession in media. You don't need the FBI recording you while you wheeze and whimper, telling Tab you need a spanking, or a butt fucking, or oral with sweetened whipped cream. His fantasy of you spanking *him* with an ancient S and M wood paddle he bought at a garage sale, with SLUT emblazoned on the back with a blowtorch is once again *not* something you want to discuss. Maybe Ruby and Verona are into that brand of perverse sex, but you're not.

But Tab doesn't believe the FBI would be interested in a girl named Daisy Rose Butterfield who works for a TV station. He firmly shook his head when you had the discussion, adamantly convinced you were just being paranoid, and that if you *really* cared about him, *and* his pleasure, you'd do what he wanted. When he tried to convince you it would be good for your relationship, you nipped it in the bud, realizing that no amount of being nice would work with someone like Tab. You think back to that night at his place:

"You know Daisy… this could make our relationship more complex, richer! Aren't those the words you like to bandy about when you talk about people and relationships and stuff?"

"Jesus Tab, how many times do I have to explain it? The FBI watching people is REAL! No! It's not going to happen. If you want fuckin' phone sex, call Ruby or Verona and pester them for it because it's *not* gonna be me."

You realized then, that you had just raised your voice and you'd never done that before. Tab scooted forward, while sitting on his restored Camelback sofa.

You recognized the wounded look. He was turned on and suddenly he wanted you. His eyes hurt, like a puppy's who's been scolded. Make-up time would soon follow. You know how much Tab loves to make up, for mostly imaginary hurts, and you love him for it. He's like a perennial teenager lost in a grey cloud of innocence that follows him around like some kind of rainbow hued curse.

"Daisy? You're yelling. Did I make you angry? Gosh honey, I'm sorry. I didn't mean to make you angry. For a minute there you reminded me of... of Blanche. Let's go to bed, baby? I can massage your back, your feet—rub lotion into your thighs—your little round fanny?"

"Is that all you think about, Tab? Fucking, I mean? I'm not complaining, but really. Do you ever get enough? Like, I said, I'm not complaining or anything." You laughed when you said that, but Tab perceived it as further mocking and assumed an even more hurt expression, which you knew meant he'd get even *more* turned on.

"Did I hurt you honey? I didn't mean to."

"Come on Daisy, let's get naked."

"Okay, Mr. Tab Hunter, you frivolous little plaything."

"Don't mock my name. Kinda like the pot calling the kettle black, you know?"

"Yeah, you're right."

After watching the phone ring for what seems like well over a minute, you get up, walk over and answer it. Your voice is low, defeated as you say hello into the receiver. Its Tab, like you knew it would be, and once again he's at it about the phone sex. That way you could feel loved and close to each other, even when you're not together, he explains brightly. You listen while he rambles on, and then silently hang up the phone. He calls back. You pick up. He's hurt, *and* determined.

"Baby, I'm comin' over!"

"What if I'm busy? What if I have someone here?"

"Yeah, right."

"Tell me what happened, Tab—was it a fight with Ruby or was it Verona this time?"

"You know baby, for the life of me, I can't figure you out. Why aren't you even a little bit jealous? Am I really that repulsive to you? And to think I used to believe I was a pretty good lookin' guy. Seems to me you were pounding on my door only last week and hanging on me like a Chimp."

"Do you want me to answer the door when you get here, or call the fuckin' police?"

"I'm sorry baby; it's just that you seem so casual about everything. You know Ruby and Verona? Those girls have had fistfights over me. Sure, it was a hassle havin' to bail 'em both outa jail at Central, but it made me feel special, too."

"Special huh?"

"I hate to admit it, but two women fightin over ya? Yeah, it makes a guy feel good about himself. Especially, when the cops were looking me over and ribbin' me about it, callin' me a fancy man and all that."

"Tab, do you even *know* what a fancy man is?"

"Well, heck! Sure I do! What, ya think I'm STOOOPID?"

"Listen; even I can't explain what happened. You were standing there in the bathroom installing the toilet seat and... I dunno you just did something to me. I've always been a sucker for a pretty face. Yes, Tab you *are* good looking. You're my physical ideal, I guess? But the reality is I don't think we've ever had a relationship that was based on much more than a sexual connection and the desire to... get off!"

"Get off? Is that all I am to you? Just a fuck? So, you sayin' you don't care for me? You sayin' you don't love me, is that it?"

"That's *not* what I said, Tab."

"You know, this ain't no back street affair, Daisy! This is a big deal to me."

"Back street affair? What does that even mean?"

"It's just an old song, but it's true. This is turnin' into a big deal."

"I know it is, and it's not that I don't care for you, it's just..."

"Then what's the problem? We love each other, right?"

"Well, yes, I suppose we do. But... I mean, you told me right off the bat that you're married to Ruby and Verona is special too... your girl on the side? Isn't that how you put it? It's only because you're a clean freak that I've even gone *this* far. I mean think about it Tab. You're fucking three women. THREE women!"

"You're making me feel less than again. Can I help it that women come after me? Can I help it that sex... well, sex is like goin' to heaven for me?"

"Are you coming over, Tab? I'm tired."

"Yeah, baby. I'll be there in twenty minutes."

"Bring over some of those potato chips you like."

"Sure thing, baby doll—and some Snapple?"

"Yeah, some Snapple, too."

"What kind?"

"You know! The *only* kind. Strawberry Kiwi!"

You open the door and Tab walks into your neat tidy apartment at The Clinton Court, east of the Clinton Street Theater. He stands in the center of the living room with that grateful smile on his face, and you feel less embarrassed about the previous week, when you were pounding on his door like a meth head looking to score. He's carrying a *New Seasons'* paper bag. It's loaded down with the special chips he likes, a natural style barbecue, and a six-pack of Strawberry Kiwi Snapple. His clean canary yellow hair is practically acting as its own light source. He sets the bag on the braided rug and puts out his arms like he did the previous week, like a sympathetic king bestowing a favor. You sigh, turn your back and walk into the kitchen, and take down two neon green glass tumblers. You turn to the refrigerator and pull out the ice tray, cracking the cubes and dropping them into each long glass. You glance over as he stands there, tall, crestfallen and adorable.

"Are you gonna be like that baby, after I drove *all* the way across town to see my girl?"

"Tab, I'm tired. You're telling me you couldn't find time to meet with Ruby or Verona?"

"I've *told* you Daisy, Ruby and I don't have sex anymore. It's been five months and over a year since we separated, with no plans on getting back together by the way. So, technically, it's only you, me and Verona—though the past eight weeks, I've only seen you, and not her. She's so bossy, kinda like how Ruby is. They're *both* bossy, and lately, I'm startin' to get tired of it. You're not bossy though, you're just… cool. You're a cool girl."

"A cool girl huh? And you wanna be with me, instead, huh?"

"I'm growing real fond of you baby doll, *real* fond."

"Fond, huh? You said you loved me on the phone last week?"

"That, too."

"Well, okay, the bed is made. Even has clean sheets. Let's go make a mess."

"That's my girl."

The sex with Tab is always magical, satisfying, and entirely luxurious. Partly it's because he always smells so good, like Ivory soap and his cliché favorite cologne *Old Spice*, which you're finding you enjoy more and more. And he takes his time. The combination of his perfect gold body, and corn fed folksy charm, along with his calm demeanor makes you feel safer and more fulfilled than you've felt with any other man. Tab is becoming a serious habit you didn't foresee happening. Are you falling in love, or merely in lust? You're not quite sure which it is, but something *is* happening, and it's becoming an issue.

****

You lay on your back afterward. He's made you come three times. When you come there is nothing else. The world, the universe is centered in your bed—the pleasure between your legs, your pink button the seeming tip of all that is joyous, beautiful, and complete. And when you come *together*, joined at the pelvis, it's so much more intense and pleasurable that sometimes you want to weep. His attitude is always generous and patient. He explained once that he's always going to "get mine" so it's important that you get yours too, and first. You lay against the pillow, smiling placidly. You've gotten over the soft

16

giggling that sometimes possesses you afterward, and you just lay there, with a dumb smile on your face. You won't weep with gratitude, but you know there *will* be other times that you will, usually late at night, after an exhausting day at work, in the dark blackness of his fragrant bedroom.

"You okay, baby?"

"Oh yeah, I'm A-okay!"

"Can I tell you about this last episode?"

"Come on Tab, please don't ruin these precious moments."

"I should quit. I'm sick of it, the way those kids smirk when I tell them they're wrong."

"So, what happened *this* time? Was it one of the kindergarten kids or an eighth grader?"

"Yeah, it was an eighth grade kid—a boy this time."

"Okay?"

"You know, the usual. "Excuse me? Mrs. Wellesley is looking for the Janitor. The sink in the Home Economics classroom is not working. It's plugged."

"And?"

"So, I say: "Okay, why would she be looking for the janitor?"

"And?"

"Kid says: "So, it can get fixed?"

"You weren't mean were you?"

"Why am I gonna be mean, Daisy? These are kids. I'm a grown man."

"Grown man. Right. Okay, go ahead."

"So, I say: "What is it the janitor does, again?" and he says: "Sweep the floors, clean, fix stuff."

"Oh, Lord!"

"Yeah! So I say: "No. That's NOT what a janitor does. A janitor ONLY cleans. I am the one who fixes stuff, like a stopped up sink, or a bad heater, or maintains the boiler down in the basement which keeps the school heated, and the electricity on. I am called a *CUSTODIAN*. You look smart, can you figure out the difference? Can you at least *spell* the difference?"

"Tab, were you mean? Jeez, they're only kids."

"He just smirked at me and walked off, sayin: "Yeah, whatever!"

"They're kids, Tab."

"Yeah, I know. I just don't know if I can stomach that job for another year. It's demoralizing, just plain demoralizing; I'm always being mistaken for the janitor! I guess I'll just never be happy. You know how long it's been since I've seen Jack and Jill?"

"I know, Tab, a long time. They know you love them, though. They have to."

"Not if *she* has anything to say about it. I was sending cards and gifts for a long time with the monthly child support, but I found out from her brother she was just tossing it all out. Telling them I didn't care none for 'em. I did that for *five* years before Stan told me the truth. She even sold some of the stuff fer money!"

"I know, but someday they'll know the truth? That you did the best you could and that you care for them—that you *love* them?"

"Maybe if I buy that replica of *The Thinker* I might feel better. I know you don't like talkin' about it but it's just such a beautiful sculpture. If only I could afford it, somehow."

"Save your money Tab, and that's the thing—you *can't* afford it. There are so many other things you could spend your money on, instead of a super expensive replica of *The Thinker!* Save your money, for a house, for Christ sake!"

"I know you don't like talking about... my dream."

"Your dream?—spending thousands on a stupid replica statue? Come on Tab, can't you spend your money in a better way? Like saving for a house? How much is it you said you've got saved, $14,000 now?"

"Why are you trying to crush my dream? I just don't get it. Haven't you ever had a dream?"

"Tab, you realize there are twenty eight monumental sized bronze casts of *The Thinker* in museums' across the country? That it's six to eight times the size of a real man, that they are seventy three inches tall? It's huge, Tab. How on earth could you do it? Have you ever considered the actual logistics? Where would you keep it? The casts are bronze, and weigh several tons, more than a waterbed, for example."

"I don't try to crush *your* dreams."

"Good God, Tab, I don't even *have* any dreams anymore. I'm happy if I can just pay my rent, eat a steak once in a while, buy a new *Dooney & Bourke* once a year, and try to keep in the black, you know?"

"God, I love it when you get pissed. Let's fuck!"

"Oh, brother!"

"Come on, baby?!"

"Sure, Tab, I'm here for ya. Scootch over and while you're at it, grab me that tube of *Slippery Stuff*."

****

You're still at work when Tab calls again. He's only called on two other occasions, because he knows he can't bother you when you're working. And he knows how much you despise Gayle, your enormous, often flatulently challenged boss who is tragically addicted to curries of any size and sort. You cradle the phone in your hand, peeking over your shoulder like a skulking criminal with a satchel crammed full of stolen conflict diamonds, and blocks of reeking Stilton cheese. You imagine Gayle banging into the office to bark at you: "You finally done with that story we need? And what in hell is that Goddamn SMELL? Daisy?! What is that SMELL?!"

Tab's voice is subdued when he tells you the news. The girls have gotten into a "tussle" outside of Ruby's apartment south of 72nd and Foster. Verona and Ruby are both in custody shivering in the downtown detention center, looking at green walls and hating each other. Ruby, surprise-surprise is the loser. This is what you would expect to hear given that she's five years older than Tab, which puts her at an even fifty seven. She's also a hopeless juice-head drunk lacking the physical coordination to do much more than walk from the *Lazy-Boy* to the Fridge for another ice cold *Pabst Blue Ribbon* and packet of chilled *Beer Nuts*, while watching yet another fun filled episode of Jerry Springer, clapping her hands and cackling happily.

Verona in comparison, is only forty, in much better condition and unlike Ruby, she's employed and doesn't live off monthly disability checks while languishing in low income housing. Verona paints the interiors of apartments for a contracting company which is how she ended up meeting Tab—with his clean overalls, canary yellow hair and bag of potato chips in hand. You know it couldn't have been that difficult for Verona to trip Ruby with her leg, pop her in the mouth a couple of times, or yank out handfuls of that color treated fluff teased into a straw-like substance that Ruby refers to as her *hair*. Though you're terrified of both of them, you generally find yourself rooting for Verona, and somehow you're pleased she beat up Ruby. Verona is five feet four like you, but skinny with bleached blond hair—scrappy like a starved cat that's had too many litters.

Though Tab has never once asked for money, you're still shell shocked because of your ex-husband and his endless requests to borrow money he never paid back. You eventually left him the contents of the apartment, (minus your closet) and a short note, wishing him luck. That he didn't see it coming and raged and wept to all his friends for months afterwards was particularly pleasing. You got tired of his endless financial woes, and flippant demands to "borrow" money he never paid back, and the occasional black eye or fat lip if you refused. You think back to those wasted years and are glad you were finally able to *scrape* him off.

Thinking back to Ruby, you realize she's an unlikely Clara Bow lookalike, but with black hair instead of red. She's slightly overweight, dumpy in her all black outfits, and a chronic adulterer, thinking that *that* is the only way to lead an exciting or interesting life. Her thrill seeking is hollow and couched directly within the transparent confines of the Electra Complex which has held her firmly within its viselike grip since she was an angsty teenager embroiled in her first sweaty affair. Tab thought Ruby was his Blanche come back to life when he started seeing her. His ex-wife, Brandi had cut him off for undisclosed reasons, and in desperation Tab fell into the lap and the bed of the nice neighbor lady who was more than thrilled to take him away from his sexy young wife and two small children.

As you hold the phone next to your ear, you're filled with that sinking sensation of dread. It rises from your belly upwards to just below your sternum. You're reminded of the film *Breakfast at Tiffany's* and the phrase made famous: "The mean reds." Because that is exactly how you feel. If your colleagues knew you were seeing a man with a wife, *and* a girlfriend who stalk and attack each other and that you basically continue to see the man anyway because he's a sexual dynamo *and* gorgeous, you'd be an instant laughing stock. Not only at the office and within your social circles but within everyone else's social circles, too. You find yourself whispering into the receiver.

"Tab, I'm trying to edit out twelve seconds of video right now. I just can't talk. I know you need me, but... you'll have to call me later on my cell."

"I tried your cell earlier!"

"Right, and I didn't answer because I'm at work. Jesus Tab, come on! That bitch Gayle is gonna be walking through that door any second now."

"It's been over seven months now Daisy and I never thought I'd find myself thinkin' about you so much. Admit it, something unexpected is happening. I *know* you can feel it. You can feel it, can't ya?" The sinking feeling changes fluidly to a calm resolve and suddenly you're transformed. It's nearly the end of the day and now you're glad Tab has called with his little quasi emergency.

"You want me to take off early? I guess I can—if you need me especially bad?"

"Oh baby, would you? I know it's a lot to ask, but I just need to be *with* you."

"Yeah, I wanna see you too, Tab. Fuck that bitch Gayle. Tiffy can do this edit."

Leaving work forty minutes early is stupidly brazen, and unprofessional. This could in time become a fire-able offense. But there's something particularly seductive about Tab's quiet, chastened voice—the voice he uses when he wants you to comfort him. And comforting Tab is always such a pleasure.

Then there's the knowledge that blood has been spilled because of Tab—that Ruby and Verona have gotten into yet another fistfight is kind of intoxicating. That Ruby sits in jail with a fat lip and an even fatter ass makes you feel smug. That Verona sits in jail, skinny, dried up and bitter, her thin lips drawn together, coated thickly with Wet-N-Wild pink frost lipstick, and they *still* have no inkling you even exist after all this time? It's doing something to you—has brought home the truth that perhaps Tab *is* someone worthwhile, that perhaps

20

you *could* be with him.

True, he is your physical ideal, and that certainly helps, and fucking Tab *is* generally a religious experience that leaves you either laughing or weeping in his arms, but he's also someone you *know* you could live with. Tab is someone who wouldn't yell at you in the morning while waiting for the coffee to percolate if you asked him to pass the organic lavender infused honey. He wouldn't violently sweep past you if he discovered you'd burned his fried egg, or slathered his stone cold toast with too much flavorless unsalted butter. He wouldn't sigh in frustration if you asked him where your purse was during halftime or told him you were out of *Tampax* pads and would he mind running to the store? That isn't Tab at all and never will be. He's tender, and dreamy, like a male Marilyn Monroe, always questioning, and innocently thrill seeking, a sensualist in the worst way. No wonder the women in his life keep forgiving him for his little indiscretions.

You're beginning to get it, and beginning to see that you too could forgive Tab almost anything. The truth is that your feelings for Tab are becoming complicated and yet, how could it work? How could you make it work, given the many differences you would stumble over on a daily basis? Imagining Tab at an office cocktail party, honest, unassuming and accommodating makes you feel more protective than you've felt toward *any* man. But Tab isn't weak, he's not a pansy. He can handle himself, unlike your ex-husband, who demonstrated he was as intrinsically angry as he was cowardly. The kind of man who got into slap fights with other guys but only in grade school. And being the insecure bully he was, he always had something to prove later on to a defenseless woman. Sometimes that woman was you.

But Tab is *not* your ex-husband.

You recall the rainy night only four months ago when you walked with Tab to his truck. You had decided to go and grab some late night *Taco Bell* but a homeless drunken man lunged at you in the parking lot. He reached for your breast, prominently displayed and milky white in a skimpy red pushup bra that showed through your light blue Nike tee-shirt. As you froze in your tracks, your arms shot up reflexively, palms out in a defensive mode and your eyes widened in fear. You distinctly remember the way Tab's face darkened, how his lower lip curled in a way you'd never seen before, and the quick easy way Tab leaned in and swiftly landed a right hand double-cross, a knuckle punch, with no pushing forward of the arm, but relaxed and potent. The man was unconscious before he hit the ground. You stood there; your jaw hanging to your collarbone, and looked at Tab in wonder, your eyes big as china plates. You waited, uncertain. He smiled, slightly smug, but not in a bad way, just pleased with himself. He reached over, and gently directed you toward the truck, his hand pressed to the middle of your back, opening the door for you, and assuring you it was all over.

"It's okay, baby, he's harmless, just a neighborhood drunk. He'll be fine."

"But... but... I mean, why'd you hit him if he's harmless?"

"No one disrespects my girl. He had to learn a lesson. It's over now."

You remember how easily Tab smiled as you looked over at the drunken man who snored, now fast asleep on the grass, his arms and legs splayed out in comical abandon, a bright green gardener snake spastically darting away from his filthy left foot. Tab's hand was still on your back as you climbed up and slid into the seat. For some reason you hadn't thought Tab was that kind of man—the kind of man who could punch someone and knock them out cold. But in the parking lot, you learned he was. And yes, you were turned on. You hated to admit it, the horrible cliché of it, but you were hugely turned on when Tab showed he could use his fists to protect you—when he showed you he could become violent.

Eating the *Taco Bell* slowly in the truck, you stole glances at Tab, thinking of him in another way, and then rushed home to fuck. You counted your blessings as you watched his yellow hair glimmer in the moonlight of his bedroom. The curtains were wide open, and the dark night sky was scattered with undulating grey and mauve clouds just outside the windows like some kind of huge abstract painting. With a light dusting of perspiration on his peach colored forehead, he hovered above you on his elbows stroking in and out. His eyes were closed, he was taking his time. And you remembered how dreamily he murmured your name, calling you *baby* and making you come again and again.

CHAPTER THREE

Ruby and Verona Going at it Again

YOUR'E AT WORK AND HE'S talking about the fight again—his chosen topic of conversation for the past week. You lean into the phone and wait for the play by play, though you know it now by heart. You don't really want to hear how they got into it, or how it ended it, or what the police said when Tab came to bail them out or what *he* said in return. But you know it's important to Tab and he's going to need to talk about it for at least a few more days. Maybe he'll save it for later, though. Right now, you're just hoping you can make it out of the office unnoticed before Gayle stomps in to bark orders and bitch and complain. Because once again, you're taking off early.

"Okay, come pick me up. Be ready to take me back to your place, okay?"

"Baby, you own my heart!"

"Okay, Tab, just take it easy. I'll wait in the back of the building, behind the dumpster. I'll be the one in the black *Goodwill* trench coat."

"A black trench coat?"

"Yeah, I got it at that Vintage shop on 28th and Burnside last week."

"Will you be wearing anything on underneath?"

"Come on, Tab, just get here!"

"What about your car?"

"We can pick it up later on. I just need to get outa here!"

You close out your project on the computer, gather your purse and new *Tumi* bag, and walk into Tiffy's office down the hall.

Poison Idea is blaring as you peek around the door, waving—a bright smile on your face.

"God, how can you listen to that garbage?" you ask as your smile dissolves into a grimace.

"Different strokes for different folks, I guess."

"Tiff, can I trouble you to finish this edit on that cat lady they found in NE? Gayle wants to keep the part about the dead cat in the front bedroom stinking up the place, but that's an additional seven seconds and we may have to cut it. I'm kinda hoping you can make the right judgment call on that. I'd sure appreciate it?"

"Again? Jeez Daisy, this is the *second* time in six weeks. What's up with you? Are you *trying* to get on her bad side?"

"Well, my mother fell again and I need to get her to the nursing home *and* get her signed in. She refuses to use the walker and I'm having a hell-of-a-time getting her to follow the rules."

"Is that the *real* reason? I don't know, that just sounds pretty manufactured. Didn't your mother die or something?"

"Tiffy, if you do this, I'll give you my new *Tumi* satchel I bought last month. I've got it right here, just lemme empty it out!"

Before she can answer, you walk over and dump the contents on her desk, gathering them together haphazardly and stuff them into your jacket pockets and purse: Two small lavender folders with field notes, a new pink Lancôme lipstick, a nearly empty bottle of *Red Door* perfume, and a slender zip lock bag filled with your nice writing pens—the kind you never loan out no matter what.

"Jeez Daisy, come on, this is my desk. God, what's gotten into you lately?"

"Do you want the damn bag or not? I paid good money for it."

"Yeah, okay—so what'd she break this time, her femur or her arm? I wanna get the story straight."

"Um… I think it was just her ankle. I can't remember. I'll let you know. Okay, thanks Tiff, you're an angel."

"Are you sure Daisy? This doesn't really seem fair. I mean, this is like a $90 satchel."

"Actually, it was $400."

"What?!"

"Don't worry about it Tiff. You know what they say, right? *It's only money!*"

"It's only money? Okay Daisy. Yeah, it's only money!"

You walk outside, and the spring air is fragrant and balmy. There's nothing like spring to make you feel refreshed, hopeful and alive—that combination of moss, lilacs and rain that seems to define the scent of Portland. You see Tab parked outside the security gate across from the dumpster. He must have been calling from his cell. You rush over, adjusting your purse on your shoulder and wave at the guard to open the gate, your face bright with a falsely cheerful grin. He asks why you're not taking your car and you smile, lying easily, and tell him there's something wrong with the battery and you'll be picking it up tomorrow to be serviced. He shrugs, opens the gate and you practically frolic through, trying not to skip across the street like a child with a lollipop and a balloon.

You find yourself smiling in spite of yourself as soon as you get within eight feet of Tab. He's leaning against the truck, his muscular arms crossed over his chest like a Calvin Klein model during a photo shoot break, and he's wearing all yellow—your favorite color on him. Custard yellow corduroy slacks you bought for him only a few weeks ago, the new Ralph Lauren polo shirt, the color a blinding chiffon, and new beige espadrilles complete the look. His feathered yellow hair is on fire and his eyes reflect the sunlight like beaten gold coins. He opens his arms as you approach, and before you know it, you're embracing him, your head pressed to the center of his chest, as you inhale the heavenly scent of *Ivory soap* and *Old Spice*.

"God, I'm so fuckin' glad to see you, Tab. I thought this day would never end."

"Awww baby, you know it turns me on when you trash talk. Come on, gimme summore!

"Let's get outa here. Do you want us at your place or mine?"

"Well? You know that bed of yours? I mean… a double? I keep asking you honey, when are ya gonna get a real bed?"

"Okay, so that means your place? Alright, let's get going."

"Yes, Ma'am!"

"Did you work out today? I see your gym bag in the backseat."

"You bet! Monday through Friday like clockwork. You should come along sometime."

"Maybe. I'm not sure."

"I'll show you some moves."

"You know a lot of moves, doncha?"

"I try not to brag, baby."

****

Back at Tab's place he regales you with another retelling of the fistfight between Ruby and Verona, and of course the aftermath down at Central. You listen, smiling, as he gets down on his knees, bending over you. He's soaping your back and scrubbing with the loofah. He takes the orange plastic juice container, submerges it in the bath water and pours soapy water over your head. You stifle the urge to protest and wipe your face instead; pressing the soap suds from your eyes as he laughs and continues with his story. He massages your shoulders with his big beefy hands, which sometimes makes you flinch.

"Take it easy now, it's only me."

"Sorry, baby, but you know that they say about deep tissue massage, right?"

"I'll deep tissue massage *you* Bubba!"

"Okay, lemme get back to the story. You'll like it."

"Alright, tell me again, but make it interesting this time."

"So, it was just so damn embarrassin' lemme tell ya! But it was funny too, you know? The cops? They couldn't stop laughing!

They said I was gettin' a reputation and if this didn't stop, they were gonna set me up with their mother-in-laws, whether I wanted to or not."

"Did they really say that? But didn't Ruby have a fat lip or something?"

"Yeah, like I told you. And a whole chunk of her hair was missing on top."

"That Verona, she's a killer."

You find yourself laughing as you reach for the wine glass on the table with the bath salts, scented oils and specialty superfatted soaps. Tab bought it all just for you, arranged neatly in three small metal baskets which he spray painted silver, gold and bronze. You throw caution to the wind, chugging the rest of the cheap red cabernet, belching lightly into your hand and giggling.

The wine is making you hot and you realize how much you want Tab, but he's still not done. He pours more Dove's Moisturizing Body Wash onto the loofa and grabs a leg, gently nudging you to recline as he lifts up your leg.

"Just be careful of my feet, okay? If you scrub my feet and it tickles, I might kick. You don't want a repeat of last time, do you?"

"Nah, baby. I'll be careful. I won't tickle you—*there* anyway."

"You're so good to me. I could get used to this."

"Well, see, that was actually my plan. Now, lemme finish, I'm gettin' to the good part."

"The good part, ah yes, the good part."

Tab tells you after he bailed Ruby and Verona out of jail, he had to pick them both up, at different times of course. That meant having to lie to them, telling Ruby it was *she* he'd picked up first, and then telling Verona he had actually picked *her* up first. During the drives to their respective apartments in felony flats and then Sellwood, Tab got to listen firsthand to their endless petty complaints and suspicion. Verona was convinced he was seeing someone new and told him if she finds out who "the bitch is" she's going to kill her slowly with a dull spoon. Ruby was less unsettling than Verona and told Tab she was pretty sure they were through. She complained he didn't seem interested in her and never made any more, "booty calls" to her place off Foster, since of course they couldn't live together anymore because they drove each other crazy. Ruby reminded Tab it had been over five months since he'd given her any "cock" and she just *knew* he'd found another woman, being that he could never go, "that long without pussy." She accused him of not loving her because she was getting old and fat. Tab denied it as he parked the car off Foster, killing the engine and leaning over the steering wheel in exhaustion.

He explained in detail how the streetlight turned on and there was light drifting in through the front wind shield, and that this was the exact moment Ruby decided to entice him.

She started acting sexy, pulling her torn shirt down to expose a flabby, freckled shoulder. She pouted, saying that if not for the neighbor intervening

Verona would have killed her. But Tab wasn't listening. His eyes were focused on the top of her head. He couldn't help but notice the pale bluish scalp beneath the bald spot. He also noticed her swollen mouth smeared with lipstick. He admitted he felt repulsed and couldn't for the life of him see the woman he'd lusted after only ten years before.

"I dunno what happened Daisy but I felt like I was sittin' next to my Aunt Florence!"

"Oh, my God, was it really *that* bad? She did nothing for you?"

"On my honor Daisy girl, I almost got the goose bumps. If she'd a touched me, I'da jumped. That's how spooked I was. I felt like I was doin' my Dad a favor or something."

"Was it because you were thinking of Verona, instead?"

"No. Not Verona either. Oh, baby it was cuz I was thinkin' of you. My smart girl. My dream girl. You, Daisy!"

"That's *not* what you said when we first started sneaking around, remember? No, don't answer. You said and I quote: "Hold on loosely, baby." You used *those* very words, remember?"

"I do, and now I feel ashamed for *ever* treatin' my baby like that. Can you forgive me Daisy? Can you forgive me for bein' a cold bastard? Can you forgive me for fallin' in love with you?"

"I dunno. I'll think about it."

"That's all I ask, baby."

Tab is pulling you up from the bathtub, lifting you up under your armpits. You're afraid you might cry again, you can feel it's headed in just that direction. It's the perfection of his wheat brown arms and the beauty of his hands, the gratitude you feel—the wine of course, and that you know what's coming next. He drapes the thick burgundy towel around you and easily lifts you up, with the soapy suds still clinging to your legs. Your hair is wet and hangs down your back, a collection of heavy glistening ropes. You curl into his arms, pulling your knees to your chest, and grip his shoulders, your fingers slipping across his slick skin, wet from your hands. You find his mouth, and start humming as your tongue meets his, bathing once again in warm toothpaste and now red wine kisses. After a moment, Tab pulls away, hoisting you, adjusting you to better hold you before he walks into the bedroom. You hear his voice echoing, but can barely make out the words.

"Baby, you didn't answer—are you okay?"

"I'm fine Tab; I'm always fine. No, it's just that…"

"You gettin' happy/sad again? Cuz you love me?"

"I'm drunk, that's all!"

"Shhhhhhhhh. Big Tab is here. Tab's gonna make it all better."

And Tab does make it all better, the way he *always* makes it all better. Later, he holds you in his arms while you weep yourself into exhaustion, quietly laughing and then crying, barely audible, trying to choke through it, trying to breathe. He murmurs baby talk, whispers into your hair and finally kisses you all over your cheeks and forehead, slow pecking kisses. You fall asleep in his arms, aware only of his hot legs and heavy lean torso, and his watching eyes— the place where all life seems to spring, the place where you feel the most centered, the safest, the happiest.

Tab looks up at the ceiling as you slowly lose focus, your eyelids falling in languid surrender to the afterglow. His pale gold eyes assume the haunted look that is now intimately familiar, something he reveals only after nightfall. He begins talking about the Sky Burials and you wonder at the man who holds you. Perhaps he *is* some kind of undiscovered genius.

"You see, baby, the sky burial is a template of sorts, of the kind of instructional learning that symbolizes the impermanence of life. It's called *Jhator*, and is thought to be an act of generosity from the deceased because their body provides food—well, *sustenance* for other living beings, you know for the vultures? Those are important virtues in Buddhism. The *Jhator* unites the dead person with the sky or within the sacred realm. Then their soul is incarnated. That happens at night of course. Sky Burials—that's what I want when I die. To be taken to the mountains in Tibet and offered up to the earth and the sky as a sacrifice, as a gift to be given back, to become one with the soil, with the earth. But that's how it works. Isn't that beautiful, Daisy?"

CHAPTER FOUR

Talking about the Talionic Night

*T*HE SATURDAY AFTERNOON YOU CASUALLY begin to discuss your plan to vandalize Gayle's office, Tab becomes alarmed. He looks at you as if he's just met you, as if he doesn't know you. His eyebrows knit together and he seems almost frightened as you calmly drink coffee at the small round breakfast table in his kitchen. The coffee is the wonderful rich Viennese blend you sometimes buy and bring over for moments just like this. You hold the hot scarlet mug in your hands, warming them, with both pinkies out, taking tiny sips. He motions to your hands. He asks: "What are you, the Queen of England?"

You ignore the comment as you gaze out the window with its violet muslin curtains, remembering they're the same one's you made by hand, heritage style, almost a year before. You recall how impressed Tab had been when you brought them over with the café rod to install them with tucked snugly under your arm. You made them the week after you first met, when you had both ended up on the bathroom floor with your bare feet in the air and the glorious heft of his hard body pressed into you.

But now, as you sit with Tab, he can't understand how your entire personality could shift so quickly and he blames himself. "Too many orgasms," Tab says quietly, trying to make you laugh, the worried look still on his face. He should learn to "dole them out" he says, looking over at you to gauge your response. But his attempt at mild humor angers you. "Tab!" you hiss, slamming your open palm on the table and looking over at him furiously. He looks down and frowns at the spilt coffee, scoots back and reaches his long arm over to the kitchen counter, grabbing a clean white kitchen towel. He lifts your mug with ceremonious patience, and mops up the thin puddle of dark coffee that rests beneath it.

"Don't make a mess in my apartment, Daisy. That's one thing I will *not* tolerate."

"I'm sorry. I—I didn't mean it."

"I accept your apology."

But Tab is still alarmed and is looking at you with restrained annoyance and

29

watchful eyes. He can't understand why the hatred of Gayle has become this all-encompassing thing. In and of itself it exists and you cannot seem to apologize for it, either. Perhaps it's some unconscious anger towards your distant mother. Or maybe it's the anger you still feel at your sixth grade gym teacher, Mr. Forester. He had tried to fondle you once, as you stood in his dim office but you'd been able to get away. When you tried to tell your mother about it later that night, she'd interjected impatiently, telling you she was too busy making dinner, and whatever it was, it would have to wait. You never told her. Years later the man was fired for allegedly molesting a seventh grade girl, but you never forgot the way he looked at you when you went to change into your gym clothes.

All you know now is that Gayle seems to represent everything in your life that has ever gone wrong and everything that is wrong with the world. You hate her. You *despise* her. And something has to be done. You have to *do* something. At the very least you have to warn her poor daughter, Mary Jennifer.

Because in a very real way you know the truth about Gale: She is the sucker of stars, the universal consumer of all things good and pure. There is evil lurking in her, evil that you wish to quell, to destroy. You will teach humility to this woman, this Queen of 70s TV News, the Vampira of the sound bite, the used-to-be-girl, the Forgotten Television Mama, the obese *Mary Kay* monstrosity, the Portland Has Been of the ever glorious Rip-N-Read.

It's not Tab's fault that he can't understand, though. His basic decency, his fundamental honesty will never completely agree with what you know of the world. He would never be able to break the law in quite the same way you can. And suddenly, you're filled with fierce remorse. You want to apologize; to beg him to forgive you, because you know how much Tab loves it when you're sorry, *and* when you beg. You've hurt him. You can see it and that is not in keeping with the arrangement you both agreed upon. You must make amends.

"Oh Tab, God, I'm sorry. Its—it's just that she's so horrible. Not just to me, but to Tiffy and Helen and a whole bevy of other unfortunate folks—all the people who have to toe the line with her. It's not your fault. It's not anything to do with you. Listen, I just won't talk about it anymore, okay?"

"This isn't like you Daisy. You're my nice girl—my relaxed girl, my cool girl. You know I didn't mean it about the orgasms. The truth is I should give you more. Would you like that Princess Daisy? Would you?"

"Like now you mean?"

"Yeah, like now."

"Okay, I guess."

"Come on, then."

Afterward, you sit with Tab at the breakfast table eating mild Brie, canned pineapple and Greek black olives from the nearby deli, fighting the sudden irritability you feel as soon as you see the china. He's arranged the food on *Desert Rose* china plates that used to belong to Blanche, part of an entire set and worth hundreds. Once again, you try to push down the desire to break every single dish when he makes a *Taco Bell* run and then innocently tell him it was all just an accident once he gets back. Once again you try to come to grips with why you feel so threatened by an old dead lady.

"What's with the granny dishes? You treat them like they're gold or something."

"Well, Daisy, maybe they are as precious as gold to me. They remind me of a very special time in my life. You realize Blanche saved my life, right?"

"I'm sick of hearing about Blanche. She was a child molester, a pervert, a pedophile. What she did to you was unforgivable, Tab."

"Blanche saved my life. I loved her. But… that doesn't mean I don't love you too, baby."

"Gee, thanks! Save it. It's not like this is a *real* relationship and you know what? I like it that way. I don't need some crazy meth head like Verona coming after me with a… dull spoon! My God, I'm a fucking professional and I'm… oh I dunno know *what* I'm doing."

"It's funny, you'd start in on this cause—well, I've been thinkin' Daisy."

"Oh Lord, here we go. How you're gonna finance *The Thinker*, or where you'll put it? Perhaps in the center of your living room, granted it doesn't collapse the fucking floor?!"

"No, baby, I've been thinking… of… well, of leaving Portland?"

"Leaving Portland?"

"Yeah, finally just leaving."

"I mean, like, why? Where would we go?"

"I *like* that you automatically think *we'd* be movin' together cause that's exactly what I had in mind."

"Are you trying to trick me or something? Wow, I can't believe I fell for that."

"You didn't *fall* for anything, baby. Stop fighting it and just admit it, we're meant to be together. You know it. I know it. And you *know* I know you know it! Wait; hold on… yeah, that's right."

"Tab, you're making me emotional again. Why do you do this to me?"

"Do what to you?"

"You can't *say* things like this. Remember, this is just a casual thing, right? That was the agreement. *That* was the goddamn agreement!"

"Things change Daisy. We both know it's been headed in this direction for a while."

"Since when? You never tell me anything!"

"I'm telling you *now*."

"Oh, really?!"

"I'm thinking Seattle, baby. Maybe a nice condo in the center of downtown, near the Sound? There's a really nice one on NE seventy fifth. It has nice big units, and isn't that old. I read it was made in 1979, and has all the amenities. We could pool our money, we could do it honey."

"Oh, really?"

"Just you and me—sleeping, cooking, working, going to the movies together, and screwing ourselves into unconsciousness every day and night? Whaddaya say baby? You and me? After my divorce from Ruby of course, cause naturally I want you to be my wife."

"Oh, Tab! Jesus! One thing at a time!"

"It's inevitable that we get married one day, baby."

"But what about that nut-job Ruby?"

"I've been putting her off. I'll just continue to put her off. Besides I'm pretty sure she's sleeping with my former brother-in-law, Stan. Once we split town, I'll… just write her a note. Slip it under her door. Wish her well, that kinda thing."

"And what about Verona? What about *her?*"

"I'll just do the same."

"A Dear Jane letter?"

"Yeah, exactly! And that's all those two deserve, anyway."

"Would that work? I mean they wouldn't come after us? They're just so… insane."

"I *mean* it Daisy! I want this!"

"But why? I don't understand why you wanna…"

"I want to look after you while you write your international bestseller. To make sure you're safe, taken care of. And you know how much I love to cook, and give you your little baths?"

"That's true. You *do* seem to be kind of a homebody."

"The truth is you're not like any other woman I've ever been with. You're smart and savvy, you've been to college, but you're innocent too, like a little girl. I need that Daisy. At my age, I need some stability, and a woman I can count on. I can count on you. You're stable… for the most part."

"Well, thanks."

"And compared to *those* two crazies, you're an angel."

"Tab, we've been fucking for ten months now. There's a lot you don't even know about me. I mean there are things I'm only just starting to discover about myself."

"I prefer to call it *making love*, Daisy."

"There's a lot you don't *know* about me. There is a lot I haven't *told* you, yet."

"What, that you're a vindictive mean bitch who wants to destroy your boss's

office after committing a breaking and entering? ˙
and I'm sure you'll get over it, once you have a
man to give stability to your life."

"You know you can be *really* condescending someth.
It's more complex than you think. You're aware she's ruining
right?"

"And what's worse Daisy, me being condescending or you talki..
breaking the damn law?"

"You just *don't* understand."

"We'll talk about breaking into Gayle's office another time. I want you to start thinking about Seattle. There are lots of good TV stations there, good newspapers, and magazines. It'd be a breeze for you to find a job, and probably for me too. Lots of good schools need… custodians."

"You're asking me to leave my home town, Tab."

"Basically, that's what I'm asking you. Portland is my home town, too. Kind of… in a way, but I'm pretty sure we won't miss it. You know how stuck up the out-of-staters can be, and they're coming in fuckin' droves now! All they do is buy everything up, jack up the rents, and tear down all the old houses and the old Tenderloin buildings from the turn of the century. You know how that pisses me off. They're ruining this town Daisy and you *know* it, just like I know it!"

"If you agree to think about Gayle's office, then I'll think about Seattle. I've thought about it before on my own anyway, just in case you've ever wondered. I'm sick of Portland, too. I've always been on the outside. Because of my *name* of course, so you're not the *only* one who's damn tired of Bridge City."

"Okay baby, have some more pineapple. It's good for you and real tasty."

"Thanks."

"Who do you love?"

"Tab?!"

"Who do you love? Come on, spill it. Who takes care of you? Who puts up with your flip outs? Who punches old drunks who try to grab yer tits? What's that guy's name? What's his name, Daisy?" After a long pause you answer.

"His name is Tab."

Talionic Night in Portland: A Love Story

CHAPTER FIVE

Torch Tremble Begs

*S*TEPPING ONTO THE TWO CONCRETE stairs, which leads to the long narrow walkway, you finally reach your front door. You're holding two bags of groceries when Torch Tremble approaches and asks to borrow more food. This time she wants to know if she can "borrow" some meat. You sigh loudly and make no attempt to disguise your impatience. Torch is your neighbor and a faded punk rock musician whose time has come and gone. Yet, she still holds onto the punk persona of spiked black hair, blood red lipstick, *Coty* face powder, and blue frost eye shadow, along with an assortment of torn black rags covering her chunky frame that seems to define her entire punk look.

"I'm sorry, but I'm not a charity, Torch. You've never paid me back for all the *other* food you *borrowed*."

"Sorry, Daisy, I'm just having hard times lately. Hey, did you wanna hang out at my place later?"

"So we can get drunk again? No thanks. I appreciate the offer but *Pabst Blue Ribbon* really does a number on me. I can't drink the stuff, gives me a vicious headache."

"I'm sorry Daisy. I know you're like… a professional reporter and stuff."

Torch looks down, defeated. You can see the steel grey as it grows out from under her dyed black hair and suddenly you feel tenderly toward this old Has Been still lost in the delusions of the 1980s Portland punk scene. She looks up at you and you see she's applied too much rust colored blush, again. You stifle the urge to laugh because as you look down at her she looks so much like a female clown that it's almost too much to bear. You bite your cheek and smile warmly instead, tilting your head to the side, sympathetically.

"I'm not a reporter. I'm an assignment editor. It's worse; we have even *more* responsibilities and get paid significantly less. Listen; maybe later we can hang out. I might need your help with something." Torch has followed you and is behind you as you set both bags down. She brightens immediately at your words.

"Sure! You know I love hangin' out with you. And I'll help with anything. There's almost nothin' I *won't* do."

"Good. Because I'm gonna need some help with something, but it won't be for a few more weeks. I'll let you know."

"You can't tell me now?"

"I'm not sure you're right for the job, but you might be. It just all depends."

"You can count on me, Daisy. You know you're my only friend, here. You've helped me out more than once, when no one else would."

"I gotta go now Torch, but think about it."

"You really can't tell me?" You pause dramatically as you put the key in the lock and turn back around to face her.

"Well… I'm gonna go out on a limb here. All I can tell you is… there's this guy…"

"Yeah?!"

"Well, he's my ex. He's been stalking me. I may need some help in teaching him a lesson. He's got a house across town, in SW. I have the key. I used to work with him, but not anymore. It won't be now or even soon but maybe in a month or so. Can I trust you to keep your mouth shut?"

"You KNOW you can Daisy! Whoa! What kinda scum bag would harass someone as cool as you?"

"My ex. He used to beat me up, too. He's got… well, he's got some old photos."

"Like nudies?"

"Yeah, that's right… nudies. You sure are a sharp one, Torch."

"Well, I been around."

You wait and are pleased to see Torch's face harden and her eyes widen in anger. Now she's your best friend. She's been asked to help, to protect you—small, slender Daisy Rose. You lean over toward her, and place your hand on her left shoulder. You look down and heave a sigh, then look back at her, your violet blue eyes big, sad and pale in the late afternoon light.

"I knew I could count on you, Torch. Yeah, I'll be by tonight. I'll bring some wine."

"I'll make some crackers with Cheese Whiz and—and cut up some fruit!"

"Sounds good, Torch. Eight o'clock?"

She nods her head militantly, her mouth a hard line of resolve, pats your hand on her shoulder, turns and marches off. You wonder if she'll spend the next two hours preparing for your visit, sweeping, cleaning, mopping and spraying perfume around her apartment. Somehow you know she will.

∗∗∗∗

When you walk into Torch's apartment, with the floor plan identical to your own unit, and can see she's cleaned and dusted. Fresh lilacs, stolen from down the street have been arranged in pink and purple Northwood Carnival glass vases. She's put them on the kitchen counter and on her glass and cedar coffee table. An old style silver 1950s breakfast table glimmers under a bright orange hanging glass lamp and you see she's gone to a lot of trouble with the spread. Cheddar, Swiss and blue cheese are cut and stacked in loose piles, and there are fancy cream crackers, and all sorts of fruit and chips, black olives, macadamia nuts, roasted almonds, fresh sliced peaches and even a bowl of expensive pine nuts.

"Wow! You really went to a lot of trouble. It's a good thing I brought over a big bottle."

"Yeah, I sold some of my old clothes at that vintage shop on 28th and Burnside. They pay pretty good money, if it's the real deal from back in the day."

"Oh, you didn't have to do that, Torch?"

"Well, I felt bad about last time. When I only had that old cheese pizza to offer you? That's probably what upset your stomach. Don't you remember; you barfed in the toilet?"

"Oh yeah, and you held my hair for me?"

"Like a true friend would!"

"Well, I appreciate this Torch. I don't get out much, or have much fun with…"

Just then, Tab calls. *The Candy Shop* ring tone on your iPhone sounds loudly and you reach into your blazer and pull out your phone, smiling over at Torch, embarrassed.

"Isn't that song by Fifty Cent?"

"Well, yeah, it's just something I did on a lark."

"Bought it on the internet?"

"Yeah, from the internet."

Tab has wanted you to spend the night at his place more and more. It doesn't feel intrusive, just natural and easy, like how you always feel when you're with him. But there's a part of you that wants to test him, to see what he'll do or say if he thinks you're with someone else. You flip open your phone.

"Yeah? What is it?"

He tells you he's spoken to Ruby and they've both agreed a divorce is the right thing to do. Then he drops the bombshell. He's told Ruby about you, and even told her your name, though only your first name. He says she seemed okay with it, but now he's not so sure. Now, he's worried maybe he shouldn't have said anything because what if she calls Verona and tells *her*?

"You told RUBY you're seeing me? Jeez Tab, are you crazy?"

"I don't know baby, it just come out. I'm so proud of you honey. I guess I wanted to show her that it really is over. She told me she's got some old fart, some new guy she met playing Bingo at the community center, some disabled veteran or something. But I *know* she's been seeing my ex-brother-in-law, Stan. I wanted her to know I'm okay. I got me a *real* lady this time—not some floozie who swills cheap beer and smokes all day and night."

"Jesus Tab, how *could* you?"

"I'm sorry. Hey, where *are* you? You sound different."

"I'm at a friend's house... my friend Torch?"

"Torch? Is that a woman... or a man?"

"She's a woman. We're with friends."

"Friends? As in more than one?"

"Yeah, just sittin' around... shootin' the shit?"

"Shooting the *shit*? You've never used that expression *before* Daisy. What's going on?"

"I told you, we're just sittin' around... talking."

"Isn't Torch that prostitute neighbor of yours?"

"Jeez, Tab, that's not true, I never said that!"

"That's it! I'm comin' over! She's in unit D, right?!"

"Yeah, D, but you can't come over. This is like a girl's night out."

"Oh, no its not."

"Yes, it is, Tab!"

"Yeah, right!"

"Tab?!"

"I'm comin' over!"

You hang up the phone as soon as you hear Tab ask if he should bring over potato chips and Snapple. You feel giddy, reckless and excited. Something *is* happening. It's your growing addiction for Tab that may or may not be turning into a certain kind of love. But it's also the stress of having to work with Gayle. It's making you unstable and you're beginning to see you either need therapy, or to take Tab up on his offer and arrange the move to Seattle. Something has *got* to give and somehow you know it will.

You also know that the night you dream about *will* happen. That one dark night you and Tab *will* indeed bust into Gayle's office and wreak havoc on her cheap furniture and nauseating collection of tedious Danielle Steel novels. It's something that is becoming more goal oriented than merely a dream, and strangely, you're okay with that. There is no fear, no apprehension, just the knowledge that it will happen. You've thought out every detail. And when the night is over, you'll both be driving to Seattle long before anyone is notified, and long after the pancake batter has hardened and the spray paint and sulfuric acid has dried to a pale toxic crust.

You glance over at Torch, who is watching avidly. The look on her face is innocent yet conspiratorial. Suddenly, you regret your move. Torch is a tramp and has confided to you already that she's taken more than one guy from a girl. What if she tries that with you? No. Tab wouldn't be *that* crazy. Torch is over forty, burnt out and fleshy, with the bad skin of an old prostitute, and the grey disintegrating teeth of the poor. Still, it will be interesting to see what happens and, whether or not Tab gets jealous.

When you hear the strident knocking on Torch's unit, you know its Tab, come to investigate this new situation and drag you back to his place. Torch walks to the door and opens it aggressively. You know she half expects to see some short, skinny bespectacled college professor or loser TV producer type standing there. That's not what happens, though. That's not what she sees. When the door flings open, you're not surprised as Torch's jaw drops and her eyes widen in dismay. It's the sight of Tab. She gazes at him, open mouthed as he stands there bathed in that glorious yellow halo that follows him everywhere, like the persistent aura of a sunny Easter morning. He's dressed in his new corduroy's and the new chiffon-yellow Ralph Lauren polo shirt you bought for him. His eyes are open wider than normal, the pupils dilated. He glances at Torch briefly and looks past her, into the dim apartment, preoccupied, searching for you.

"Where's my girl, Daisy?" Tab demands in a terse voice.

Torch turns, and looks back at you, then mouths: "Oh My God!" to indicate she's shocked at how good looking Tab is. Looking at Torch as she turns back to Tab, you lean back imperceptibly into the overstuffed chair, and with the calculated logic of a predator lizard, you realize you've had enough and will now introduce Tab as… your boyfriend. You have to—you have no choice. You stand up, walk over and introduce him.

"Hey Tab, this is my neighbor Torch. We're just having a little picnic inside with some wine and goodies. Torch, this is Tab, my… boyfriend!" Tab steps inside as Torch opens her arms in a welcoming gesture. Her face communicates instant disappointment. She closes the door and turns into the living room, motioning for him to find a seat.

Your casual words were not lost on Tab. As you walk back to the chair and sit down, crossing your legs seductively, his eyes follow you. His eyes soften and he smiles at you dreamily as you sit there, gazing up at him with a nonchalant expression on your face. Torch doesn't understand the significance of the moment and seems confused when Tab doesn't look away, but instead continues to gaze at you with love in his eyes. You smile in spite of yourself as Tab approaches, and bends to kiss your cheek. His mouth lingers near your temple and you know he's breathing in the smell of your hair and neck. He turns to Torch perfunctorily, and thanks her.

"Torch? Nice to meet you. I've heard of you. It's nice to meet a friend of my Daisy. This sure is a nice picnic you've got here!"

"Oh, please have some; it's some of the stuff I know *Daisy* likes. *She* brought the wine."

"Yes, I brought the wine, Tab, and the food is just delicious—all exotic little tidbits that anyone would love." You smile becomingly and tilt your head flirtatiously. You're teasing Tab and enjoying it. He seems to know, but doesn't care. He's delirious with happiness only because you called him your boyfriend.

For the next hour, he digs into the food and compliments Torch incessantly about how delicious everything is. You move to the sofa and snuggle next to Tab, leaning your head on his hard shoulder, and listen to Torch brag about her days when she was a singer with a punk band called *The Rose City Wankers*. She's brought out a big photo album and crowds herself next to Tab as you sit on her stained, brown faux leather sofa, with Tab ensconced between you. You can tell Torch is jealous. She wants a man just like Tab for herself and now you're starting to feel secretly irritated. What nerve you think, and after everything you've done for the annoying little nitwit. After over an hour of Torch flipping through one photograph after another, and Tab being polite and "Oooooing" and "Ahhhing" over her short lived career, and blurry Lloyd Center *Glamour Shot* photos, you tell Torch that you and Tab really need to get home.

"Are you sure you wanna go, Daisy? I mean, you can both stay over? You know we could have fun together... just the three of us?" You ignore the suggestion, smiling sweetly and looking away.

"Oh, that's so generous Torch, but I'm just beat. Maybe another time? Hey, this has been great. You take care. I'll call you soon, okay?"

Tab looks confused and doesn't quite get it. He doesn't understand that Torch just suggested you all have a threesome. You know Torch would be thrilled to get naked with you, especially if it meant she could crawl under Tab and kick you off the bed. The thought fills you with a quiet rage, and you feel the pressing urge to get to Tab's place and into a hot soapy bath and then into bed as quickly as possible. The time will come for you to contact Torch again, but it won't be for a while. And in the end, you see the value of paying her. A good $300 in cash stuffed in an envelope would be a fitting way to help her feel less used, and you in no way beholden to her.

You walk out the door with Tab behind you, onto the stoop, and turn to see Torch standing in her bare stocking feet, her black tights torn and fashionably ripped... for 1983. Her oversize black baby doll dress is higher in the back than the front and the hem is coming out with frayed threads hanging forlornly just above her thick dimpled knees, which you notice is the exact color of maggot flesh. You notice her dark pits; the perspiration soaking through the black cotton pullover she's wearing. Her red lipstick has gathered in the corners of her mouth and there's a thick smear of it across her two front teeth. You stifle the urge to laugh by biting your tongue, and smiling instead.

"Hey, thanks Torch. This has been fun. I'll be in touch."

"Yeah, *anything* you want Daisy. And I'll help you with that *thing* we talked about earlier. Absolutely, you know you can count on *me!*"

You smile, turn and wave goodbye, and walk with Tab to the truck where you stand for several minutes talking in hushed tones. You can see he's amused. Somehow he knows it was a ruse to make him jealous, and you can tell he's excited and looking forward to getting you back to his place so he can get you undressed and onto his California King.

"You just wanted to get my blood up, didn't you, Daisy?"

"I have no idea *what* you're talking about."

"Lying is not a good thing, baby. It can ruin a relationship. You need to remember that."

"Tab, I'm not lying…I'm…"

"Yes, baby?"

"And coming from *you*, that's kind of a funny thing to say. You've had lots of experience with lying, haven't you?"

"Yes, I have, so I can recognize it. I don't want that for us. Not now. I'm past that kind of thing. I'm just too old for it anymore."

"Well, okay, maybe it was a little bit of a game. I was bored and you didn't call me yesterday, remember?"

"I was beat from work. One of the eighth grade girls locked herself in the smaller bathroom near the back of the school, and I had to go with the gym teacher and pull her out by her ankles. She was threatening to kill herself because she thought she was fat. It was a total scene, just awful."

"Oh, my God, really?"

"Screaming, yelling, on her hands and knees, hysterical, wouldn't get up. Then after the gym teacher got her to calm down, she proceeded to puke all over my work boots. I told Jim I was gonna quit. I just walked out."

"Jim?"

"Yeah, the gym teacher. After the ambulance came and carted her off to the hospital Jim ran to get the principal to come in and talk me down as I was hosing down my boots in the back, by the tool shed. Took Mr. Klee a good half hour to get me to agree to stay on the job, and a crisp one hundred dollar bill from his very own wallet."

"Oh, Tab! That's horrible."

"Yeah, it was. Just another day at the office, I guess. Let's focus on the present, though. I made a low fat tuna casserole and pear spinach salad for dinner. We'll have a nice long Saturday morning in bed, okay? I wanna sleep in. And then I'll take us to breakfast at the Pancake House. Maybe we'll run into Gus Van Sant, again."

"When did we see Gus Van Sant?"

"Never, but that's the rumor I hear—that he goes there."

"You know it's funny you called. I was starting to worry she was gonna hold me hostage. I'm really glad you called. She kinda gives me the creeps." You laugh mildly and look over at Tab as he unlocks the passenger door to his Ford truck.

"You said I was your boyfriend. You've never done that before. You're starting to love me, aren't ya, baby?

"Maybe a little."

"Nah, I'd say more than only a little."

"Shut up, Tab."

"Sure, baby. Sure. Anything you say."

CHAPTER SIX

Strident Declarations of Color

S ITTING AT YOUR DESK YOU hear the distant roar of Gayle yelling in her office. She's arguing with her interior decorator about her house, which is always in the process of some new renovation or repair. The monstrosity that is her home is all about being pink and grey, not quite as bad as Jayne Mansfield's *Pink Palace* but definitely close.

"What in the hell do you MEAN 'strident declarations of Color' would benefit the living room? Who are *you* to judge me that I like only pastels? That's not your job, Maurice! That's not what I'm *paying* you for!"

Gayle stomps to her office door and slams it shut. You continue to hear her muffled obscenities as they drift under the door jamb and her clicking heels as she paces across the tiled front entrance of her office, avoiding the carpeted sections so she can stomp and make noise. You hope she slips and breaks her neck as you sit alone with your elbows on the desk and your face slumped into your palms. You smile evilly, envisioning her like a fish out of water, dying of oxygen deprivation while she does "the chicken" on the floor. In the fantasy she's clutching her throat, shitting her pants and twitching pathetically in violent death throes, before finally croaking, her eyes locked in Optical Poptitude as her corpse cools on the floor. You snicker to yourself—oh if only.

Earlier in the day she called you into her office and as you stood there, trying once again to explain the importance of working collaboratively *with* the other TV stations and newspapers, she barked that you weren't paid to *think* but just to do what she tells you. That and to keep the young reporters in line and on task. At the very moment she was wiping a stray string of spittle from her oily chin, her daughter Mary Jennifer called. You listened to her weeping daughter as a resolute part of yourself promised the girl you would at least meet with her one day and warn her about her demented mother. That it would never be worth it to try to please such an impossibly narcissistic woman. And that she would have to escape Gayle's toxic influence once and for all if she ever wanted a chance at happiness or at least peace of mind, or any form of muted, medicated contentment in this world.

As you listened, you were able to ascertain that Mary Jennifer was distressed over some issue involving a young man she had a class with, but of course you couldn't pick up all the specifics. Gayle was impatient as usual and finally told Mary Jennifer she'd have to call her later, that she was busy making money to pay for her university education and all her psychotherapy bills. You cringed as you watched Gayle slam down the telephone receiver while her daughter continued to fret and weep. And then there was the melancholy silence of the line going dead.

Taking a deep breath, you had walked to the left of her desk, and plopped down on the mauve sofa next to it, as you began plotting effortlessly, like water passing over a polished black stone. It was instantaneous and the cold clarity of it surprised you. You wondered why you hadn't thought of it before. If you could convince Gayle that you sympathized with her, and get her to talk about Mary Jennifer, then you might be one step closer to finding out where the girl lives and goes to school, being that Gayle never discloses that kind of specific information about her daughter. You inhale deeply, feeling somewhat thrilled to be taking such a risk. You relish the premeditation of it, the boldness of it— the sneakiness. You'll be offering an angle to Gayle that she would never think to suspect is untrue. And you know you're doing it for the right reasons—for that poor child Mary Jennifer, named after a dead girl.

You begin speaking: "Kids; I don't know how parents do it, today. My aunt Colleen has three kids and she's always complaining about how she has no freedom and they use up all her resources, you know, all her money? Sometimes I'm glad I never had kids. It must be tough."

Gayle looks at you suspiciously, but she's surprised, too. There's a part of her that *wants* to unload the guilt she drags around with her, knowing on some deep primal level that *she's* the reason her daughter is such a mess. You sigh, stretch your legs and run your hands through your hair as you lean back and continue speaking.

"I have a cousin, Melody? She's a few years older than me. She had a kid, turned out he had learning disabilities. She gave him up for adoption when he was three. Later, she found out he turned into a criminal. She told my mother just the other day: 'I'm sure glad I dodged *that* bullet!' Gayle watches you, you know she wants to confide in you, but she's not sure. She's teetering on the edge, so tempted but still uncertain to take that precarious leap.

"I never knew you felt that way, Daisy. But it makes sense, considering what I hear from everyone at the office. They say you don't date since your divorce— when was that, about 2003, right?"

"Yeah, it was 2003, not my favorite year."

"I don't blame you. Men are pond scum. At least you have peace of mind. And parenthood is a chore. I've *never* enjoyed it."

"My ex and I are both better off. I can't imagine the sense of *crushing* responsibility of being a parent. That's what would really kill *me*, I think."

Gayle looks at you with a sidelong glance. She wants to say something but still she's just not certain she *can* trust you. You have to make her feel she can trust you, though. You have to make her think it was a sincere and genuine admission, something spur of the moment and real. You have to stop talking about it, and *end* the discussion.

"Well, anyhow Gayle, I should probably get going. I really gotta do that school thing? For the high school kids at Lincoln? You can't get Tiffy or Helen to do it?"

"No. It has to be you. You're more attractive Daisy, besides you know what a kick people get once you tell them your name." You cringe and fight the desire to pop Gale in the mouth.

"I was just hoping someone else could do it."

"Nah, Daisy, it hasta be you. But we can… we can, you know, talk later?"

"Okay, gotta run. Hey, do you know by chance if that intern finished the story on that *bumicide* down under the Burnside Bridge? If not, I'll give her a call and tell her to step up on the filming and editing. Citizens are already calling in and asking about that one."

"I haven't heard yet, but I'll send you a memo when I find out. I'm probably going to be leaving early today. Maurice and I have been having problems with the new living room renovation."

"Okay, Gayle, I'll head out now."

"Yeah, that little presentation thing at Lincoln has gotta get done. One of the parents is a neighbor of mine and I don't want Tiffy doing it, you know she has no poise, and Helen's just too damn old to make a good impression. I need *you* there Daisy. Everyone seems to like you, anyway."

"Okay, I'm on it."

As you walk out of Gayle's office, a part of you feels infinitely smug. She fell for it. You're a better actress than you thought. Sooner or later, in one way or another, you'll find out where Mary Jennifer lives.

Driving across town to Lincoln high school you feel a positive surging confidence in yourself that makes you sit up straighter and grin wildly as you drive too fast, flying across the Hawthorne Bridge in your new "pre-owned" Lexus with the rose leather interior. The class demographic is a group of juniors and seniors. A couple of them are writers for *The Cardinal Times* school newspaper and they want to get into either TV reporting or become journalists of some sort. You're going to give them a prep talk about what it's like working in TV news. You're going to encourage them all to stay in school, go on to college and take the world by storm, becoming productive members of society, who pull their own weight and "give back" by contributing to their community and happily doing service work.

You walk into the classroom and can immediately tell that none of these kids has ever gone without, not in any real concrete sense. They're all either blond, red or auburn haired with blotchy freckle stained faces, designer clothing, and metal in their mouths. And it's clear they're about as in touch with the real world as Leona Helmsley was in touch with the importance of honestly doing her taxes.

You approach the front of the classroom and set down your *Fossil* purse on an empty desk to the left, just as the teacher smiles and welcomes you to the class with a graceful wave of her hand and a few kind soft spoken words. The students look over at you eagerly, hungry for any information you might have about the glamorous world of TV news and journalism. And in Portland, Oregon, no less! But suddenly you feel naked and realize your lipstick is fading. Your presentation won't go well if you're not behind the mask, and a thick layer of lipstick always calms you. You excuse yourself briefly to go to the restroom down the hall. As you enter the dim restroom you see a tall, emaciated blond girl from another class. She's sporting a severe bob and covered in makeup. She's bending over the sink, and touching up her rose-beige lip gloss with a long wand, dabbing it into the gloss container daintily and smearing it across her mouth in a thick layer. She talks to her equally blond friend, who stands to her right, her arms crossed over her chest and a bored look on her face. As you walk toward the large mirror to the left of them, to apply a fresh layer of peach frost lipstick, the first girl complains to her friend.

"I hate my fucking MOM. She's *such* a slut. A fucking whore, really!"

"Why do you say that? She seems pretty nice."

"She's fucking cheating on my Dad again. I hate her guts."

"Wow. I wouldn't know about that kinda stuff. My parents are divorced."

You cringe as the two girls continue to talk, seemingly oblivious to your presence only feet away. You look down, close your eyes tightly, and take a deep breath, hating the sight of both of them. Tucking your Lancôme lipstick into your purse you walk back to the classroom feeling grateful you never had to attend such a fucked up high school as Lincoln.

You stand in front of the students and answer questions for ten minutes, giving them the conventional rehearsed answers you know you should about colleges and journalism and communication majors. You end the presentation by delivering the speech you now know by heart, inspired only by your bitterness and cynicism, the speech you've been working on for months, waiting for just this chance:

"As for being a TV news assignment editor, think CHEF. The good ones manage to balance competing elements to create a satisfying sense of place. They largely decide what gets covered after judging story ideas from reporters, show producers,

46

news managers—even tips from the public. The assignment editor puts reporters on task, keeping in mind the time and effort needed to get the story investigated, photographed, written, reviewed and produced with graphics in time to reach the air. This is hard work if you refuse to take the easy way out—meaning you make that extra phone call, you develop another source, you follow another fresh lead, so you can satisfy your skepticism before finally saying: "It's ready!" Along the way too many news operations from the top down are satisfied with stealing the contents of the local newspapers front page. This is called a Rip-N-Read. This kind of news leads to sloppiness, rumor mongering, and propagandizing without any penalties for those sins. Distressing, too, is the fact that we see TV news with too many under-trained people more interested in becoming colorful TV news actors than in making sense of a confusing and dangerous world. As a result, we're not seeing a chef at work, only a hack with an uncritical bunch of line-cooks turning out cheeseburgers! With the decline of the print newspaper there's a shrinking pool of material for these characters to steal from, and unfortunately, that's the truth! So, you have to ask yourself kids, do you wanna be a CHEF or a line-cook churning out cheeseburgers?"

You take a deep breath and sigh heavily. You're world weary but you're still young enough, thin enough and well-dressed enough to project the image of a totally with-it hipster. It helps that you *know* you look great. As you gaze out at the teens sitting around spellbound and silent, you realize the students don't know what the hell you're talking about. You feel satisfied being able to unload on them, and get some of what you *really* think off your chest. Fuck the pimply little bastards, they'll find out soon enough their lives are doomed. You glance over at the young auburn haired teacher and are pleased to see the look of confusion and utter fright plastered on her pretty painted face.

You reach over for your purse, smile and say: "Thanks kids! This has been great! Hope ya learned sumthin!" No one moves. No one says anything. You could hear a pin drop. Then a loud chorus of heavy applause breaks out just as soon as you turn your back and waltz out the classroom door. You flip your hair over your shoulder as a smug goodbye just before the door slams shut. You can still hear them applauding as you turn the corner and head out the front door toward Salmon Street.

Talionic Night in Portland: A Love Story

CHAPTER SEVEN

Silent and Ashamed

*Y*OUR HAND IS A BALLED-UP FIST as you pound on the door. Is it even necessary to do that, since he knows you're coming? You hear Tab jog over in his bare feet. The door swings open quickly with a swoosh and Tab looms impressively in the doorway, standing just behind the threshold. The golden light from the vintage Alfred Chambon floor lamp behind him darkens his face, and illuminates his yellow hair making it seem as if a halo is floating just above his head. He looks like some kind of ascending Angel as you prepare to stumble inside, exhausted.

It's late again, after midnight, because once again you had to edit a story at the station until long after your shift, before heading over to Gayle's second office downtown to discuss the details and when it would be aired. You step over the threshold and stand there, dropping your purse to the floor with a soft thud. You look up at Tab and before you know it, your hands are firmly pressed over your mouth. Your eyes sting as you burst into tears on the spot, silent and ashamed. You look up at Tab, and then down at the floor and then back up, not knowing what to do or say. Frantic eyes search the room, trying in some way to convey something you can't verbalize. The growing sensation of panic rises steadily. It's surging up toward your sternum in waves and you don't know why. Fat tears make their way down, drifting over your thin fingers. The tears wet your sparkling nails done up in gold frost polish and filed to a sinister point only that afternoon at the nail salon—because you always have to look your best and the technician suggested you try a different look: "Something a little Cruella de Vil!" she had said with a cackle that made your skin break out in goose bumps. You choke out his name. It comes out in a broken sob. You look up at Tab, and see the searing concern spread across his face. His eyes are wild with it.

"Jesus, baby, what is it? Are you hurt? What's happened?"

"I don't...I don't know how to..."

"Come inside, sugar, let's get you inside."

Tab grabs your wrist and forearm with both hands, and pulls you to him like a rope. Reaching behind you, he closes the door, turns the deadbolt and latches the chain lock in one deft motion. He turns back to you quickly, his eyes focused and intense, his hands gripping your shoulders to steady you. He leans forward, bent over, searching your face, looking over your body as if to find the cause of your distress. Your hands drop and you fall into him. His body feels as substantial as a newly shaven log, immovable and set in stone. You grasp him around the waist, pressing your wet face sidelong onto his bare chest, and into the blond-grey hair that covers it like a carpet. Still, you make no sound as you grip him with both arms. Tab returns your embrace, fiercely pulling you to him, crushing your collarbone and neck as he presses into you. He supports the back of your head with his right hand, gripping your hair in his fist. His arms are all around you, moving fluidly, encompassing you like a curious octopus trying to gain leverage.

"Is it the panic again, Daisy? Is it the fear?"

"I—I don't know what it's about. I'm sorry."

"Don't *ever* apologize for something like this. That's what I'm here for. To be the man you lean on. Let's get you into a bath."

"Okay. But I think I should tell you something. I hope you won't be angry. This isn't like me, but I... I need to get this out."

"I'm here? I'm listening?"

"I think... Oh, God! I'm starting to love you!"

"Daisy, is that what this is all about? That's it?"

"I know it sounds like the most pathetic cliché. And it is, it's so fucking pathetic, but I'm scared. I can't go through another... my ex and what he did to me? I just can't..."

"Come on, baby. Let's get you out of your clothes and into a bath."

Tab directs you down the hall and into his squeaky clean bathroom. You stumble against him, following, sniffing and hiccupping. Your arms are still around his waist, hanging on as you dog his steps awkwardly, whispering apologies over and over— hating yourself.

"I'm no good, Tab. You'll discover that soon enough—that I'm just no good! I'm all messed up inside, all tangled up. I promise you, there's a lot wrong with me."

"Stop it, Daisy."

"It's true, Tab, I'm... "

"Now, I said *stop* it!"

"Don't waste your time on me. Look at me; I'm almost forty and a complete failure!"

"Daisy! You won't be forty for another three years! You are *not* a failure. Jeez, honey, what are you so *worried* about?"

"Well, if you must know, I'm worried about the future. You talk about

Seattle, and I'm tempted. I'm really tempted but… there are so many considerations. And then, well, you know I've just *got* to help that girl. I've just got to! Gayle's daughter?"

"Yeah, I know who the girl is. Okay, listen. Everything's gonna be fine. Let's just get you into your bath and get some food into you. You'll be as right as Portland rain after that."

"Are you *sure* everything's gonna be okay? Ruby and Verona won't come after us?"

"No."

"No?"

"No! I'll have them arrested if they try *anything*. Trust me; I'm not gonna let those two psychos hurt you. They're *not* gonna jeopardize our future, baby. Listen, you're probably my last *real* chance at happiness. I *want* you! I want you more than I ever wanted either of *them* or any woman for that matter… heck, even more than Blanche!"

"Really? Even more than Blanche?"

"Even more than Blanche."

"Wow…I never thought I'd hear you…"

"Would you just *stop* that kinda talk?"

"I'm sorry, but I told you I'm no good, didn't I?"

"Enough with that!"

Tab begins to undress you, and you raise your arms so he can pull off your sweater. You step out of your slacks as he pulls them down to your ankles, nudging them aside with his foot. Still behind you, he loosens the clasp to your bra and leans down to kiss your neck and murmur *baby-baby* into your ear as he pulls it off, tossing it on the white wicker chair next to the table. He reaches around and kisses your neck and temple. His left arm wraps around your waist, as his right arm drifts over your chest, locking you within his long gorilla arms. You lean into him, dizzy and vague. Tab turns you around, his hands on your shoulders and helps you step into the bathwater, steaming and bluish opaque from the bath milk he bought the previous week. You ease into the hot water and start feeling your sense of equilibrium returning. You exhale a long shuddering sigh and the sense of relief you feel being with Tab is palpable as you watch him pour body wash on the Loofah, gently push your hair aside, and start in on your arms and back.

Tab is uncharacteristically silent as he gently moves the loofah across your back in circular motions, and suddenly you feel ashamed again, unworthy of his attention. What were you thinking dropping in on him like this to unload your childish insecurities, and after he'd worked a full day? What if another girl tried to kill herself, and Tab and the gym teacher, Jim, had to pull her out of the bathroom stall by her ankles, and stuff her into another waiting ambulance?

What if he'd been mistaken for the janitor, again, by another snickering student?

You drop your head and sob silently, your shoulders hunched and shaking with the effort of containing an avalanche of accumulated sorrow and fear. Tab stops scrubbing and drops the loofah into the water between your knees where it lands with a wet plop. Your vision is blurred but you focus on his huge hands. You focus on the sensation and the visual of both of his hands. His left hand rests on your right thigh, while his right hand cups your left knee. He says nothing as you continue to weep and gaze at his beautiful hands in front of you. You can't remember ever seeing hands quite as exquisite.

"You have *such* beautiful hands, Tab."

"My... hands?"

"Yes! You have beautiful hands!"

"Have you... been drinking, Daisy?"

"I... I don't think so?"

"You don't *think* so?"

"You know, you don't always have to do this. I'll love you anyway, even if you don't. I know it must get to be a burden, thinking that *every* time I come over, you have to... to... do this, give me a bath and everything... feed me?"

"Don't worry about it, I enjoy doing it. Stop fretting, Daisy Rose. Besides, I like seein' you naked. I enjoy the privilege of lookin' at your little shapely body. You give me everything I want. You never say no, you're not a nag, and you don't *talk* my ear off all the damn time. You have *no* idea how much I appreciate that."

"I don't like conflict, either. Not really, anyway. I *try* to get along?"

"I know you do, baby."

"I guess I'm not really much of a drinker, either. Helen asked me out for drinks after work and, I hadn't eaten. I don't know why I went with her. I only had two but I guess I've just always been a lightweight. I'm sorry to stress you out like this, coming over half drunk. And I drove, too. I *shouldn't* have. I shoulda called a cab."

"Yes, you *should* have called a cab or me. Just don't do it again, okay?"

"Okay. I promise. I promise I'll never do it again."

"Good. But no, you're not stressing me out. It's Ruby and Verona who took the enthusiasm right outa me."

"Really?"

"Yep. That is until *you* came along. In a very real sense you restored me, Daisy."

"Do you mean that?"

"You bet I do. I was gonna swear off women for a while, thinking they were all disagreeable control freaks. Like Ruby and Verona and even my ex-wife

Brandi. But you're not like them at all. You're easy going, sweet, and agreeable... for the most part. And that's what I need. At my age, I need someone like *you* Daisy Rose."

"I like it when you call me Daisy Rose... cause I know you mean it. I know you're not just makin' fun of me—makin' fun of my name."

"Why would I? Your name is not a joke to *me* precious girl. It's beautiful and besides, I was named after Tab Hunter, so... I *get* it. "

"I don't know *why* it makes me feel so guilty when you do this for me. You're just always so good to me and..."

"And why wouldn't I wanna treat you right?"

"I just want you to know that... if you ever got sick; I'd take care of you. You know that, right? If you ever *did* get sick, Tab, I'd take care of you."

"I know you would. I believe you, honey."

"Okay. I just want you to know that."

"Here, lemme help ya up. It's time for bad girls to go to bed."

"Oh Tab!"

You reach over and grasp Tab's hands as he pulls you up. He wraps the big burgundy towel around your body, and prepares to hoist you into his arms. You look up at him with chastened, adoring eyes, the tears still glistening on your dark eyelashes.

"I'm going to carry you to bed. You're going to feel better in no time. I'll bring you the rest of that spinach pear salad I made the other night. It's still good and fresh."

You sit Indian style in the middle of Tab's California king, with the salad bowl resting on a pillow in your lap, and stab the spinach leaves with a fork, eating them and looking over at Tab as he watches you.

"I like to watch you eat, baby. You know you really *are* a little too thin."

You smile and say nothing in response. He's sitting in the chair next to the bed, leaning back with that magnanimous paternal smile on his face. Neither of you say anything while you continue to eat, eagerly digging into the salad, hunting for the sugared walnuts and big chunks of Gorgonzola cheese covered in tangy raspberry vinaigrette.

"You always seem to know what I like."

"I do. I *do* know what you like."

When every last morsel of the salad is gone, you hand Tab the large bowl without a word, scoot off the bed, and walk naked into the bathroom. He watches appreciatively, leaning forward, smiling and preparing to rise from the chair. After you brush your teeth with his tooth brush, *you* spray the bottle of *Red Door* perfume you keep at his place all over your neck and breasts in a faint mist. You brush your dark ringlets down your back, pad into the bedroom and crawl onto his huge bed, pulling the comforter over you. Tab flicks off the light, as he stands in the shadows. In the dim light he unhooks the buttons to his jeans, and pulls them off. He drops them to the floor, where they land with a gentle swoosh. He crawls onto the bed, lifting up the comforter and crawling under. He's on his left side, facing you, his head on the pillow. His smiling topaz eyes, like beaten gold coins sparkle with that interior light that seems to emanate from every gold cell in his body. Tab could not be happier and you know why. Your sudden tears and inexplicable fear were all the confirmation he needed. He reaches over and kisses the tip of your nose, the only man to ever do that to you, in all your life. Then he rolls away, laying back, a smug smile gentle on his mouth.

"Crawl over to me, baby. You come to *me*, now," Tab whispers smoothly.

You scoot over and settle within the circumference of his wide arm span. His hands stroke and squeeze your thin shoulders, and cup your small breasts, and he smiles, dreamy and sensuous. After a moment, he leans back on the pillow, once again putting a small distance between himself and you. He smiles, waiting for you to inch closer and find his mouth with yours. You take the hint and silently lean in, turning onto your knees.

"You don't want to lose old Tab here, do ya?"

"No, I don't."

"How much do you love me, baby?"

"Soooo much!" you murmur. You're becoming delirious and drunkenly vague. Leaning into him, still on your knees; with your back arched, you try to place your lips over his, only millimeters away from his mouth. He turns his head away, just out of reach, teasing you.

"Do you love me enough to beg?" Tab asks with his head turned away from you and the coy smile still on his mouth.

"I'll do whatever you want. I promise. Just tell me what to do."

"Okay, then. I want you to beg. Beg, Daisy girl. Beg."

You beg, you whine and plead—you giggle and whisper. You breathe out the words he wants to hear. Begging excites him. His breathing picks up and he pulls himself up and lays over you, covering your hips with a long heavy leg, as his mouth presses hard against yours. His tongue pushes inside, insistent, sweet, bubble gum pink.

CHAPTER EIGHT

Blaze Handle Sells Drugs

*Y*OU'RE WALKING TO YOUR CAR, trying to get to work before Gayle pounds into the office at 9:15, when you notice Blaze jogging down the block to hassle you again. Blaze Handle is a young white boy of about seventeen. He has lanky ginger hair and ashen grey skin that makes you think of rickets, kidney failure and other tragic childhood diseases. He fancies himself the neighborhood coke pusher, but you've never seen *any* evidence of this. Blaze is determined to get you to buy some of his "product" promising you that its quality stuff and will actually enhance your life, your working career and even your health. You've heard it all before, but decide today you'll have to take a different tactic if he becomes excessively pushy again.

"Hey beautiful, how's it hanging?"

"Blaze? I mean Howard? I've told you before I'm not interested in any of your "vitamins." You're just going to have to get used to it. Why don't you hassle Torch? She's always looking for company."

"What makes you think I haven't tapped that old fart, already?"

"Howard, I'm just not interested, and really, you shouldn't talk about her like that. She's told me she thinks you're cute. She could be your girlfriend!"

"Yeah well, I've already got a grandma. And stop callin' me Howard, I've told you my name. Just call me Blaze, like everyone else."

"Okaaay! Blaze it is."

"You know, I don't appreciate you snoopin' around about me and my mom either by the way. Some people get killed fer that kinda shit."

"It wasn't hard. I just made a phone call Blaze, and found out you and your mother's vital statistics. It was easy as pie, really."

"Yeah, well you better keep yer mouth shut about my name. I got a reputation to protect around here."

"Around *here*? You mean SE *Portland*?"

"Yeah, this is my hood, or didn't you know that?"

"Oh come on, all I've seen you do is sell a little weed from time to time. You don't have any real coke connections. I'd know if you did. I *was* a reporter before I became an assignment editor, you know. I can smell bullshit when I see bullshit, especially when that bullshit is standing right in front of me."

"Why do you think yer better-n-me Miss DAISY?!"

"I've never once done or said anything to give you that idea, but I *am* old enough to be your mother and in my book that's not cool. I'm not a cradle robber, son. So, you really need to put the idea *out* of your head, cause it's never gonna happen."

"What's up with that? I never done nothin' to make you..."

"Oh yes you have. The flirting? The constant innuendo?"

"Enu-what? What are you talkin' about?"

"Seriously Blaze, you're a child to me."

"I ain't no child, I'm a MAN!"

"Right. Listen; do you want me to bring my boyfriend around here to have a word with you? I'll do that if you want. I'd be happy to."

"You don't even *have* a boyfriend. You're always alone when I seen ya."

"Actually, I do. He's about seven inches taller than you, and about seventy pounds heavier, and it's not fat that makes him heavier, its solid muscle."

"What is he like some college kid you picked up at PSU campus er sumthin? Some guy my age?"

"Not even. He's FIFTY TWO Blaze. Old, like me. You've seen him, he's the maintenance man who comes by periodically to fix toilets and spray for bugs. The blond guy who looks like a body builder? The one who's always in overalls? He's my boyfriend. THAT guy."

"You mean TAB? The maintenance dude, Tab? Shit man, that's the fucker that punched my uncle Darrell out cold when he was homeless fer awhile, livin' over by the Taco Bell! Tab? I don't believe it. Not for one minute. You'd never be boinking... that dude?"

"Its true Blaze. He's my old man now and if you don't stop hassling me, I'll have him visit the manager of the apartments here and have a chat. About *you* and your mom? What's the manager's name again? I think it's Adarsh, right? From the East Indian family? He's such a nice guy, so professional and friendly. And a real stickler for the rules as I recall."

"Come on Daisy, I was just kiddin' wit ya. Shit man, can't you take a joke? I just like to hassle you sometimes, cuz you're cute, for like, an older lady and stuff."

"I knew you'd come to your senses. Listen, maybe if you're a nice boy, Tab and I might invite you and your mom over for dinner sometime, but right now I have to get to work. Its 8:38, or didn't you notice? I haven't even had my coffee yet. Don't you crave a hot cup of coffee this early in the morning?"

"Nah, I generally drink somethin' else, even *this* early. Somethin' a little stronger."

"Is that right?"

"Yeah! Anyway, it was nice chattin' wit ya. I'll tell Mama you say hello."

"You give Penny my love. She's good people."

"Yeah, whatever."

"That's right, Howard."

As you walk to your car, and open the door, you smile at how easy it was to get Blaze off your back. You should have decided to play hardball sooner. You think the next time Tab comes over in the daytime you'll make a point to hang around out front, canoodling in the off chance Blaze might walk by and see you straddling Tab, sitting on his lap in the cab of his truck, and Frenching in public. The thought of Blaze seeing you with Tab, lying across his lap with the door open and Tab's legs spilling out onto the street in all their beautiful long legged, jack-booted glory gives you a delicious tickle. Then you remember the magazine article you read that stated women lose sixty percent of their authority once people learn who they're fucking, but that's only in a professional setting, so it wouldn't really apply to Blaze, or would it?

As you drive north, you notice the homeless man who tried to grab your breast stumbling down the street heading south. He's wearing the same filthy green army jacket and torn up Nike sneakers. You idle by the corner and watch as Blaze runs up and hands the old man some crumpled up cash. They turn around and begin ambling north, and you realize the man must be the "Uncle Darrell" Blaze was talking about. You also realize they're probably going to walk to the local *Plaid Pantry* on Division and buy a bottle of either fortified wine or *Old English 800* to start the day—*breakfast of champions* you think to yourself, cynically.

Though Blaze wants people to believe he's an up and coming drug pusher, the reality is, he's turning into a drunk like his mother Penny and apparently his uncle Darrell. As a high school dropout Blaze has been diagnosed with a learning disability and he and his mother live well enough on two disability payments and food stamps. This allows them both ample time to drink and loiter and con passersby for "short term loans" as Blaze calls them. They do this so they can buy groceries since they're not "eligible" for food stamps, even though they are and you've seen them many times in the Plaid, handing over their EBT card for expensive chocolate bars and cans of chili and black olives.

You shake your head while contemplating Blaze's indefatigable optimism and complete inability to think of the future and actually use his time on earth to accomplish something worthwhile. His only real concern is in staying in supply of cheap booze for his beloved mother. Penny is a vague, sweet tempered woman in her fifties, with a mop of white hair. She's lived most of her life as a victim of domestic violence and predatory men, and she also happens to be completely deaf. She reads lips and she and Blaze know American Sign

Language, which totally surprised you when you first saw them doing it.

The good news, if you can look at it that way, is that now Penny is missing most of her front teeth and so undesirable looking that even homeless men don't want anything to do with her. Her son Blaze acts as her doting servant and fierce protector. Her only real agenda is keeping their little apartment spick and span and entertaining herself while making the one meal of the day—supper, for she and her son. You've discovered it's usually something good like homemade beef stew or Jambalaya with lots of paprika and sautéed onions and Bell peppers. You've watched them for over a year now and realize they are doting companions and that as long as Penny has Blaze to make sure she doesn't get involved with any possible "stepfathers" then she and Blaze will likely do just fine.

Maybe sometime this week, you'll make a quick three cheese Lasagna for Penny and bring it over when you know Blaze is home for the night. If you could show him that you're not the enemy and extend a simple kindness to his lush mother, then perhaps he might back off and stop bothering you every time you walk out your front door. Because the reality is, if it's not Blaze, then it's Torch and frankly, you're sick of it.

You had thought the Clinton Court Apartments were charming when you drove by them three years ago, but it only took about six weeks after moving in to notice the water marks slowly appearing on the ceiling, the leaking faucet in the kitchen sink, the loose cabinet doors and the slugs as they slimed their way under the back door once the fall rains began in real earnest. The poor heating and the mildew on the old windows is something you've learned to live with, but now you're starting to seriously consider the idea of leaving town and moving to Seattle with Tab. If you give him the seven thousand or so you've saved and he pools those funds with his money, you could put a down payment on a condo or small house somewhere near the city center. You *could* make it work. And anything would be better than living with the constant mildew, the forlorn wandering slugs, the water stained ceilings and unreliable baseboard heat. Anything would be better than living in the waterlogged and disintegrating Clinton Court Apartments.

CHAPTER NINE

Stale Coffee and Young Reporters

*Y*OU SAIL INTO THE BUILDING at five to nine and fly to the elevator. Once at your floor you jump out, still in your pink fuzzy slippers, and sprint to your office, carrying your favorite black pumps in the crook of your left arm. In your right hand you hold the office key sticking out like a dagger, ready to plunge it into the lock. After opening the door you fly to your desk, kick off your slippers and stuff them in your bottom desk drawer.

You slip on your pumps, and muss up some of the papers piled on the desk, mountain like, finally setting up your purse, briefcase, and 1970s vintage *Brunette Barbie* lunch box in their usual spots on the large windowsill behind your desk, with the great view of glorious sodden Portland. Grabbing your empty mug you sprint to the break room, spilling the ice cold coffee from the day before on the counter as you pour it in your cup. You splash in some cream from the refrigerator and then dump half the coffee in the sink, drinking a small sip as you power walk back to your desk. It's all about appearances and making Gayle *think* you've been in the office since before eight.

You sit down and prepare to send dozens of emails to the young and ambitious fresh faced reporters you oversee. With their acne and excessive cream concealer smeared on their faces, you regularly grill them about deadlines, and making sure they consider the "entire process" of a good story. And of course you have to remind them of the obvious, telling them to step things up and follow every possible lead, or they'll never "make it" in TV journalism. Some of them are retained and inevitably, some are let go. Fortunately that relished duty is left to Gayle, who seems to take real pleasure in it, laughing later about the girls who burst into tears, with their mascara running down their cheeks, or the young men who huff and puff and then storm out.

Sitting at the computer, you remember the other night when you made a fool of yourself. You had stood in front of Tab and bawled like a child about how you love him. You cringe remembering how you'd had only two drinks with Helen after work at the Benson, and then ended up at Tab's door—tired, boozy, hungry *and* worked up—never a good combination. As you stood outside his doorway, you had the strong and unreasonable fear that he might have been killed on his drive home from work, and if it didn't happen *that* night, what if it happened *another* night? The mental image of Tab's handsome face, and his golden topaz eyes widening in fear of the impending collision suddenly broke your heart and you felt a lump rising in your throat. What if you lost Tab, what then? What would you do? How would you go on?

When Tab answered the door, you could see he was alarmed but also annoyed at your pounding. The sight of his face melted your drunken heart and you dissolved into tears, telling him what had been in your mind for weeks but you couldn't face up to. That you loved him, *and* that you were scared.

You cringe remembering the emotional scene.

What you had really wanted at that moment, as you stood outside his door, was just to feel him, to hold him and *smell* him. But as you fell into him, grabbing him around the waist and holding on, you couldn't stop the tears. Your face contorted as you sobbed wetly against his bare chest in resolute silence, because at least you don't make any noise when you blubber. Looking back, you hate yourself for your moment of deplorable weakness for the simple reason that now he *knows*. He knows you *need* him. And you realize this knowledge may give him that smug, abusive edge men sometimes get when they know the woman they're involved with is falling hard and falling fast.

How could you have been so stupid to reveal your hand? And so soon? But will it even matter with Tab? He's not like the other men you've been with. He's genuine and kind, and full of empathy. Only time will tell, but you're hoping he forgets how you fell into his embrace, and how he practically had to hold you up to keep you from collapsing onto the hard wood floor, a quivering collection of insecurities and fierce unapologetic *need*.

As you chew another pencil, biting into it and leaving sinister vampire teeth marks, you hear Gayle exit the elevator and stomp into the office. You hear her bounding down the hall and know she's coming right for your door. Oh God, you think, let it not be anything important. Let it be Gayle wanting to confide in you about her no account daughter Mary Jennifer and her latest suicide attempt. Let it be Gayle and another new fangled diet that gives her "the gas." Or one of the reporters broke a leg and can't make it to work, or ate bad macaroni salad and can't stop shitting. Let it be anything but what you fear. But as usual, you're not so lucky. Before Gayle even turns to make her lumpy body visible in the doorway, she's already yelling your name.

"Daisy?! Daisy?!"

"Yes, Gayle, I'm here?" Suddenly, she looms in the doorway, dressed from head to toe in… Biscayne Blue! As you gaze over at her, wide eyed, all you can think of is the little girl in *Charlie and the Chocolate Factory* who turns into a huge blueberry. But then her booming voice brings you back to reality. The giant blueberry has begun to screech.

"What were you thinking doing that stunt at Lincoln? That teacher was really alarmed. Giving the kids a rant about how journalism is going downhill and the print newspaper is dying? And what were you talking about when you started in on CHEF'S and LINE COOKS making cheeseburgers? What in the damn hell is WRONG with you Daisy? Just when I think I can trust you, you pull a stunt like that? Well? What have you got to say for yourself? Anything?"

"Gayle, if you'd just lower your voice and give me a minute to…"

"Hell NO I won't lower my voice! Don't you talk to ME like that, young lady! I'm the boss around here… I'm the one who…"

"And I'm pushing FORTY Gayle, and frankly, I'm sick to death of you talking to me like I'm a goddamn child. I've been working in media and television since I was twenty two. I'm not a fuckin' INTERN, so don't treat me like one!"

"I could fire your ass in a New York minute! Do you realize that?"

"And maybe you should, Gayle. Maybe we'd all be better off with you tellin' the kids to go ahead and rip the front page from the Oregonian every day! Yep, that's real journalism for ya, at least around here—the good old Rip-N-Read. But I have a question for you; are you EVER gonna catch up, Gayle? To modern times I mean? You realize it IS 2005, right?"

"You get your skinny ass outa this office, Daisy! I want you OUT for the rest of the day, until I decide what to do with you!"

"Gladly, and if you need me, you can reach me on my cell."

"You really think you're smarter than me, doncha? You know Daisy; I was reading the news when you were still in diapers!"

"Uh huh? And you're *not* reading the news *anymore*."

"How dare you! How DARE you, with your mop of black RINGLETS! Who has RINGLETS in this day and age, anyway?"

"My hair is not black, it's BROWN, also known as BRUNETTE and at least *my* hair color didn't come from inside a bottle! As to my curls? They're natural!"

"Get out! I want you OUT!"

You brush against Gayle, as you storm out of your office, shouldering her lightly. She gasps in disbelief as you toss your purse over your shoulder. You turn into the hall and see the shocked faces of Helen and Tiffy, and a couple of the young interns, one of whom looks like she might cry. They're off in the corner, near the break room watching as Gayle sashays to her office and slams the door. You can tell from the noise that Gayle is throwing things and this fact pleases you immensely. You walk down the hall and smile back at Helen, giving her the thumbs up as you pass her, a crazy grin on your face, your eyes wild.

"Hold on, Daisy? Oh my gosh, are you gonna be okay?"

"Don't worry yourself. It's just Gayle's daughter, Mary Jennifer. I think she tried to kill herself by drinking too much hot sauce again."

"What? Hot... hot sauce?"

"You should go and console her. I hear they had to pump her stomach. Can you imagine? Be sure to tell Gary over at KOIN. I think *he* should know. His kids knew Gayle's daughter, went to Catlin Gable together or something. He should definitely know. But keep this between us. Don't tell him I told you."

"Oh, okay. Sure, yeah, I'll let him know. My god, that's terrible. Yes, I've heard her talk about her... her daughter. What are you gonna do for the rest of the day? I mean, if you wanna hang out later, we could go get drinks with Tiffy again... if... if you're up to it?"

"Would that kid be there?" You ask the question meanly, motioning impatiently with your head to the teary eyed University of Portland intern standing next to Helen, wide eyed and terrified.

"Oh, no, she's not old enough to drink yet. No, Martha wouldn't be with *us*. Come on Daisy, you sound like you don't wanna go? What's up?"

"What's up? Probably my boyfriend's penis, but that won't happen until later. I still have to go and check with him as to what our plans are going to be."

"What? You have a boyfriend, Daisy? For how long? You didn't *tell* me? Oh my god, I'm so happy for you. Hey, we need to double date! You, your new man and me and Phillip! I'll have to see when he can make it; he's still finishing up at Lewis and Clark law school, as you know, my little egghead nerd."

"Well, I don't know Helen, maybe. I'll have to think about it. We're both very private people. Anyhow, I do have to get outa here before *The Creature* comes out and starts throwing things *at* me."

"Oh Daisy, I love your humor. You know, you're the *only* one who can talk to her like that. Anyone else would be fired on the spot."

"If I'm lucky, that person will be me!"

"Oh, come on! But hey, I want you to know how happy I am for you. I bet he's a lawyer or a doctor, huh?"

"Uh, yeah... *something* like that."

"Well, of course, I mean he's with *you*, right?" You look hard at her and don't answer, as you turn on your heel, and head out the main door, to the elevators. Suddenly, you despise Helen, knowing in your heart that you always have.

"Daisy? Daisy? Hey, I'll call you, okay?"

You don't answer, but casually turn around to watch the elevator doors close with you standing there and Helen across from you, looking fearful and uncertain, as you gaze at her stone faced. Walking to your car, you feel relieved, as if a huge weight has been lifted. You've got enough in savings to pay rent for over a year if needed. And if you ever *really* hit rock bottom, you could always rely on Tab. If Gayle fires you, it wouldn't be any great loss. You could keep busy partying with Tab for a few glorious months while you look for work, a kind of mini vacation with endless sex and long lazy mornings in bed. You could also toy with the idea of going back to school and finishing that master's degree in fiction writing you've been periodically chipping away at over the years.

What you *do* know is that you can't wait to get to Tab and spend some quality alone time with him. Watching Tab as he strips and climbs into bed with you is the highlight of your day and you crave him with a sudden rapacious hunger that makes your knees rubbery and weak, and the back of your neck hot and tingly.

As you slip into the Lexus, you consider Helen's comments about Tab and the double date. How could that *ever* work? You know her well enough to know she'd be shocked to think you were involved with a man who hadn't graduated from, or even attended college. She'd think he was an ex-con or some type of criminal, maybe even a serial killer, and later she'd try to convince you to break it off, earnestly telling you not to waste your time with someone "common" and "pedestrian" as only a custodian could be. She would never see the gentleness, the beauty or the heart of someone as rare as Tab.

She would only see the overalls.

Talionic Night in Portland: A Love Story

CHAPTER TEN

The Melancholy Hush

*A*S YOU WALK INTO YOUR place, swinging the door shut with a gentle shove, you feel the melancholy hush of being alone in your tastefully decorated 'single woman' apartment. The faint notes of Roberta Flack's rendition of *"First Time Ever I Saw Your Face"* drift over to you from the kitchen radio, which is always tuned to KINK. It's mid-afternoon and the dappled sunlight is filtering through filmy mauve curtains.

Somehow it feels like an intrusion, though. You're almost never home at this hour and it feels wrong in some way. You feel as if you're being watched, like there's a ghost in every corner—faceless invisible creatures you can't see that refuse to leave. But you *know* their fingers are pointed directly at you, judging you, whispering that you're a loser, a slacker, on the way down and on the way out, irrelevant and pushing forty. And of course, you hear your late mother's voice. That subtle disappointed tone that lets you know no matter what you do, it's just always short of the mark. That no matter how hard you try, it's just never quite good enough.

Looking around you see the sofa, the love seat and overstuffed chair, the end tables and the lamps, the TV in the corner with the fifty inch screen, all used from *City Liquidators* and all still quite nice. The walls are covered in forgettable floral framed prints that look like they came from a pediatrician's office. You realize you could pack two suitcases and a couple of boxes, toss them into the back of your spacious Lexus and just split. You have nothing here, nothing of any value and no one would miss you. You have nothing to *tie* you to Portland. All the family heirlooms you inherited from your parents passing you gave to your younger sisters Rose, and Pansy, and your brother Leaf. You didn't want them, or to be reminded of the past, so you just gave them away.

You think of your siblings and feel the ache of not seeing them, but they're busy with their own lives, now. You consider your relationship with all of them represents only the occasional email. Every three months or so you send an email, ask how they're doing and maybe tell them you love them, and wish you could get together. That's it. But you feel the loss of something, the ache of how you've gone your separate ways with no expressed regret that you're all drifting in a sea of indifference and unspoken nostalgia. You remember the old days, those distant grey times, colored by the romanticism of the loneliness you feel nearly every day. But you don't have a solution. You're adrift and too tired to care much one way or the other, despite your regret.

You dig in your pocket for your cell and see that Tab has called twice within the last hour. Tab has that uncanny sixth sense when something's wrong. If you're feeling sad, scared or afflicted with "the mean reds" he'll just call as if he's in tune with something no one else can pick up on. You wish he'd call now as you look at his name flickering on the screen of your cell. But there's nothing, and you realize he's probably still at work, slaving away in his custodian uniform, and enduring the snickers of the children with their razor sharp understanding of who is high, and who is low on the adult food chain of school employees.

You want to be with Tab, but you know you need to unwind and maybe even take a nap. You haven't been getting enough sleep lately and it's starting to show. You walk to your bedroom, stand at the threshold and look beyond the purple shadows into the darkness where you see the bed made to military precision with the hospital corners your mother taught you. You remember how she forced you to learn the correct way to do it, and how she sneered: "Yeah, I know. It's not *important* to learn how to make a bed. *You've* got better things to do. Well, one day, you'll be glad I made you learn hospital corners and how to do them properly. One day, you'll be glad!" It's been three years since she died and you feel the loss every day. The ache of not being able to say goodbye, how she died in her chair dressed in her pink house dress, emaciated, with a bowl of half eaten rice pudding sitting neatly in her lap. How you wish she'd at least once told you she was proud of you and all that you'd accomplished. But that's not how it was in your family. There were no hugs, no heart to heart talks, no saying, I Love You, and now, it's too late.

You stand at the threshold of your bedroom, debating whether to take a shower or just lie down when you hear someone knocking on the front door. You turn and tiptoe down the long hallway and into the living room. Walking over, you peek through the thin curtains on the living room window. It's only Torch, come to ask to borrow more food or invite you over for a *ménages à trios*. She doesn't see you as you peer though the curtain, so you turn around and silently walk away.

"I know you're in there, Daisy. Please answer!" You stop for a moment and then explode.

"Fuck off Torch! I'm trying to sleep!"

"Please Daisy? I really need to talk with you. I think I'm gonna get evicted!"

"Fuck OFF!"

You continue to hear her pleas but ignore the growing desperation in her voice. Her pathetic beseeching becomes more and more distant as you walk into the bedroom, close the door and lay down on the bed, pulling the simple patchwork quilt your mother made over you. You look at the pretty squares of pastel calico fabric and recall how she made it by hand in the year before she died. You drift off almost immediately, falling into a fitful and troubled sleep, wishing once again you'd been able to tell her goodbye and that you loved her, wishing once again that things had been different.

While you sleep, you are oppressed by dark meandering dreams. They're characterized by an oppressive feeling of endless overcast shadow. The world is encased in dim blue darkness, and white ash is drifting everywhere. You find yourself in an abandoned tennis court that has gone to seed. The birds have stopped singing, the robins have disappeared and you become one of only thousands of people left. More than half of humanity has died of disease, pestilence, and military genocide. Fat golden rats scurry here and there among severed heads lying all around the tennis court in varying stages of putrid decay. You walk out of the exit, and see piles of dead uniformed soldiers in rotting heaps, victims of mass poisoning by rebel civilians smart enough to fool them with *Kool Aid* on a hot day.

Men, women and children lie everywhere, their bodies' ravaged, their desiccated purple tongues, stick limbs and empty eye sockets all that's left of them. They were the fortunate ones, shot through the head, the illiterate civilians whose organs were harvested for the criminal elite. The elite live high up in the hills with their armed guards inside abandoned mansions with no electricity or running water. Harvested as replacement organs for the sick or as dinner for those who used to enjoy beef liver, the elite are the only ones with handguns and rifles and everyone else is at their mercy hiding in the abandoned buildings all through downtown and the industrial areas of NW Portland.

Iridescent green June bugs crawl around, slowly consuming the heads and bodies bit by tiny bit and you can *hear* the sound of their jaws working, the incessant clacking on the desiccated flesh. You carefully step over them as they glimmer like scattered jewels. They cluster around hundreds of rotting heads and bodies, while the sour odor of decay lifts up into the warm drifting winds. Wandering along, surveying the evidence of man's inhumanity to man, you see that the human race has ceased to operate as it once did. There is *no* rule of law. Street justice is the only justice. Groups of people hover over camp fires, couples fight, children cry forlornly among the mounds of rotting heads, but as you wander, no one seems to notice you. It's as if you're invisible. Despite that feeling, you cannot escape the sensation of constant jeopardy and dread. You are alone, completely alone—like a tiny Island floating on silver water, an abandoned barge with no directed course and no land in sight—and most terrifying of all, you can't remember your own name.

Tab is nowhere to be found, because of course you *are* looking for him. You wander aimlessly, searching for his tousled head of canary yellow hair, like a beacon of light that will guide you. You can *feel* that the humble, kind and interested light in his eyes has been extinguished somehow. You *know* he's dead, that he'll never return to you and as you awake, hot and damp with perspiration, you feel the pain of having lost Tab. The emotion enters you like a rock careening inside your guts. It's fallen inside to some pit of Bottomless Sadness that you know will always exist within you, and never leave. You lay on your bed, your eyes blinking, trying to leave the dream world behind. You try to enter the reality you know of as your *real* life, but the dream world hangs on, like a stifling vapor, a hand across your throat, a foot on your chest, and it's hard to shake the fear and despair. Your hair is damp and tangled with clotted perspiration, when you suddenly begin to weep, turning your face to the dark wall. Because you can barely acknowledge how hard it is to hang on anymore and least of all to your solitary self who knows the truth already. The charade seems almost over when you have these kinds of dreams. You're running out of steam, losing the strength to continue the circus of this life you've chosen, and knowing it, you're terrified.

As you fully come back into the real world, you realize you *do* still have Tab. He's not dead. It was a dream, only a dream. He's still here. Tab is still in the real world of the here and now, and maybe he's right. Maybe you both *are* meant for each other, to find each other this late in life, the equal to your unique sum of parts that complements the other so perfectly, so harmoniously. But with that erotic edge you require—that edge that brings you the pleasure and the sublimation—the *spiritual* fucking you crave and must have. As your face is still screwed up in grief and the tears continue, despite your relief, slowly slipping onto your neck, and into the crevices of your ears, you hear the unique rattle of Tab's ring tone. You pick up the phone, breathless and say his name, barely audible, not a question, just a statement.

"Daisy? Are you okay? What is it?"

"Just a long day. And I might be out of a job."

"For real?"

"I guess I kinda did it to myself, but I can't stand her. There's just something *about* her."

"I took off early today. You want I come get you? Take you back to my place?"

"You don't mind? I just... I just don't feel like driving right now."

"You know I don't mind, baby. I'll be there in fifteen. Traffic won't be bad."

"I look forward to seeing you, Tab."

"I know you do, baby. I'll be right there. Hang tight."

As you lay in bed, you think of the first time you and Tab fucked, right there on the floor of your tiny bathroom. You had both felt the attraction and you recall how overpowering it had been, intoxicating like a generous shot of whiskey or the mellow rush of a Valium dissolving in your empty stomach. He had just finished installing the toilet seat, and stood there awkwardly in front of the sink, his long arms hanging at his sides.

"Well, that's it, I guess."

"Thanks so much for coming out. I *do* appreciate your help."

Tab looked you in the face and scanned your body from the top of your head to your bare feet. He was completely obvious but boyish and humble at the same time, and utterly charming. His eyes were wide and uncertain, and you felt as if you'd always known him. There was an easiness to his presence but an excitement too, and the appreciation of his appearance—the beauty of his face, his long legs, his teeth, his wonderful musky smell and the strange glow of his yellow hair. He asked if you were single and you said you were, nodding your head and smiling. He said he was single too, separated from his wife and preparing for a divorce. That it was no kind of life being alone like that and he missed life with a woman. He missed the day to day, sleeping, shopping, and cooking together, going to the movies. You nodded your head in agreement at his earnest declaration, knowing that if it had been anyone *else* saying those very words, you'd probably have smiled politely and walked out of the room to wait uneasily by the front door, happy to show them out. But it wasn't anyone else. It was Tab, so you smiled the wan smile that people often remark on when they say you have "understanding" eyes. You both looked at each other, for a long while it seemed, gauging the other's response, body language and what was being said with both sets of eyes. He reached over wordlessly then and brushed a stray dark ringlet from your forehead, murmuring: "Gosh, I really like your hair. It's so pretty."

Impulsively, your hand reached up. You covered the back of his hand with yours, and pressed your cheek into his palm, closing your eyes sensuously. Just as quickly he stepped forward, cupped your face in both hands, bent down and looked directly in your eyes as if he was searching for an answer. You didn't object, you looked up and smiled. He bent to kiss you as you reached up. Your arms went high, going for his neck, something to latch onto, climb up, and cover him like a vine. Mouths joined and tongues met. By then he was already taking off his jacket with one hand and trying to drop his tool belt with the other. Hearing the heavy thud of his tool belt hit the floor, you fell against him, your small bare feet lightly stepping onto the tops of his steel-toed work boots. He pulled you into him, pressing you against his front, twisting your neck into his left shoulder, and bearing down hard on your mouth. You felt the beautiful scary erection press against your belly, long and fat through the fabric of his overalls, and started humming quietly. His tongue was in your mouth as he manipulated your body in the ways he wanted. Your legs flexible and fluid like a ballet dancer, he hoisted you up, and pressed you against the wall.

Five minutes later, those same overalls were down around his knees, and you were flat on your back, your pink lace panties in the corner in a minuscule tumble as you rocked against each other, breathing hard, and in no hurry to end it. Your feet were in the air, his pelvis thumping against you. In that moment, you couldn't wait for the building orgasm. But he was taking his time. He was waiting for you to come first. You started to come and then saw him finally left go. His eyes closed and he grimaced as if he was in pain. You both came together, and it was unlike anything you'd ever experienced.

As you came down from the waves of pleasure, the emotion began to rise up, and you had to bite your lip. You watched Tab slowly come back to reality, and the pleasure dissipate from his face, replaced by an unmistakable look of boyish embarrassment. You were leaving the shadow ghost behind, until the next time, when scrambling limbs, and hungry eyes would start the race all over again. You had both cleaned in silence with wet washcloths, silent with your heads down, still strangers to each other. Tab gathered up his tool belt, hastily pulling up his pants and zipping, he tried to compose himself long enough to search his wallet and hand you his card, sheepishly asking you to call him. You walked him to the door and smiled, running your hands through your hair, acutely aware of what had just happened, and how unexpected it was.

"I'm sorry, I don't... I don't usually do that."

"I know. Me neither, it's just... well, I guess I can't say why we..."

"Can I call you tomorrow, Tab?"

"Yes, please do?" he said, his eyes eager, almost desperate.

"We could... go to dinner?"

"Yes, dinner. I'll wait for your call, Miss Daisy."

"Okay, thank you Tab."

****

When you hear Tab's heavy work boots on the concrete walkway outside your apartment, striding forward quickly, you rush to the door, tiptoeing, turn the deadbolt, and let him in. He looms in the doorway, tall, and long legged. Your mouth starts watering as soon as you see him. Tab sees you're upset, tired, depleted. He walks to you wordlessly; pushing the door closed behind him. He cups your face in his hands, and bends to kiss you. His tongue is inside your mouth as you lean into him. You reach up, and embrace him around his broad ribs, holding on. After a moment, he pulls away and kisses your temple. You press your cheek into the hollow of his right shoulder breathing in the scent of

Ivory Soap and *Old Spice* and close your eyes as you begin whispering.

"Tab? Let's fuck on the living room floor. Please? I need you to fuck me."

"Absolutely, baby. We'll go to my place after. Come on, let Tab make it better."

"Please, make it all better?"

"What's wrong? What's happened?"

"Nothing. We can talk about it later. Just fuck me."

Talionic Night in Portland: A Love Story

CHAPTER ELEVEN

The Meeting with Gayle

G AYLE CALLS THE NEXT DAY. She wants to meet and talk. She says she doesn't want to lose you, and feels if you can hash things out, then maybe your "working relationship" can be restored. You agree to meet at the Georgian Room on the tenth floor of the *Meier & Frank* department store. After you get off the elevator, you walk through the oval front entrance, past the green velvet rope and into the large room. You notice the tall thin cook lounging against the wall next to the kitchen door, and he gives you a friendly nod. You head toward the table next to the green and white walls with the large square mirror and once again marvel at the ornate décor of one of the best kept secrets in Portland; the lovely Georgian Room. As you brush against the grand piano to the right, and step up onto the higher landing, the cook motions over to the lone waiter to serve you, whom you notice is also leaning against the wall next to the kitchen door, lost in thought. The lunch hour is almost over and there are no other customers in sight but being a regular, they serve you anyway.

The gay waiter with the dark brown mustache waits on you and once again you enjoy his elaborate formality of movement, the graceful and ceremonious way he sets down your coffee cup, pouring the steaming hot coffee and setting down the small silver container of cream, as if you were royalty. You look up at him and smile, and quietly ask for lemon wedges to go with your ice water, while you look over the menu, finally deciding on a small green salad and a side of cottage cheese.

Gayle is late, but it gives you time to think. You try but can't single out one character flaw Tab might have. He seems like the perfect man. That he's not been to college feels irrelevant. His other qualities are priceless and rare in comparison to something as mundane and ultimately unimportant as post secondary education. His habit of being unfaithful is not a big deal either, not really, as you know it's a common occurrence, especially among handsome men. And for a man like Tab, you see that at fifty two he may have matured, and may be more committed to making a relationship work than when he was younger and more capricious.

In your mind's eye, as you gaze onto the flat black surface of your coffee as it rests motionless in the cup, you see a sunny kitchen, spilling with light and green hanging plants next to bone colored muslin curtains. The walls are cheerful yellow and from the large kitchen window, overlooking an entire tree lined neighborhood, you see the silvery agate-colored water of Puget Sound as the sun reflects on its glassine-like surface. Somehow you *know* this is the kitchen you and Tab will be living in. You push the thought from your mind though, as soon as you hear Gayle's deep contralto barking orders from the restaurant foyer.

"What happened to the coat rack that used to be here? I'd really like to be able to hang my coat on a rack, rather than the back of a chair. Its camel hair, ya know!"

"Yes, I see, I'm so sorry, I'm…"

"I realize you guys are having financial problems but really!"

"I'm sorry; the coat rack was taken to a different part of the store. They've been moving things around a lot lately. I do apologize…"

"I'm waiting for a woman with long, dark Shirley Temple ringlets. Have you seen her?"

"Oh, yes, you must mean Daisy. She's one of our regulars, come this way."

You cringe as Gayle brushes past the waiter, stomps over to your table and then imperiously drapes her taupe colored coat over the nearest chair. "Honestly, why can't they get a coat rack for this dump?" The waiter gasps and walks away, in search of a menu and a glass of iced water. You wonder if he'll spit in it.

"They're not doing very well, Gayle, what with the opening of the *Red Star* down the street and there's a rumor they might be closing down, too. This is an historic place though, and still quite popular."

"That's no rumor, they're history, and so is Meier & Frank's. Anyhow, here we are!"

"Yes, here we are. It's… nice to see you again."

"Well, I suppose I should say it's nice to see you too, or that I'm *happy* to see you but frankly, I'm just a little fed up. What is going on with you lately, Daisy? That you seem to think you can shirk your duties onto Tiffy and Helen, leaving work early—multiple times? I mean, come ON! And I've heard some scuttlebutt you have a new man, too. So, who is it? Anyone we know?"

"It's not important. It's just… you know… just a sexual thing."

"Oh really? So, he's younger than you, is that it?"

"Uh, yeah, he's younger, a younger man."

"Well, in that case, bravo. I approve. Ya know sometimes it's just a matter of needing to… cop a nut once in a while. Isn't that what the men say—copping a nut?"

"Well, I wouldn't know about that..."

"I have a guy myself, I pay for him but I like it that way. I can tell him to get the hell out once it's over, ya know? He comes over every eight weeks, on the button. Knows just what to do, never asks me what I'm *thinking* or if he can borrow money for a new coat, or to help pay his damn rent. Are you paying for it too, Daisy?"

"Well, uh..."

"No, I guess you wouldn't have to, would you?"

You look away to the far side of the room, mortified, and try to pretend it doesn't bother you—her callous murderous talk. She notices and laughs, grabs your glass of iced lemon water and chugs it noisily. After she's drained the entire glass, you gaze at the iridescent water mustache bubbling on the surface of her oily upper lip, mesmerized.

"What are ya lookin' at Daisy? Looks like you're goin' into a trance again!"

You quietly tell Gayle she has a water mustache, and look down at your fingernails, suddenly exhausted. She laughs, and wipes her mouth with the back of her hand leaving a smear of orange foundation on the back of her wrinkled, spotted blue-white hand. She burps loudly, and seems surprised, yet nonchalant.

"Oh! Excuse me! I've been dealing with excessive gas lately, because of my new pinto bean diet. My naturopath will probably arrange another high colonic for me. Have you ever had a high colonic, Daisy? It's amazing how much better you feel afterwards... I had my first one when I was..."

"Okay Gayle, can we please just get to the point, here? I'm on a time crunch right now. I've got an appointment later with my... chiropractor."

"Your chiropractor, huh? Are you sure it's not your *new* man? Tiffy says he's a doctor or lawyer. So, what *does* the guy do for a living? You don't wanna end up with some no account bum do ya?"

"My personal life is no one else's business. Let's cut to the chase. Do I still have a job or not?"

"Probably. But what I'd like to know is why you're so intent on getting yourself fired? Why are you so quick to dump me with a bunch of stupid interns and first year reporters who don't know shit from Shinola about media *or* how to conduct a proper investigation? I need you *on* task. I need you to oversee all the stuff I can't get to. You know the job description; you've been doing it for years."

"I know."

"Then what's going on, Daisy?"

"I'm just going through a slump right now. I don't know—I'm just discouraged."

"Well, everyone's discouraged, so what! That's just life. You know, one of the interns, Martha I think, says she saw you with some guy in overalls eating Taco Bell somewhere in southeast. On 82nd I think she said it was? Now, what would you be doing over in *that* part of town?"

"I have no idea *what* she's referring to."

"She said he looked like a Ken Barbie doll and that he was a few years *older* than you. She said he looked like a maintenance man or something. What's going on, Daisy? Is that the new man you told Tiffy about?"

"We were… we were heading home from a costume party. He was playing the part of a maintenance man and I was playing the part of… of Blanche Dubois from *A Street Car Named Desire*."

"A costume party? It's not Halloween for a few more months!"

"He's an old friend of my brothers. It was a costume party for… for the birthday party of my younger brother. He's a theater geek, that's all—my brother—not his friend. "

"Seriously? I dunno, that sounds kinda fishy. Martha said you were looking at him like he was the Messiah or something, all wide eyed and smiles, touching his knee, giggling, calling him Mr. Blaine this and Mr. Blaine, that!"

"Martha huh? Yeah, well, I've been getting complaints about *her* performance. I'll give her a call tomorrow and talk to her about her duties at the office, and they certainly don't include spreading falsehoods about *my* personal life!"

"Daisy, you can't leave work early and you can't sass me anymore, either. I've got to run a tight ship. If those girls see you disrespecting me, I'll lose my authority with them. Now, you've been with us the longest and you're damn competent, so I put up with more from you, but I can't have those stupid nitwits seeing me being disrespected, even by you. Am I understood?"

"Yes, Gayle. I understand. And I apologize for…. for being sassy. It was a really bad day. I was just lashing out. It was wrong of me, though. "

"Okay, I'm glad we had this discussion. So, what are you buyin' me for lunch? I can't remember what's good here."

"They have an excellent BLT, if you're into pork."

"What, you don't eat bacon anymore either, Daisy?"

"It aggravates my joints and doesn't make me feel well. I gave it up about two years ago. I generally have the liver and onions or a green salad and cottage cheese."

"Liver and onions? Good God, no thanks. I'll have the BLT, but I want extra bacon on it, and extra crispy! Where's that damn waiter?"

You motion the waiter over and he takes the order. With Gayle gazing into the large plastic menu and oblivious, she also decides on a dessert. It's at that moment that you discreetly slip the $20 bill into the right hand pocket of the waiter's uniform. He notices, looks down and smiles at you with love in his eyes. He seems to understand Gayle is your boss and the empathy is immediate and genuine. Who would want to work for such an *awful* woman, his eyes seem to say. You know the next few times you come in he'll give you a free tart, or extra cottage cheese, or a free coffee, as he often does when you tip generously.

After the waiter leaves, you sit across from Gayle watching her eat the BLT with the reckless abandon of a starving teenager. She smacks shamelessly as chunks of crisp bacon drop from her mouth onto the plate. She pinches them up greedily between her fingers and stuffs them back into her mouth as if someone might try to snatch them away if she doesn't get them quick enough. So much for her pinto bean diet, you think, as you watch her gulp 7-UP, belching loudly. Suddenly, you lose your appetite for the small green salad and side of cottage cheese that sit innocently below on the table, untouched.

Watching Gayle eat is like watching a sea monster consuming an uncooked giant squid still alive and fighting for its life. There's such an angry violence to it, but it seems in keeping with Gayle's voracious attitude toward everyone and everything. She's stopped talking though and that's a temporary blessing. She's immersed only in the process of consuming the BLT as quickly and as viciously as possible until there's nothing left but a single wilted shred of iceberg lettuce on the plate. You know the BLT pleases Gayle by the thin dribble of bacon grease slowly sliding down her chin, and the way she smacks unabashedly.

As she swallows the last bite, Gayle finally wipes the grease from her face with a green linen napkin, taking along a generous smear of orange foundation makeup with it. You look down at your hands as she begins a short tirade about her ungrateful daughter Mary Jennifer, with a full mouth of course, as she has now begun eating her dessert—a large slice of chocolate cake. The dark frosting becomes encrusted in the corners of her mouth and you wonder if you should tell her. You decide against it. The brown seems to mix nicely with the hot pink of her lipstick. You remember once again that you've got to find out *where* the girl lives, so in time you can warn her about her mother, and tell her to save herself and run as far away as she possibly can. After the last swallow of cake, Gayle burps again and you're not sure but suspect the baritone timbre of the belch has made the silverware on the table jingle.

"Where's that damn waiter? I need my coffee refilled!"

"Yes, Gayle."

Talionic Night in Portland: A Love Story

CHAPTER TWELVE

The Silk Nightgown and the Spectacle

*I*T'S SATURDAY AND AFTER WAKING up and enjoying a hot soapy shower with *Dr. Bronner's Pure-Castile Liquid Soap*, you towel dry and smooth *Johnson's Baby Lotion* all over your body. You stand in front of the sink and slowly brush your teeth with *Tom's Toothpaste* while the lotion absorbs into your skin and then carefully floss your teeth. After you dress, slipping on new panties and bra, you walk down the long hallway, lifting up your new silk nightgown in the front just above your ankles as it drifts behind in the back, trailing across the floor like the train of a wedding gown. Tab bought it several weeks before and as it was made for a woman five feet six and not five feet four, it's too long. But you wear it anyway, loving the texture of the thin silk, the delicate lavender color, the fact that it fits you perfectly everywhere else, with its scooped neck and half length sleeves—but mostly you wear it because Tab bought it for you, spending far too much money on it than he should have.

You go into the kitchen to make mint tea and buttered toast with lemon curd but after you put your favorite red mug into the microwave, you hear something ominous outside your apartment. It sounds like the crunching of leaves and a kind of anxious murmuring. You turn and listen, and that's when you notice a dark shadowy figure lurking outside your living room window. The mop of bleached blonde hair looks dangerously familiar. Claw like bony hands, with long nails painted bright purple press against the glass as the person attempts to gain purchase on the soft flowerbed they're standing on. Your heart sinks when you realize its Verona trying to step behind your exquisite *Charles de Gaulle* heritage rose bush in order to peep into your window. The curtain is not transparent but it is sheer and if it were evening and there was a lamp on in the living room, she'd be able to make you out as you walk around the apartment, going from the living room into the kitchen or from the hallway to your bedroom. But because its morning, a little after eleven with the bright sunlight behind her, she can't see inside.

Your heart jumps in your throat when you realize there's someone else with her. You're not certain but you think you hear Verona sneer the name *Ruby*, and realize in that instant that Tab's estranged wife Ruby and his "girl on the side" Verona, are both outside *your* front door, and probably mean to do you harm. You tiptoe to the door, silent and terrified as you strain to hear what you can. Verona begins talking first, the sound clear and strident as a church bell, and the violent hatred in her voice drips with pent up rage and irrational jealousy.

"Lemme tell ya, I'm gonna kill the bitch. Some stuck-up *TEE VEE* slut, thinkin' she can take *my* guy? Ah, hell no! Man, I jus wanna git my hands around her fuckin' throat!"

"Why'd you ask me to come, Verona? I'm still pissed at you fer coming over to my place and slappin' me around last month. Just cause I wouldn't share my beer and listen to you bitch and complain? I don't care *what* Tab does anymore. He's just a big dumb meathead."

"You know you're still hung up on Tab!"

"No, I'm not! I got me a new man, now. His old brother-in-law, Stan. How's that fer gettin' revenge? And I know *you're* probably fuckin' at least three other guys. I mean that is yer MO, right Verona? Didn't you used to be a prostitute or somethin?"

"It don't matter if I *am* messin' with other guys. A girl's gotta make a living. But Tab is still my main man, or at least that's what I thought. Sides, what does it matter, Ruby? We're friends, now. Heck, we could even party together one of these days. I wouldn't throw *you* outa the bed. I know *you're* game."

"I appreciate that, Verona. I really do, and I'll take ya up on that later. But this is crazy. I don't wanna get in trouble. That girl probably knows important people. She could call the po-lice and they'd be here in a minute. I mean, she works fer a TV station. She's like one of them bosses er something right?"

"Ah, she ain't nuthin. Jeez, Ruby, don't ya know anythin' girl? Why'd she be livin' in a dump like the Clinton Court Apartments if she was somethin' special? Man, this place is practically fallin' over. I can just imagine the mildew and mold growin' inside a shithole like this. The manager probably blasted the heat for two days before he showed her the place, and she probably thought, 'ah, what a nice charming place' and moved right in. You oughta know she's just a rich bitch who never worked for anything. She's probably been handed it all on a silver platter her whole life."

"If'n she's been handed it all her life, then why's she livin' here? Just like you said, why's she livin' here then? You ain't makin' no sense Verona, as usual!"

"I'm tellin' you Ruby, you better shut yer trap before I pop you in the mouth again. Here, I'm gonna start bangin' on this window. That'll wake the bitch up."

Verona starts rapping on the window as you creep back into your bedroom and close the door. You turn the heavy deadbolt, grateful for its presence and that now you'll be safe. The second you look over at your cell phone on the oak nightstand it rings. The ringtone sounds for only a moment before you scoot over and flip it open.

"Hello Tab?" Your voice is a whisper and you're terrified.

"Baby... is everything alright? I was just gonna come get you when I found a note outside my door. Please don't tell me Verona is at your place... is she?"

"Tab? I'm really scared. It's not only Verona, but its Ruby, too. They're right outside my apartment. I think I'm going to need you to come over?"

"I'll be there in ten minutes, just as soon as I pull on my jeans and run out to the truck. Do NOT answer that door. You understand?"

"Yeah, I got it. Trust me; I'm not gonna answer it. I'm in the bedroom and... I locked the deadbolt you installed last month. Oh God, I really don't need a scene, but I'm scared, I *need* you!"

"I'll take care of those two crazy... Aww, how did I *ever* get tangled up with those two crazy fuckin'... Listen, you'll be fine Daisy, as long as you stay inside the bedroom. I'm so sorry. I love you precious girl. I love you *so* much!"

"I love you too, Tab. I love you so much, too!"

As the phone goes dead, you hear Verona and Ruby yelling at each other as Verona continues to knock on the living room window. She moves to the front door and starts jiggling the door handle, but it's unmovable with the new deadbolt Tab installed the month prior when he did a complete safety upgrade to your entire apartment. Verona redirects her attention and starts pounding on the door with her fist. The pounding stops and its quiet for a moment and you wonder if they've decided to leave. Then you hear one of your terracotta planters crash onto the sidewalk, then another one, and then another. You envision the huge mess of broken terracotta, the scattered potting soil and the innocent little pansy's, with their tender purple faces that you planted only the week before.

"How do ya like that, you bitch? Yeah, how do you like *that*? You cheated with my man! Only a whore does that!"

"Yer no better, Verona. You cheated with Tab when he was MY husband. You're no better than that girl he's screwing!"

"And wasn't he married to his wife Brandi, the mother of his two kids when he met *you*, Ruby? You took a father away from his kids, so don't act all high and mighty with me!"

They both start yelling but its Verona's gin and cigarettes voice that dominates as she yells at Ruby to shut up. Then she's bellowing full force into the door about how she's going to find you if it's the last thing she does, how you'll never escape her long reach, how no one cheats on her with some "TV anchorwoman slut" and how you and Tab are both going to pay with your lives. You hear Ruby continue to tell Verona she's no better and to stop making a scene and drive her back home. Then you hear the unmistakable sound of a hard slap and the thud of a human body falling on the concrete walk. Then a low wail, followed by a spew of more colorful profanity and insults by Ruby and more yelling from Verona.

"I done TOLD you to stop, Ruby. I done TOLD you!"

"You crazy bitch. No wonder you can't keep a man. Yer nuts, totally and one hunerd percent nuts!"

"You want I take off my belt, Ruby? You wouldn't be the first woman I done whipped! I'll whip you good and you'll never forget it neether!"

As you can hear every word, even behind your bedroom door, you decide that perhaps you *can* venture out. The front door is solid wood and has two locks, including the new deadbolt and a chain lock. You start to feel ridiculous thinking Verona, at 130 pounds could break down your door. You slide off your bed, walk to the door and unlock the deadbolt and then stride into the living room, delicately carrying the front of your lavender silk nightgown in your hands like a lady of the manor. You stand back in the center of the living room and look out the filmy curtains, taking care not to get too close. Ruby and Verona are on the front lawn, which separates the two sides of the bungalow apartments. They're standing on the grass, screaming at each other. Ruby is bent over, her arms hanging limply at her sides as she begins wailing— a high pitched animal sound. Verona is yelling at her to shut up, and threatening to slap her again.

You peer to the left and see that Torch Tremble and Blaze Handle are running over to enter the fray. Oh, great, you think—Torch and Blaze to the rescue! Torch is in her bare feet wearing a huge black tee shirt with bleach stains, and Blaze is shirtless, wearing only black pajama bottoms with big red hearts all over them, his tender grey flesh otherworldly and strange. He's rubbing his eyes and yawning, while Torch demands to know what's going on.

"What in the hell is this? Why are you tryin' to hassle my friend, Daisy?"

"You know that bitch?"

"Don't you talk like that about my friend, or I'll knock *you* on your ass!"

"Tell her to get her butt out here so I can rip her apart. She's been fuckin' my man!"

"What man? You mean her *boyfriend*, Tab?"

"Tab ain't her man. He's MY man!"

"How can he be YOUR man, when he's *my* husband, Verona?" Ruby demands.

"You shut the hell up old woman, before I give you somethin' to *really* cry about!"

You watch as Torch tries to make sense of things. She's quiet and just stands there when she literally begins to scratch the top of her head, looking infinitely confused. Blaze starts dancing around, laughing. He's bent over and laughing so hard he can't speak, tip toeing around like a boxer dancing in front of an opponent. He staggers over to Torch and starts hanging on her arm, pulling her to him. Then Torch starts laughing too, leaning into Blaze.

"Oh my God, this is so fucked up, Blaze! I never knew Daisy was a badass. Stealing another girls' man? Oh my GOD!"

You notice one of the neighbors opens their apartment front door and stands watching. The older woman is tall and emaciated, a human skeleton wearing an old flowered house dress of pink and beige calico that hangs on her like a tent. You notice she's got pink curlers in her sparse grey hair as she yells over the lawn that the police have been called and *someone's* going to jail.

"Get back in your dump, you old bitch!" Verona yells.

"Don't you call ME an old bitch, you white trash meth head!"

"Aw, fuck you!"

The sound of Tab's truck pulling up onto the street and the screech of the brakes echoes through your apartment, along with the slam of the truck door. Suddenly, he's jogging over, and standing in the center of the lawn, facing Ruby and Verona and breathing hard. He's looks into the front room window of your apartment, a frantic look of concern on his face as he takes in the scene. Ruby has fallen on the lawn, damp with morning dew, and is bent over blubbering. Her legs are spread, her head is hanging over her chest, and her flip flops lay askew next to her as she shakes her head from side to side and bawls, asking no one in particular:

"What happened to my life? What happened to the wonderful life I used to have?"

"You shut yer damn mouth, Ruby!" Verona bellows.

Verona is standing directly in front of Ruby. Her shoulders are hunched; her fists balled up in rage as she contemplates Tab standing on the lawn looking like a bewildered fifty something GQ model. He's wearing Levi jeans, a white tee shirt, an old denim jacket, and white Keds deck shoes, and looks as if he just fell out of bed.

"Verona? I know it's *you* who done this! If you touched one hair on Daisy's head, I swear, I'll…"

"You'll do what? You'll do what, Tab?"

"Why don't ya love us no more?" Ruby wails. "I was willin' to share ya!"

"You shut yer mouth old woman. He was done with you a long time ago!"

"How about I tell you that I'm done with both of ya? How about THAT?"

"Oooweeeee, look at this. The man *does* have passion. I bet you'd like to hit me wouldn't ya, Tab? Well, you go right ahead. Go right ahead and hit me. Come on! Be a man! Hit me!"

"Verona? I am *done* with you. And I'm done with you too, Ruby. You're both nothin' but a couple a drunks. Nothin' more than bottomless pits a NEED with cigarette breath and too many bad habits! It ain't never enough. No matter *what* I do for either of ya. And let's face it, neither one of you can be trusted. You're both a couple a pathological liars and... and narcissists!"

"Well, well, did ya learn a new word from your college graduate girlfriend there, Tab?"

"Maybe I did! So what Verona. Daisy's clean, and sweet. She don't smoke or drink. And she's not a slut, but that's all both a you are! Nothin' but a couple a goddamn sluts!"

"Well, then why don't you take better care of us?" Ruby demands.

"Shut up Ruby!"

"I ain't shuttin' up Verona! And if you took better care of us Tab, we wouldn't *be* sluts!"

"Oh GOD, Ruby, would you just shut up?" Verona yells.

"Ruby, it would never be enough. I don't have enough in savings to buy you all the booze, smokes and Beer Nuts you live on, *and* service you into the bargain. And that goes for you too Verona. It's over! I am DONE!"

"Do you really think you're gonna be *happy* with that snooty Snow White rich bitch? She's just usin' you man. She's not one of us. She's not from the streets, like *we* are!"

"But see that's the thing Verona, I'm *not* from the streets. Maybe *you* are, and maybe Ruby is, but *I'm* not. Neither one of you basket cases can hold a candle to my Daisy! Neither one of you, but especially not *you* Verona!"

"*WHAT* did you just say to me?"

"You heard me."

Verona rushes at Tab, with a guttural howl reverberating in her throat and tries to punch him. She's like a wild cat, but Tab is faster. He grabs both her wrists and maneuvers himself behind her. With his hands gripping each wrist, he pulls them to the opposite side until Verona's trapped. He yanks hard to secure his grip. She's helpless, breathing heavily and trapped in a prison of her own scrawny arms crossed over her chest like two bars. She falls into him, whimpering, her tone changing just that quickly. She looks up beseechingly, and begs him to take her back. Her tanned face is deeply lined, and the pink frost lipstick she wears is not attractive. She's layered it on so thickly it does nothing to beautify her thin lips but only makes their thinness stand out even more.

"What does that girl got that *we* ain't got, Tab?"

"Would you shut yer damn trap, Ruby?" Verona hisses still breathing heavily.

"I want you both to get outa my LIFE! I'm done!"

"You can't just throw me away, Tab. *We're* still married."

"Not for long, Ruby!" Tab says.

At that moment, sirens can be heard several blocks away howling in the distance. Tab shoves Verona forward with such force she goes flying through the air. As she tries to right herself, hurtling through space, her legs pump frantically under her, but she loses her footing and slips, landing on her butt with a dull thud, and skidding several more feet as if she were on a summertime Slip-N-Slide. After she rights herself, she sits there bent over, out of breath and scowling as three Portland Police officers jog over. The men approach the scene just as Tab growls under his breath, but loud enough to be heard.

"I love DAISY! And that's not EVER gonna change!"

"We're still married, Tab. I want you back. I want you BACK!"

"It ain't' never gonna happen, Ruby. Besides, you've been gettin' busy with Stan, my ex-wife's brother. It's over Ruby. I shoulda dumped you a long time ago."

"Did you hear that Ruby? He said it's over!"

"Yeah, well its over for you too, Verona!"

The three officers approach Ruby and Verona and help them up, separating them. After they speak with a small crowd of gathering neighbors, both Ruby and Verona are arrested, cuffed and placed on the wet grass to hurry up and wait. The bottoms of their jeans get soaked from the morning dew as the police officers continue to take statements from witnesses, jotting down details in their tattered field notebooks. Ruby blubbers loudly and you notice a long string of snot hanging from her nose as you gaze out the filmy curtains of the living room window, safe from the tumult and a world away from danger behind the locked door of your clean perfumed apartment. Verona is seated only a few feet from Ruby, and tries to kick her in the butt, but ends up slipping onto her back instead. Ruby begs the officers to put her out of her misery.

"Just shoot me. I wanna end it all. Just kill me! Put me in morgue! I don't care anymore!"

They ignore her and turn away, trying not to laugh. Ruby then announces she's just wet her pants and doesn't care if the whole world knows. She repeats herself and tells the entire block she's wet her pants, yelling loudly that it's all Tab's fault. The crowd of neighbors titters with laughter, nudging each other and snickering. The tall skinny old woman doubles over. She's laughing so hard she starts to cough and reaches into her pocket for a hanky to wipe her eyes. Ruby continues to blubber, wailing wildly while greenish snot gathers thickly under her upturned nose.

"I pissed my pants. I pissed my pants, god damn it! Nobody cares, I pissed my pants!"

You've watched it all unfold like a terrifying, nightmarish bad dream, a soap opera disaster where every bad thing that could happen *does* happen. But now you know it's time to make your appearance, your grand entrance so to speak.

You couldn't have it any other way. They *have* to see you, so they can both understand that Tab means it when he says it's over. Once they see you, they'll understand how they ruined such a good thing. How Tab *was* that good thing, and that they have no one to blame but themselves, and can no longer make any claims on Tab. He belongs to you, now.

As Tab continues to talk with the three police officers, his voice low and his demeanor humble and respectful, and Verona continues to grumble profanity under her breath, and Ruby continues to wail, you walk to your purse and take out your pink lip gloss and sterling silver compact with the Gibson Girl etched across the front. You flip it open, and apply a glossy pink layer, drop the lip gloss and compact back into your bag and then walk to the door. You stand tall, arch your spine, stick your breasts out and take a deep breath. You unlock all the locks, turn the handle slowly, and let the door fall to the left, opening all the way. As you stand triumphant in the doorway, the *Charles de Gaulle* rosebush is at your right, the rose-mauve color of the blooms as vivid as a neon sign at night. Bright sunlight filters toward you, coming out from behind a cloud at just that moment with you standing in the shimmering spotlight.

Your dark ringlets cascade down your back and over each delicate collarbone. Your vibrant eyes sparkle like ice cold Blue Hawaiians. You give your head a little shake, flipping the longest ringlets over your left shoulder. You know you look as enticing as anything Hollywood has to offer. You lift up the silk nightgown in front, exposing pale calves, milk white ankles and slender bare feet, and step down onto the concrete landing just beyond the threshold. Standing there, with your chin high, you gaze directly at Ruby and Verona slumped over on the wet grass.

They lift their weary heads, notice you, and both their jaws slowly drop. You're still holding up the front of your nightgown, daintily, when you nod to each of them and smile serenely. Their bleary eyes widen, becoming as big as saucers as they take you in, just as their eyebrows knit together almost simultaneously in pained awareness of the stark reality. And the reality is that they don't stand a snowballs chance in hell of *ever* getting Tab back. Not when he has a woman like *you*. Not when he has his very own Daisy Rose Butterfield. Your breasts are high and firm, your nipples hard as they poke through the thin silk. The three police officers look over and say nothing, dumbfounded, silent and appreciative as only straight men can be when looking at a scantily dressed, gorgeous young woman. As soon as Tab turns around and sees you, his face melts, and his eyes mist over, a helpless smile forming on his matinee idol face.

"There she is. That's my girl."

"*That's* your girlfriend?" one of the officers asks in disbelief.

"You bet she is, just look at her. My tender loving baby."

"Excuse me, miss? Can you tell us what this is all about?" You flutter your eyelashes before speaking, hesitating and adopting your most endearing little girl voice as you begin speaking to the officers.

"Tab can explain it. If that's okay? He's my fiancée. He was going to pick me up today and we were going to spend the day at his apartment, preparing for our wedding."

"Can you just tell us what happened?"

"What happened? Well, he has to divorce that... that *woman* over there first, but we were going to spend the day together and then I heard these two... these two women fighting on my front lawn and breaking all my terra cotta planters? With my little pansies still inside? Well, you can see the mess. I called Tab right away and he said he'd come over and protect me. Tab can explain everything for you, if that's alright of course?"

"That's fine miss, but if you wouldn't mind coming out here, we'd appreciate it?"

"Well, I'm... I'm just really scared. Tab, what should I do?"

In an instant Tab is walking toward you, and then past you into the apartment. He grabs your pink kitten slippers by the baseboard heater, just inside the door and comes back out. He steps down to the concrete sidewalk, bends over and reaches up offering you the first of the two slippers. He extends his large hand for you to hold, to steady yourself and you take it. As you extend each tender foot, he brushes off the bottom of your feet, and places each slipper on. You stare pointedly at Ruby and then Verona, making sure they have an unhindered bird's eye view.

You're Cinderella and *he's* Prince Charming, and *they're* the two ugly stepsisters.

After the slippers are securely on your feet, you pretend to lose your balance, reaching out for Tab, and he quickly steadies you with an indulgent smile, steps onto the landing and places a protective arm around your shoulders. You turn to face the officers, bring your slender hand to your throat, like a heroine in a romance novel, and begin apologizing.

"I'm so sorry, I'm just; well this has just been so upsetting. Tab and I are... well, we're planning our future and they just can't seem to accept that it's over. Tab wants to be with me, now. He loves *me*. Is it wrong for two people who love each other and have so much in common to be happy together? I mean... *we're* in love!"

"Oh, no, that's not wrong at all" one of the officers says. "You both have every right to be happy!" he concludes as he gazes brazenly at your breasts. You shiver, and look up at Tab helplessly standing next to you. You don't have to say a single word to make him understand. He quickly takes off his denim coat and wraps it around your shoulders, pulling you to him, protectively.

"Would you look at this shit?!" Verona demands abrasively. You turn briefly, looking down your nose at her and then dismiss her just as quickly.

You look up at Tab, eyes wide and then back to the police officers. You're playing the part to the hilt but you can't stop, now. You *want* Tab, and the sight of Ruby and Verona makes you want to demonstrate more than ever before that they are *nothing* in comparison. Not when he has you—younger, fresher, prettier Daisy Rose. Ruby and Verona continue to watch, but now they're more composed. The reality is becoming clearer and they're beginning to seethe with jealousy and resentment. Verona glares with unadulterated hatred and Ruby suddenly begins to wail once more.

"Its cause I'm OLD, isn't it, Tab?"

"That's not it, you drunk whore," Verona begins, "its cause you piss your pants every day!"

Ruby looks at Verona, wide-eyed, and then begins to shriek forcefully, over and over as if she's being eaten alive. Tears and snot glisten on her red contorted face as you look over impassively at her huge gaping mouth, noticing for the first time that she's missing several back molars. You lean into Tab and clutch him around the waist, looking up at him. Your eyes are frightened as you glance over to the police officers, pressing your cheek against Tab's firm pectoral, snuggling in and batting your eyelashes as he pulls you into his arms.

"You know, I just never knew people could be so... so savage? Can you *imagine* what my poor fiancée has been put through by those two awful women?"

"It does look pretty bad, I'll give ya that," one of the officers says philosophically. "But I think alcohol and drugs are probably a daily part of *those* women's lives. Hopefully, they'll both get the help they need. Do you wanna press charges, miss?"

You look up at Tab, your eyes questioning and unsure. He bends down and kisses your nose, murmuring encouragement. You sniffle and a single tear makes its way down your right cheek, which is still pink and glowing with pristine cleanliness from the hot soapy shower.

"Officer, I really need to ask my fiancée what I should do. I consult Tab on everything. We're a team but I always ask his *permission* about important matters."

The three officers smile simultaneously, incredulous, and nod their heads in happy approval. A woman who consults her man—how novel their faces all seem to say. They're liking you and Tab more and more by the minute. You look up at Tab, eyes wide with unabashed adoration and childlike trust.

"Daddy? What should I do?" The oldest officer snickers and looks away, laughing quietly and shaking his head in disbelief.

"You need to press charges. They both need to be locked up for a few days. To teach 'em a lesson. Baby? I want you to press charges, okay?"

"Yes, Tab. I'll do as you say." You turn to the police officers and nod your head in agreement.

"My fiancée has decided that we need to, I mean... I mean *I've* decided that I need to press charges. So, that's what I'd like to do. For harassment—threatening my life *and* destruction of property!" you conclude smoothly.

"And Verona assaulted me. I wanna press charges, too." Tab announces firmly.

"Okay! That's all we need. Let's go get started on the paperwork. Looks like you two lovely ladies will be going back to Central—your new vacation home!"

Ruby and Verona begin to loudly protest, groaning and complaining and thinking up new colorful insults to hurl at each other. Inexplicably, Ruby accuses one of the officers of grabbing her butt earlier while she and Verona were being cuffed, but the man merely laughs at the notion. He seems genuinely amused, shaking his head in disbelief as if to say that could not possibly have *ever* happened. Ruby looks over at the officer, interprets what his incredulous laughter means, and begins to wail once again, begging the question: "What happened to my life?! What happened to my happy life?!"

The officers help them up off the lawn and as Ruby is nearby, Verona once again tries to kick Ruby's butt. This time she's successful. She lifts her foot and kicks Ruby squarely in the ass. Verona's big toe goes right up Ruby's butt cheek, her anus protected only by the denim of the jeans she's wearing, and the possible presence of a second hand thong. Ruby is propelled forward; her hands still tightly cuffed behind her back and is face-planted into the wet, velvety lawn. She lifts her head, gasping and begins to howl like a mournful starving coyote.

"Save me! Save me, Tab?!" Ruby wails.

"Oh Christ!" Tab mutters in disgust.

"Would you stop yer constant belly aching?" one of the officers mutters, reaching down to help Ruby up. He shoves her ahead of him, while the other two officers help Verona to her feet, reefing up her arms from behind until she squeals. Both women stumble to the patrol car angle parked by the curb in their bare muddy feet. Their butts are soaking wet from the grass (and urine in Ruby's case) and their heads are down, with Verona continuing to grumble and Ruby bawling loudly, her face covered in tears and snot.

"I pissed my pants! I pissed my pants!"

"Shut up! Can't you just shut up, you old whore?!"

The party is over for Ruby and Verona, but its only just beginning for you and Tab. You stand next to him as he waves goodbye to the officers, thanking them for their help and apologizing for the terrible trouble. You notice Blaze and Torch long ago disappeared and wonder if they went back to Torch's apartment to fuck. Probably, you think to yourself bemusedly. Tab looks down at you as you look up at him, and you can read his mind, just as he can read yours. You're both red hot, more turned on than you've *ever* been.

"Damn Daisy that was some performance. I started gettin' a hard on right there, as soon as you opened your mouth. I had no idea you were such a great actress. You sounded just like... like Marilyn Monroe!"

"It was fun. I took two years of drama in high school. It's come in handy a couple of times. I had to do my part, but you know none of this would have happened if you hadn't told Ruby about me."

"I know. That was a stupid move on my part."

"Oh well, I guess it was bound to happen, sooner or later, huh?"

"That's right baby, it was. Now, it's outa the way! We're a team now, aren't we? Just you and me. You love me though, doncha, baby?"

"I do love you, but then you already know that, you big gorilla!"

Tab smiles as you step into the apartment and he closes the door, turns the deadbolt and secures the chain lock. He turns to face you, and sees your eyes are sad and adoring as you approach him, placing your hands lightly over his chest, as you look up at him. He gazes down at you, the expression on his face purposeful and filled with intensity.

"And I love you, Daisy, completely and with my whole heart. Are you *my* girl, now?"

"I'm your girl."

He bends down, grips you under your armpits and scoops you up. As you rise into the air, you pinch up your nightgown, to free your legs so you can wrap them around his waist, hanging on like a monkey. You lay your head on his shoulder as he carries you down the hall without a word. You spend the next hour in your bedroom with the deadbolt locked, and all the lights on. The antique metal bed frame bangs against the wall as the neighbors yell for you to keep it down, but you don't care *who* objects, anymore. You and Tab will do exactly what your bodies demand.

CHAPTER THIRTEEN

Confidence and Aplomb

WHEN YOU WALK INTO THE office, it's with the easy confidence and aplomb of someone who simply doesn't care anymore. And you *don't* care. You swing your hips loosely, relaxed, noticing how tender and bruised you feel from the night before, when Tab was holding you down and fucking you hard. But you *have* dressed for the part and look fine in your new black skirt suit, pink silk blouse, black pumps and sheer black nylon stockings.

As you walk into the office, you feel it's become only a burden—this profession you used to love so much. It's lost all its former discovery and joy. There's no pretending now. You've changed. You're not the same girl you used to be, when it was so important to be the first on the scene—the first to investigate some despicable crime or horrific disaster, which had everyone questioning the existence of God and screaming at the sky. Now, you just don't care. You don't miss the depressing interviews, sitting down with broken people, Blood Simple from trauma, and having to ask the same dumb questions, or listen to the same stupid replies: "He was a loner who kept to himself," or "He seemed to really love his mother, I just can't imagine he'd kill her like that," or "I honestly didn't expect my ex-wife to stab me with a salad fork in the middle of the Spaghetti Factory." Once it was important to be the first to pitch that timely story idea to the assignment editors or producers who used to be your superiors—but now it's just not the same, because the thrill is gone. You no longer care about ratings, or finding that special scoop, because nine times out of ten the credit goes to some man anyway, whether he deserves it or not.

You were glad when the time came for you to leave the streets and become an assignment editor. You've never missed a single day of the hustle and bustle of chasing down that ever elusive story, or the tedious burden of dragging along some overworked stressed out cameraman going through yet another messy divorce. Gayle is right though, no one can keep the young reporters on task as well as you can, you seem to have the magic touch. But lately it just feels like so much babysitting. And you're sick of it. Always having to call them up, cajole them into getting the stories investigated properly, following every lead and then filmed. Then there is the dreaded editing process, the constant task of cutting time, trying to trim those annoying ten seconds that always need to be scrapped. It feels like you're caught in a Halloween corn maze and after searching for an exit for hours, you *still* can't find your way out.

Like you told Gayle, you're in a rut, and perhaps even ready for that drastic change you fantasize about. What she doesn't seem to understand is that you're feeling reckless—reckless enough to force her hand just to get it over with. Despite the meeting at The Georgian Room, you know it's not destined to last. Your promise to do better, not sass Gayle in front of the interns or skip off early will eventually come to naught.

You know it's only a matter of time before she fires you. You'll be sitting at the computer some dim afternoon with the gunmetal clouds hanging over the Portland landscape like a shroud. You'll be trying to help one of the new copy editors cut out a sound bite, trying to edit those interminable ten seconds that are always there, and always in need of trimming, and then you'll think of him—Tab. His image will come to your mind, his unlikely yellow hair and topaz colored eyes. And the expression on his face, so boyish and tender you'll get teary eyed just contemplating the very idea of him. You'll think of his legs, how long and beautiful they are and his thick lean torso. The perfection of every inch of Tab's body will come to you in a visceral rush of sensation, and then you'll *want* him.

You'll feel the ache only his presence and body can fill. You'll be sitting there at the desk, and suddenly you'll be a million miles away. The editor-in-training will call you by name, once, twice, maybe three times until you snap out of it, and return to the present moment. You'll laugh, excuse yourself, go to your office and call Tab on your cell. You'll whisper into the receiver like a criminal. You'll ask him to come and get you, sweetly, knowing he loves it when you beg. You'll tell him you need him to spirit you away to his apartment and the California King you know is waiting in his darkened, sweet smelling bedroom with the box fan and the Egyptian sheets and the dark purple and blue shadows.

You'll beg him to fuck you, and he will. Tab will pour wine for you, and light patchouli incense. He'll smile mysteriously as he sits in the tall backed chair next to his desk, shirtless and waiting for you to come to him, unzip his jeans and climb on. Tab will wait for as long as it takes, requiring it, demanding it of you—that you come to *him* now. And you'll do it, without hesitation, without pride, needing your hour of worship more than anything—your hour of worship in his darkened bedroom, with the black curtains, the lit candles and all the costly Buddhist sculptures and trinkets lying across every flat surface, like a second rate antique shop from 1930s Hollywood.

You see it all as clearly as the old carpet under your feet while you slowly walk down the long hallway to your locked office, silently lamenting the fact that you've got another eight or nine hours ahead of you, and you're not sure if you can make it.

There's such a continuous feeling of anti-climax when you're away from Tab, as if the world is spinning slower somehow, as if nothing's happening, and why should you care? But when you're *with* Tab, there's that feeling that anything is possible, coupled with the delirious sensation of forward momentum that leaves you breathless and eager for more. The atmosphere around Tab smells different, like spring even when it's not. Its only when you're *with* Tab that you notice that special scent so unique to Portland, of rain, wet trees, violets, moss and lilacs. It seems to drift through the air as you sail down Albina in his Ford truck, with the windows rolled down, and Tab smiling big. He's always glad to be at the wheel with you next to him, your hair wild as he speeds to his apartment across from Peninsula Park. You can see it all playing out, just like you know it will, if not tonight, then some other night, or some night after that.

And when you're with Tab, if he's not quietly discussing some aspect of mythology, or some Buddhist ritual that fascinates him, then he's suggesting a ride in his truck to the Rose Garden overlooking the city, or perhaps Kelly Point Park, a place you've both been to twice already. You'll walk on the cool sand in your bare feet, holding hands like you always hold hands, like a couple of high school kids. Or he'll regale you with another sad tale of his job as an unappreciated grade school custodian, knowing his stories make you laugh. Or suggest a movie, and dinner, followed by the sex that only *he* can give you, because there's always *that*. There's always the fucking.

Getting through the workday is becoming harder and harder. And today won't be any different. The singular torture of your day will be hearing Gayle's heavy stomping feet once she bursts into the office, and pounds down the hall. You know it will only be a matter of time before she's walking in your door, ready to bark some order, or make some asinine comment about her daughter or even your appearance and the clothing you're wearing. She'll demand to know why something's not been done to her satisfaction and what will be done to change it. Or she'll demand that you join her for lunch in her cluttered perfumy office, shoving another smelly curry in your direction and telling you to eat all of it, because God forbid we waste any good food when children are starving in Ethiopia. As if you don't already know that.

You walk into your office, sit down at your desk and toss your keychain into your open bag. You gaze down at the stale coffee from last afternoon sitting squarely on top of a manila folder from the Crank File you'd been perusing the day before, just for kicks. You shrug and take a long swig of the stone cold brew.

The taste is still sublime as the cream spreads across your tongue, coating it in a luxurious layer of milk fat. You lean back and guzzle the rest, closing your eyes in pleasure and fatigue. After slamming the mug down on your desk, you hear the unmistakable far off rumble of Gale's three hundred pounds as she turns in the hallway and stomps to her office. She's early, which might be good, or bad for that matter, but at this point, you're not sure which, or even that you care.

It will only be a moment before she's tossing the door of your office open, to stand there, a corpulent pink confection dressed in mauve, grey and fuchsia. And she'll either be a raging beam of sunshine, or a sullen hound from Hell, depending on her mood of course and whether or not she's eaten and her blood sugar is low. You're not sure which is worse, the happy Gale or the angry Gale, as both personas make you want to get up and run screaming from the room. The bizarre endless energy that she seems to put forth into both her personalities seems completely exhausting, and you still can't fathom how or why she's so driven. You hear her walk, somewhat tentatively to your door and strangely she knocks this time. You don't answer right away, surprised that she didn't just barge in. She knocks again in the same respectful nonaggressive way, and you answer, calling out for her to come in, thinking she might have changed her tune, or perhaps she'll make an effort to be civil. But as soon as Gale opens her mouth, you realize nothing has changed.

"Well hello, Daisy. You look lovely—for a funeral. I just thought I should tell you I got a call from my good friend Stella—she's one of the Lincoln parents... of the kids you gave your little speech to?"

"Oh yes, the little speech. Yes, I do recall the little speech."

"Don't get smart!"

"Yes, Gayle."

"That's better. Well apparently, you were a huge hit with her son, Devin. He's a senior. He's decided instead of pursuing a degree in English Literature or poetics at University of Portland, he wants to study journalism and get a job working for one of the *great* TV stations or newspapers here in town!"

"You're joking, right?"

"Well, actually, I'm NOT joking!"

"Okay? So, how does this involve me?"

"His mother is eternally grateful to you. Apparently, he wanted to be a poet or something equally moronic, and now he's decided on a more realistic major. I'd be grateful, too!"

"Is this good news? Have you encouraged his mother to talk him *out* of it?"

"Daisy, I'm trying to be positive! Why are you always so negative all the time?"

"Okay, so the kid wants to be a journalist. Okay. And?"

"And Stella wants to *meet* you. Her son Devin wants to meet you, too. I would be expected to come along of course as she's *my* friend."

"Well, I really don't have a lot of time to meet for coffee, I'm supposed to…"

"No, it's not like *that* Daisy. This would be a formal dinner at her home. She lives somewhere on Southwest Prospect Drive. She's loaded. It's a huge place overlooking the entire city, with a ball room and all that other 1920s crap from a bygone era."

"A bygone era, huh?"

"This would be a *formal* dinner at her estate. I'm *requiring* that you accompany me. This would be… a *business* dinner. I hope we understand each other?"

"Just tell me when and where." You slump down into your swivel chair, defeated as she glowers at you, triumphant, her mouth twisted in a wry smile.

"You know I know quite a few people in this office who would be THRILLED to go with me. But not you, oh no, not you."

"I'm just tired, that's all."

"Oh, you've always got *some* excuse."

"Generally, yes."

"It should be in about a month. I'll keep ya posted."

"Yes, Gale."

"You'll have fun, if you *allow* yourself to have fun. This is important too, so no freak outs or raging about the death of the print newspaper, how technology is changing everything, or any of those *other* tangents you like to go on, understood?"

"Yes, Gale. No tangents. No freak outs."

"I've ordered another curry for lunch. I'll expect you to join me. The interns aren't invited this time. Three hours from now. Okay?"

"Yes, Gale. Another curry. Thank you Gale."

"I requested it medium spicy this time, instead of extra spicy. Curries are good for your digestion, you know. Hopefully, you won't vomit like last time."

"I'll do my best. I promise."

"What you don't finish, you can take home. Waste not, want not, remember!"

"Yes, Gayle."

"By the way, is that story on the public masturbator done yet? We need to get pumping on that one… so to speak." You wince as Gayle snickers at her own joke.

"Martha and I are still working on it. I'm assisting with another cut."

"Well, get on it. We need it done before the end of the next century damn it all to Hell!"

You don't answer as she turns on her heel and pounds out the door. You can almost feel your stomach begin to churn thinking of the bi-weekly curry she's been demanding you share with her for the past three months, and the fact that she always orders them spicy just to be hateful. She *has* to be doing it on purpose, there's no other explanation. Whether she's aware of it or not, she's *trying* to push you out the door. With hope, things will begin to implode before the dinner on the hill with Devin, the teenaged journalist wanna-be from Lincoln with stars in his eyes.

The thought of meeting some pimply, humpy, repressed kid who wants to take Portland by storm as a journalist is about as appealing to you as scarfing down the curry that will soon be steaming under your reluctant nose. The stench will likely induce dry heaves as you delicately fork out bits of chicken and dip them in sweet-n-sour sauce to mask the heat, washing them down with iced lemon water, and trying your best not to vomit all over Gale's desk. You remember the scene, and how she had screamed obscenities and then dissolved into malicious laughter at the sight of you bent over her desk, dry heaving with pink and yellow vomit all down the front of your bright green turtleneck sweater, and gasping for breath as if you were dying.

As you sit at your desk, you pick up the office phone to start tracking down reporters, absently thinking of the emails, queries, memos and follow up messages you still have to attend to. But out of the corner of your eye, you're distracted by one of the Crank files. It's your favorite, from an old man named Spencer Mulroney, who's convinced that a sad hungry Big Foot lives in the SW Hills near his home, and communicates with extraterrestrials bent on saving Planet Earth from the evils of air pollution, landfills and global warming. Glancing down at it with an indulgent smile you pick it up, noticing once again its glorious heft and girth. You flip through the worn pages, forgetting the phone calls, the reporters, the queries and the follow up messages you're supposed to send, and begin to read just for the pure enjoyment of it.

The Crank Files—one of your truest guilty pleasures. Perhaps that should be the title of your first nonfiction book: *The Crank Files: How to Survive the Portland Literary Scene in an Age of Small Town Bias*. And you'd be the perfect one to write it you think to yourself with a smile, you'd be the perfect one.

CHAPTER FOURTEEN

Black Curtains and Incense

*T*HE SUNLIGHT DRIFTS IN LIKE vapor, a watery peachy aura meandering from behind Tab's black curtains as you stretch and yawn, pushing the slate grey silk comforter off and kicking your legs out. You're gloriously naked and feel wonderful, stretching like a cat lying in the warm shade on a sun dappled afternoon. You turn to see Tab; he's on his side, watching you, and smiling.

"How about we better get up?"

"I guess."

His hair is damp, as he swings his legs out of bed and walks over, nude, to close the pull-shade from behind the curtain which immediately darkens the room to a pale bluish charcoal.

"Why do you like it so dark in your bedroom? That's a funny quirk with you."

"Oh, I don't know. After my years with Blanche, I just got used to it. It's not important, baby. I just like it to be dark in here, I guess? Do ya not like it?"

"No, actually it's restful. I was just wondering. Blanche. Of course, *she's* behind everything, isn't she?"

"No, not everything, but a lot—you know we both have our histories. I'm no spring chicken."

"You're not old either Tab, so get off it."

"Sure, baby, whatever you say."

"Why are you up so early? It's not even ten yet."

"No reason. Just preoccupied I guess, worrying a little, too."

"Worrying? About what? You have nothing to worry about, Tab. Or do we?"

"I thought I should let you know, Daisy, I've contacted a Seattle realtor. We need to start seriously talking about Seattle. And I've put in my sixty days notice with the school." You sit up in bed, alarmed and give Tab your full attention.

"Sixty days? Jeez, Tab, do you think that's wise? We shouldn't rush things."

"This is something we need to do, baby. Do you really think Ruby and

Verona will give us any peace? To live our lives the way we want, or be happy? Because if you believe *that* then you're the one being naïve."

"I am *not* naïve... but do you really think they'll come after us?"

"As long as we stay in Portland, I can promise you they will. They're both crazy swingers. Took me a while to figure it out, but I did. But they're also addicts. With Ruby its booze, with Verona it's... other stuff. Plus, they're both vindictive as all get out. I don't have to tell you that."

"As all get out, huh?"

"As all get out."

"I dunno, I mean, can't we just..."

"Daisy, we need to start making preparations. It's inevitable we leave."

"But what would you do for employment? Another... custodian job?"

"Not exactly. I've been making arrangements to start with the Washington State Ferry service. They need new men and I've already got a commercial driver's license. It would just be a matter of training, but there's nothing I can't learn, especially if it means how to operate a big rig or a machine. I mean, how hard can it be working for the Washington State Ferry service? You just turn on the engine, and you steer!"

"What's it called again?"

"Technically, it's called the Washington State Ferry Company. It's a ferry service. I'd be navigating a Ferry across the sound, back and forth. That kinda thing."

"Well, that sounds... you know, fun and respectable, yeah!"

"Why, thank you my lady. You approve?"

"Of course I approve, come on!"

"I don't want you to be embarrassed to be seen with me since I'm only..."

"Stop it, I'm not embarrassed... it just took a while to get used to how... you know, how different we are. But I'm *not* ashamed of you. And I don't care who knows it either—you know, now that we're a couple."

"I'm glad to hear you say that, baby."

"Yeah, I need to start looking into something else, too."

"Like maybe a Seattle TV station?"

"No, I'm thinking I might apply with the *Seattle Post Intelligencer*. But, I mean I'll have to apply with multiple places obviously, but I don't anticipate much problem finding a job. I've been working for Gayle for nine years now, and I've been in media in one way or another for over fifteen. I'm just thinking I wanna get away from the pace of TV work, and settle into the more reasonable pace of... well, it's more than that, too. Most print newspapers are going belly up. I think it's important to keep the medium alive. It's a sacrifice I'm willing to make."

"Would it involve a pay cut?"

"No doubt it will, but so what. I wanna make a difference for a change."

"I know you'll do fine Daisy Rose, whatever you decide to do."

"I hope so. I don't know what's been wrong with me lately. But I think something *is* wrong, you know? I just feel so stagnant and trapped and, sometimes just so... sad. I can't stand my apartment, either. I hate being there. It feels haunted somehow—that old damp depressing place with hardly any sun, the windows in all the wrong places and the constant condensation on the glass. I have to clean those windows at least once a week. I hate being there alone most of all."

"I know, honey. You know you don't have to stay there. You can *always* stay here with me?"

"You wouldn't mind, or feel crowded or anything?"

"Of course not, and it would give you time... to think about what the issue is, why you're feeling the way you are. What the origin of your distress is?"

"The origin of my distress? Listen to you, like a doctor and everything."

"It's just something I remember from a book I read along the way."

"I can't figure out where it comes from, like what the source is, you know? It feels so deep and so... profound, this *sad* feeling. Like it's always been with me."

"I understand. It took me years to figure out I was depressed because of... well anyway."

"If you mention that dead woman's name again, I swear, Tab!"

"It's true, though. I don't know why she impacted me the way she did. Maybe it was cause I was so young and it was all so new and exciting."

"You mean when she started raping you at only fourteen?"

"It was sex Daisy, not rape."

"That's what I'd say too, if I was *you*."

"That's not what I was referring to. It was more after she died, all during my twenties. I spent years trying to replace her, trying to replicate that feeling—the emotions I felt with her, when we were making love, kissing, holding each other? I thought with Brandi maybe it could work."

"How could *that* have worked? Isn't Brandi younger than you?"

"Only four years younger but she *reminded* me of Blanche—with her dark humor and her good nature, her big booming laugh, her deep voice. But after the second baby was born, little Jill? Brandi just turned off, like a switch. Didn't want me to touch her—she'd cringe if I came near her. Then one night she told me it was cause... well, she'd had a relationship with her father's brother when she was in her early twenties, and it was all coming back to haunt her."

"Are you serious? Her *uncle?*"

"She'd never known him growing up and met him for the first time when she was twenty three. Within a month, they were fucking. She showed me the photos, hundreds of them. He looked kinda like Sean Connery. She told me he was "the love of her life."

"How long did it last?"

"A bit over six long years until her mother found out.

"Jesus!"

"They were at some lodge once, to go skiing, but really it was just so they could spend the weekend together and fuck nonstop. Some friend of her mother's seen 'em together and ratted 'em out to her mom, who put two and two together."

"What happened after that?"

"Her mother told Brandi's father who then confronted his younger brother, whose name was *Knut* of all things."

"What was it?"

"Knut. Ya pronounce it Ka-nooot. German or something."

"Sounds like a dog's name."

"They were half brothers, but still the guy *was* Brandi's half uncle. It was a huge family scandal. Her parents disowned her because she and the guy kept seeing each other on and off for several months. But it wasn't the same I guess, not after everyone *knew* about it, wasn't exciting anymore. Then I met her and I think she thought I could make it all go away. Like, I could save her?"

"I can only imagine."

"She never told me the truth a course. We got married and her uncle got super depressed. Left the country, started drinkin' and visitin' underage prostitutes, he even contracted venereal disease at some point."

"My God. I thought my family was fucked up. You never knew the truth?"

"No, a course not. She decided to spring this boatload of crap on me *after* little Jill was born, maybe a month later. I'll never forget the day she brought out the photos. It felt like a punch in the gut, like my stomach had gone into my throat somewhere. I felt sick."

"I'm sorry, Tab."

"She had all these photos, *Glamour Shot* photos of them together with their watches and jewelry and her hair and makeup done. Him with his polo shirt, his tan and perfect teeth, both of them smiling so big, so happy, just like regular people. Then there were the porno photos, of them fucking and kissing? She kept them in a locked strong box and told me they'd all been scanned and the negatives were in her safety deposit box at the bank. She told me if I ever destroyed 'em, she'd be able to have copies made, so I better not even try."

"Wow."

"She told me she'd die loving *only* him. That no other man could compare to the love she felt for her uncle, or all the great sex they had, how everything *he* did was perfect."

"In comparison to what... you Tab?"

"I dunno. I walked in on her one time, though, after she'd told me the truth, a few weeks later? She'd had her mother take the kids for the day so we were alone and I thought maybe I could get through to her, maybe we could make love and reconnect somehow."

"So, what happened?"

"She was in bed, leaning up against all the pillows, masturbating with a big red dildo I'd never seen before. She was holding up this huge eleven by fourteen of Knut fucking her. There were glossy photos everywhere, like fallen leaves all around her—dicks and cunts and tits and tongues everywhere, all over the bed. And she was crying, with tears all over her face while she crammed that dildo in and out. It was so weird. I just stood there, bug-eyed, ya know—trying to figure out what to do"

"That's actually really sad."

"She turned on me then, snarled at me to get the fuck out. I turned around and left. As I walked out the front door I could hear her coming, grunting like an animal and sobbing. I Left the apartment, spent the night in my car. That was the last time I *ever* came near her. I never touched her again after that. The sight of her sickened me. She packed up and left a few months later, taking the kids with her while I was at work. She had been planning it for weeks."

"Why'd she cut you off, though?"

"She said I started lookin' like her father, can you believe it? I was only four years older than Brandi and she accused me of *that*. She said havin' sex with me felt too much like incest. It was then I knew she was nuts. Blaming *me* for the affair she had with her uncle before I even knew her? Jesus! I can't remember feeling as hurt as I was when she gave me *that* crazy line."

"That's like... totally certifiable!"

"The following week she told me that my touch had always filled her with repulsion. That's how she phrased it—repulsion, but that she knew I'd be a good provider so she figured why not? By then the marriage was over. I'd tried for months to get her to see a doctor, but she refused. I went over eight months with no sex, beating off in the bathroom and then I met Ruby in the apartment elevator, and I just... I just couldn't say no. She was right there in the same apartment building, up on the sixth floor and I knew she was good for it. The first time I fucked Ruby, man, I came like a papa bear. I thought I'd pass out it felt so good. To be with a woman again?"

"So, then Ruby reminded you of Blanche?"

"With her it was cause she kinda *resembled* Blanche, in her face, her hair and how she dressed and did her makeup. But in time, ya know, I realized I'd never be able to replace Blanche and I kinda came to a place of rest with her. I stopped... looking."

"And then what happened?"

"Then I met you, baby. Then I met you."

"So, you're saying I've replaced Blanche? I'm the new Blanche, is that it?"

"Okay, take it easy. Don't get upset. No, you're *not* the new Blanche. You're the furthest from Blanche of any woman I've ever known. You have a little Minnie Mouse voice, you don't drink or smoke And your tits—I mean your *breasts* are more of a normal size, not huge?"

"Well, at least there's that."

"And you're educated. Blanche wasn't educated, she never made it past eighth grade, which is why she wanted *me* to finish high school and always read what I liked reading. She read worthless romance novels, while I read mythology. She was always so impressed by that."

"Wait, you said Brandi was crying when you walked in on her. Why?"

"Well, that's where it gets hairy. The guy hanged himself—Knut? He committed suicide and she blamed herself. She felt if she'd just not worried about what anyone said and gone with him, they coulda been happy together and he wouldn't have done it. He even gave her all his life savings, like fifty three thousand dollars or something. He worked for a travel agency his whole life, and that's what he had saved so he gave it all to her. He had an ex-wife and a young daughter then too, but he wrote them out of his will. Naturally, Brandi didn't give the ex-wife or the guy's daughter a dime, but that's how she was— always thinking only of herself."

"That's so selfish."

"They *both* were, like selfish children. He wrote her a ten page suicide letter that partly blamed his brother and partly blamed society for why they couldn't have their love be out in the open. He wrote that he wanted to marry her and father her children. Can you believe that? *Father* her children?! He was nuts, just like her, nuts! He told her she was the love of his life and that no one else could compare, so he might as well just die. He was only fifty when he hanged himself. Fifty!"

"Did you ever try to contact him, call him on the phone after you found out?"

"I didn't know what I'd *say*! If it had been any *other* man, I'd have been jealous. I'd maybe fought for her, but her *uncle*? How do you approach that? How do you solve a riddle like that? I never did a thing. I just let our marriage die. Or maybe I should say I let *her* let our marriage die. Then Ruby came along and the rest is history."

"He really committed suicide?"

"The fucker hanged himself in his hotel room in Thailand, after spending the afternoon fucking an underage prostitute. He offed himself with the girls pink tights. After that all Brandi had were all those photos, close ups of them fucking and kissing that they'd taken with a tripod and a timer. Hundreds. Close ups of his dick, close ups of her pussy, close ups of his dick going in her pussy. That was what turned her on. Her fuckin' uncle! After she cleaned out the apartment while I was at work, I literally couldn't believe I'd ever been stupid enough to get involved with her. We knew each other for only three months before we got married, but by the time she left, I was *glad* she was gone."

"Jesus, that's just… biblical somehow."

"It is kinda biblical. It's one of the reasons I get sad too, Daisy. I think of my kids and how screwed up Brandi is, how tormented she must still be. How she'll *never* be happy. How she'll never be… normal? And it makes me sad."

"I know it does."

"But like you, I try to deal with it. Like you, I just try to… swallow it. Push it down."

"What was it about her that you responded to? I mean, what did she *have*?"

"Brandi was really beautiful and fun, at least in the beginning. She was like the opposite of you in appearance. She wasn't so pale, as you. She was tan, sporty, with reddish auburn hair, and light green eyes. She dressed really nice, cracked jokes, laughed a lot. She'd walk in a room and everyone would turn and look at her. Kinda how people turn and look at *you* when you walk into a room, but you're way more feminine looking than Brandi ever was. You have a gentle baby face, a kind face, and kind eyes."

"You're layin' it on pretty thick."

"It's only the truth, baby. Anyhow, Brandi seemed to enjoy sex, at least for a while in the beginning. Then she *didn't* and she dumped all her secrets on me, and it just… well, it just killed our marriage."

"I'm sorry."

"That's why I think a fresh start away from Portland would be so good for us—to just leave all these ghosts behind… in the past… in Portland."

"I don't remind you of Blanche in any way?"

"No, not in any way, baby. She had a deep voice, like Verona. Gin and cigarettes, they call it. Your voice is soft and you squeak like a little girl when you come."

"Would you shut up?"

"Come on, Daisy. You *know* I love you. I wanna be with you and no one else."

"Is that right, Mr. Blaine?"

"You know damn well it is!"

"You wanna take a shower, now? We need to get started on our day."

"That's exactly what I was thinkin' baby."

"Maybe, you can massage my shoulders, they're tense."

"What else can we do in the shower? Any suggestions, Daisy girl?"

"You still have that shower seat you like to sit on, sometimes?"

"I got it. What'd ya have in mind?"

"If you get some of that water proof lubricant you have, on your nightstand? I could sit on your lap and we could, you know, comfort each other like how we do?"

"I like the way you think, Daisy. I'll get the lubricant."

"Tab?"

"Yeah, sugar?"

"Do, I… you know, do the things you like?"

"You have no idea how much you please me."

"Really?"

"No foolin' Daisy. I don't have to negotiate or make plans with you. I don't have to bribe you with dinner or jewelry. You're always game. Just like me, you're always game. So, don't you worry. You please me to the moon and back."

CHAPTER FIFTEEN

Spinach and Red Wine

*F*OR A LATE LUNCH YOU decide on spinach and pear salad with gorgonzola, sugared walnuts, and raspberry vinaigrette. It's your new favorite salad Tab introduced you to and you can't seem to get enough of it. Later, for dinner you'll prepare vegetarian lasagna, sautéed spinach along with fresh raw mushrooms and red wine, so you and Tab decide to head out early to go food shopping. As soon as you get outside the bright sun stuns you with its unforgiving light. You shade your face with your hand, and agree Tab should probably drive your Lexus rather than his Ford truck. He's parked the Ford several blocks away in the driveway of a sympathetic neighbor named Randy, who knows both Ruby and Verona, having seen them in action himself in a downtown tavern, a smelly dive called, The Dirty Duck.

You quickly skulk down the walkway to the car, clutching your purse to your chest. Tab looks from left to right, making sure Ruby and Verona aren't squatting nearby, lurking behind a French lilac or blue hydrangea with a dull spoon or fork in hand waiting to attack. He quickly unlocks the door, slides in the driver's seat, reaches over and opens the passenger door. You slip inside, looking around like a furtive criminal as you pull the seat belt on, and Tab shoves the key in the ignition and locks the doors.

You do all this in an effort to avoid Ruby and Verona who have both been bailed out by family and friends and have begun calling Tab and making various threats. Though Ruby is now fifty seven-years-old, and hasn't had sex with Tab in months, she's already called twice to inform him, amidst tears, that she's pregnant and simply doesn't know what to do. Fortunately, Tab saw through the lie and didn't respond. In fact, when the call took place, only the day before, he changed his number on the spot, calling the phone company and telling them death threats from his ex-wife's new boyfriend have put his life in jeopardy. They didn't charge him and within five minutes he had a new cell number. His fear then was that if they can't reach him by phone, they'll both ratchet up the harassment and start swinging by his place in person in one fashion or another.

As Tab drives to the New Seasons it gives you time to talk, and strangely, you find yourself wondering about his obsession with *The Thinker*, by Rodin. It's been bothering you for as long as you've known Tab and perhaps if you ask him, you'll be a little closer to understanding him, because as much as he appears to be a straightforward person, he's not. He's complex and sometimes secretive, able to hide much of what he doesn't want revealed behind a demeanor of placid agreeableness, good cheer and politeness. If it's the last thing you do, you want to get to the core of the ultimate mystery that is Tab— the man who appears to have no secrets, but in reality is full of them.

"Why do you love *The Thinker* so much? There *has* to be a reason. It's not like I'm gonna judge you. I've just always wondered."

"No real reason, I guess I just like it, that's all."

"No reason, huh? That doesn't make much sense, Tab."

"Do I have to have a reason for liking the damn thing? It's just a beautiful sculpture."

"No. There's more to it than that. Fess up. Tell me?"

"Tell you what? Why I like it?"

"Hasn't that been the question all along?"

"I dunno, I just like it."

"I had no idea this would make you so upset."

"I'm not upset, Daisy, okay?"

"Cough it up, Tab. I wanna know. TELL me!"

"Jesus, alright! I guess… I dunno, I personify the thing. Isn't that what they call it, personification?"

"Right? Continue?"

"It's just that maybe… maybe I see some of myself in *The Thinker*. He's a good looking guy, tall, lots of muscles, women like him?"

"Lots of muscles, okay. And?"

"He's in good shape, and it's his body is what makes him who he is, right? But he's not dumb. He thinks! He's a thinker, bent over with his head in his hands."

"He does seem to be thinking, I'll give you that. Go on."

"Well, that's what I like about it, okay? It shows that even if you are a good looking guy, just cause you've got a good body and… well, in my case, really light blond hair? It don't mean you're stupid."

"I see."

"He's got things on his mind. Unsettling things, like how I do. I guess there are lotsa reasons I like *The Thinker*. Mainly, I guess I like how I feel about myself when I'm looking at him."

"*Him*? Huh. Did people ever try to say you were stupid, like, when you were younger? Is that what's at the core of this?"

"Everyone did, Daisy—the teachers, the kids, the damn neighbors!"

"Why?"

"Cause I was dreamy and vague, cause I saw things different. Cause I loved lookin' at the girls and they mostly seemed to like me, too. Boys called me faggot, but the girls were all over me, even then. They'd dress me up, put make-up on me, try to curl my hair. Teach me kissing games when I was ten, fondle me, things like that."

"Fondle you?! When you were ten?!"

"Well, you know? They'd tell me their secrets and stuff. Promise me to secrecy. I never told the other boys, though, even when they begged. Even then, I knew how to keep a secret. But basically, they *all* said I was dumb. Even when I was gettin' good grades in writing class and English in high school they said I was dumb. The girls never did though. The girls, they liked me—even some of the popular girls."

"So, when you look at *The Thinker* by August Rodin, you feel… better about yourself?"

"Who?!"

"By Rodin, by *August* Rodin?"

"Daisy? It's Augoooste Rodin. It's pronounced Augoooste Rodin, not the common August like what comes after July!"

"Well, well, Mr. Fancy."

"It's important to show the proper respect for the man. He *was* a genius."

"Okay, okay. Whatever you say, Tab. I don't wanna offend you or anything."

"Well, pronouncing another person's name correctly is important."

"Are we almost there, yet?"

"Are we almost there, yet? I love how you ask me that, like a kid. Yeah, baby, we're almost there. Let's buy some extra stuff. I want dinner tonight to be a real feast. If… the girls come over, we can always split and spend the night in a motel somewhere. We won't have to hide from them forever, you know?"

"A motel? That might be fun, okay."

"I'll pay for it, of course."

"We could go halfsies if you…"

"No Daisy. I'll *pay* for it. Don't worry about it."

"Okay. Whatever you want."

"I try to be a gentleman."

"You are a gentleman, Tab."

"Okay, then, I'll pay for it."

After you finish the shopping, drive back to Tab's place and park in front of the apartment, you quickly time your departure from the car and hustle the bags up to the landing above the concrete stairs. Tab quickly slides the key in the lock of the main foyer door, and pushes it open as you both bend down to grab the paper bags by their handles. You're standing back up, when you hear Verona yell from across the street and you both freeze.

Verona's voice is as gravelly and evil sounding as you remember. Instantly goose bumps cover your entire body and the fine transparent gold hairs on the back of your neck stand up. You both look over and see her standing next to a bush of daphne odora, with her hands planted firmly on her hips, dressed in ratty blue jeans, a dingy purple tee shirt, and neon orange flip flops. She'd been hiding in front of a house, watching as you got out of the car and scurried up the front steps to the door. Verona continues yelling in that loud gin and cigarettes voice that sounds like it comes from within a tomb in some, ancient cemetery somewhere in the Deep South, in a forgotten nightmare of a town populated with only bigots and racists.

"Tab?! You and your new CUNT are never gonna work. You'll cheat on *her* just like you did on Brandi and Ruby and me! It's always gonna be in your nature to cheat, because *that's* what you are. You're a cheater and you'll never be happy either, you worthless son-of-a-bitch!"

Tab is silent, but his face darkens, and his jaw begins to clench. He's standing just behind you, and it's at that moment you see Ruby scamper out from behind Verona, brushing off some dry leaves from her discolored, spotted, bare arms. She's wearing a short red mini skirt with black stockings, a hot pink tank top with no bra underneath, and old-looking, scuffed ivory colored pumps. She looks like any garden variety streetwalker you might see loitering on Sandy Boulevard late at night clutching a Big Gulp, and drunkenly singing to herself. Tab groans as soon as he sees her.

"God, Ruby really has gone to hell."

"Let's just get inside, Tab. Then we'll wait them out and head to Beaverton. I'm sure there's a Motel 6 we could find. "

"Good idea," Tab murmurs.

Ruby struts into the street walking behind Verona, with her head high and a defiant look on her heavily made-up face just as you dive into the foyer, then into the hallway to the right, and finally to Tab's unit on the first floor, number 7. He plunges the key in the lock and then you're both in the living room, lugging in the bags of heavy groceries. Tab is behind you, and quickly sets down the bags he's carrying. He turns, closes the apartment door, turning the deadbolt and locking the chain lock. You both sigh once inside the relative safety of the quiet, still apartment.

"Oh thank God. At least we made it inside, huh?"

"What's wrong, baby? They'd never hurt you. You know that, right? I'd *never* allow them to lay a finger on you. You understand that, right?"

"I know honey, it's just…"

"No, you need to understand that. You need to have faith in me, that I'd protect you!"

"Well, they're both so... intense and angry. How could two women become so angry at life?"

"With those two, easy, that's how."

"I know if they ever got me alone, they'd probably—you know they'd probably kick my butt!"

"I'll tell you what; juggling those two was a full-time job. There were times I could just feel the energy draining from me. They're both psychic vampires—total psychic vampires."

"Isn't that where the person sucks all your energy, and positivity from you? I think my ex-husband was a psychic vampire."

"Well, I'm done with both of 'em, and I want you to know that, baby! I'm never gonna look somewhere else again. I have no reason to, now. You are all I could ever want or need. Okay?"

"I believe you, Tab. Don't worry. *They* can't change my opinion of you."

"Good, cause I want you to know, cheating is not something I'm comfortable with. It doesn't come second nature to me. I never really *enjoyed* it, if that makes sense."

"I hear you. Don't worry."

You both walk to the bay window and look out, fascinated and wary at the two morbid spectacles out on the street. Ruby and Verona don't venture past the sidewalk leading to the apartment; they just stand in the gutter, their feet almost touching some pooling water with the rainbow sheen of heavy motor oil undulating across it. They seem to know not to cross *that* line. They hang back and start yelling obscenities and strutting up and down the gutter, next to the sidewalk, like a common *strawberry* would—a hooker trying to display her most advantageous angles to a hungry audience of horny men with fat wads.

They continue cursing and you can see they're perspiring and waving their arms, pointing and making obscene threats. Tab pulls the draperies fully open and walks with you to the window, standing directly in front of it. He takes your hand and gently pulls you in front of him, as if he's putting you on display. He places both of his large hands on each shoulder protectively, possessively as he stands behind you. Finally, you turn and see the defiant look on his face and how his chin is held high and he's looking disdainfully down his nose at them as they stand outside in the street. He's challenging them in his own way, in that silent way he sometimes adopts that still mystifies you. Knowing intuitively that he wants to give them a performance, you turn and look up at him. You wrap your arms around his waist as he glares out the window, disgusted, and nuzzle your face into his left arm pit.

"God, I wish they'd just get the hell outa my life!" Tab mutters.

"You wanna give 'em something to remember?" you breathe, giggling up at him.

"Yeah, look at 'em, just standing out there like a couple a old bag ladies. Let's give the crazy wenches a thrill."

"*Wenches!* That's funny!"

Tab glances down at you. His eyes soften as he gathers you up, leans down, bending his knees, and kisses you on the mouth. You're swaying in his arms while hearing the distant roar of Ruby and Verona outside screaming obscenities and wild comical insults about rape, broom handles and ending up dead in a penitentiary in Caldwell, Idaho. Tab reaches down and picks you up *Gone with the Wind* style. He continues to hold you like that for another full minute, and then looks out the window, a placid smile on his handsome face. Your left arm drops and your head falls back, as if you've just lost consciousness. Your pale neck is exposed and particularly vulnerable looking, your pert breasts point to the ceiling, the nipples hard through the thin fabric of your pink Nike tee shirt. You giggle thinking how dramatic it must look from their frame of reference outside on the street looking in, with the bay window acting as a silver screen of alluring voyeurism. They can look *in* but they can't *enter* your world. Tab chuckles looking down at you, limp with surrender as he holds you easily in his beefy golden arms.

"Damn, Daisy, you're like a regular ham, you know that?"

"Just shut up and play along. They need to think about us every day, all the damn time. I want it to torture them!"

"That's downright evil, baby, but somehow… I like it!"

"Of course you do. Now take me to the bedroom and show me you're the boss!"

"You got it bossy girl. I'll sting yer butt for that."

"Get moving, Tab!"

Ruby and Verona were silent for only a moment, just as soon as you played the limp lover having a fainting spell, but as soon as Tab turned around and began walking slowly to the hallway, away from their view, dismissing them, and heading to the bedroom, the distant roar of their screaming started up all over again.

"Tab, do you think one of the neighbors will call the cops, like last time?"

"Probably, but that's okay. By the time they get here in the next half hour, we'll be done messin' around and we can talk to them if we have to. Right now, we need to comfort each other."

"Yeah. We need to comfort each other."

CHAPTER SIXTEEN

Preparing for the Talionic Night

*T*HE FOLLOWING MONDAY YOU WAKE up and realize that getting Torch on board for your big night is your next serious priority. You've got to explain the details, and what you'll be expecting of her. Of course, you'll *have* to lie. But that's not a problem. Lying to people like Torch has never been a problem—not for you anyway. It's an absolute necessity in fact, as Torch is not someone you could trust. She'd rat you out to a cop or perhaps another journalist if she was given enough of a reason—so what she doesn't know can't hurt her.

And for right now her options in life are limited—so you know she's good for the favor. She wants to be your best friend and you've got to play along and let her think you are. If you tell her you'll pay her $300 for her help, she'll be as good as gold. Letting her think it's your ex-husband you're getting even with is the lie that will make her comfortable with breaking the law. But you suspect this won't be the first time Torch has broken the law.

Your biggest current need is creating a rock solid alibi if Torch is ever questioned. You've planned it down to the last possible eventuality. If all goes as planned, you and Tab will slip away on that dark night and be gone and in Seattle long before the police are ever called to report the damage to Gayle's interminably pink office early Monday morning. You call Torch on the phone and give her the details. You promise to bring her dinner at her place, cheesy pasta, green salad, with Green Goddess dressing, and toasted garlic bread, and that Tab will be there too, but she has to keep everything top secret or it won't work. Toying with Torch on the phone turns out to be more enjoyable than you imagined. She's like a child in that she believes you and makes all the right sounds at all the right intervals. As you speak to her, you marvel at your easy ability to deceive. She's among the kind of people who think *they're* the deceivers, and not the other way around. No doubt there's a part of Torch that thinks you're not only soft but also dumb. She couldn't be more wrong.

"Torch? I need to get some stuff back from my ex-husband. He stole one of my diaries, from when I was a teenager and into my twenties? There were some photos I'd taped to some of the pages, about forty eight of them. It's a photo album, photos taken back when Instamatic cameras were all the rage, remember those? I need to get them back. Do you think you can help me?"

"Dang, Daisy, I told you, I'm on board. And we already discussed your nudie photos, remember? I still can't believe you loaned me that $279 for the rest of my rent. You saved my fricken life!"

"Don't worry about that. Consider it a gift. Tab and I will swing by with dinner sometime later tonight. He'll show you how to do the Hustle. He's really good at it and a pretty good dancer."

"He likes to dance?"

"Oh yeah. Tab's a hoot. We'll have fun."

"Sure! You know, I've been so alone the last five years, and you've been, like, my only friend."

"I get it, Torch. I can relate better than you think. So, how about 7:30, right around there?"

"I'll be here. In fact, I'll start cleaning up my place now. I don't wantcha to be grossed out by my disgusting mess."

"Sounds good, girlfriend. See ya then!"

When Tab arrives to your place, he's been prepped on the evening. You have to meet with Torch and he may have to flirt with her just a little, teach her how to do the Hustle, joke around, lead her on a little bit. He's angry, of course. He's against the night you're planning, explaining that it's too dangerous, that its overkill. He's not convinced Gayle is really that bad a person. He tried to talk you out of it on the phone before he arrived, but failed to convince you: "Why do you still wanna *do* this? You haven't given me a good enough reason." He was angry and frustrated but still you dismissed his concerns.

"I told you Tab, I *know* she's going to fire me. And it's payback for all the years of her bullying me—not only me, but others too, including that poor child of hers, Mary Jennifer?"

"Let's be honest, baby, you're going to make *sure* she fires you. You're going to make sure that happens, so don't blame her. It's *you* who will make *that* happen."

"Do you really think you're qualified to psychoanalyze me?"

"You're not that hard to figure out, baby."

"Oh really? And what's your background, Dr. Tab?"

"Stop being coy. I know how this game is played."

"What game?"

"You think I haven't done it myself, Daisy?"

"Well, I dunno! I don't know everything about your past, you know!"

"Remember I told you I worked at the Prime Rib up on Sandy years ago, and how much I hated it? I got myself fired when some old woman complained about my service, called me stupid or slow, or something. I walked over to the station, picked up the plastic ice water decanter and walked back to her table. I poured that whole damn container of ice water onto her hot lap. Cooled her off right, quick. They fired me on the spot. But I knew what I was doing, that's why I *did* it."

"This is different Tab! Listen, if you don't wanna be a part of it, fine. I'll do it alone, with only Torch's help. At least I can count on *her!*"

"I'm trying to reason with you. It's too risky. What if you were discovered in her office, committing criminal mischief, not to mention the charge of breaking and entering? They could arrest you—it'd make the papers. Can you imagine? Competing news agencies love stories like this, and you should know that. You'd be the fuck-up who burgled her boss's office and tore the place up. You'd be a laughing stock, Daisy!"

"That's not gonna happen!"

"Remember that one cop who was stealing presto logs from the old Thriftway in NW? Officer Callahan, I think? Made the damn news, didn't it? They even had the dumb jerk on camera. Now, can you imagine how embarrassing that would be for you, if you made the news? It would ruin any future career prospects."

"No, it wouldn't! I'm not gonna get caught!"

"You know, I've never been arrested Daisy. I made that choice myself—to always be polite, to always cooperate, even when I was a little buzzed, out driving when I shouldn't have been. If I knew I was in the wrong, I apologized—I acted right. And I didn't break into someone's office. There were at least a couple times I coulda been arrested but I wasn't. Because I wasn't out lookin' for trouble!"

"What for buzzed driving?"

"Yeah! For buzzed driving which is basically the same as driving drunk!"

"Well, good for you!"

"And now, I'm glad I've never been arrested. I'm fifty-two-years old. Staying in steady and good employment becomes more important and more of a challenge the older you get, Daisy. You're gonna learn that. I'm fifteen years older than you, baby. I don't like to pull rank about our age difference but right now I feel like I need to. There are certain things I know that... well, I guess you don't."

"Stop trying to talk me out of it. And stop talking *down* to me. I'm gonna do it whether you approve or not. I have to. I have a moral obligation to stand up against that horrible shrew of a woman. Besides that cop didn't even get fired. He was only suspended and then a few months later, he got promoted to sergeant! That's how it generally works at PPB!"

"Baby, please listen!"

"I'll do it alone. You don't have to be a part of it, mister holier than thou!"

"Got-damn-it Daisy!"

"Just shut up, Tab! I'm done talkin' about it!"

"Baby, let's fuck? That'll make you feel better. I'll come right over and we can fuck!"

"I'm sorry Tab, but we've got an engagement in only a few minutes, with a certain Torch Tremble—my neighbor and an educated woman of quality!"

"If she could hear how you talk about her, she wouldn't be your friend."

"Yeah, well, the tramp *can't* hear how I talk about her so problem solved!"

You hang up the phone and wait for Tab to arrive. You're still dressing when you open the front door and he walks in, sullen and quiet, following you to the bedroom like a little boy who's being punished. You pull on the Khaki shorts you've chosen to wear; pulling them up over your shapely bottom covered only by a tiny pair of French-cut black lace panties. You glance over at Tab as he watches, his eyes filled with bitter resentment and sorrowful lust.

You slip on the new halter top, made from pink and green calico, tying it in the back. You're wearing heavy sterling silver hoop earrings and your dark ringlets look particularly pleasing as they bounce around your shoulders. You adjust your breasts, shoving them up into the halter top and look at your reflection in the ornate beveled mirror on the bedroom wall.

"Look at that hot tramp!" you murmur, glancing over at Tab brazenly.

"Come on baby girl, lemme undress ya and make ya happy? We can get naked right here. It's been three whole days since we been together. I need your pussy."

"Tab, she's expecting us. My gold plated pussy can wait. And remember, you may have to teach her how to do the Hustle."

"I don't want *anything* to do with that diseased skank! Why are you pressuring me like this?"

"I'm expected at my friend's house!" you announce blithely as you stride out of the bedroom, flipping your hair over your shoulder. Tab follows, stopping just as he steps beyond the threshold, his arms limp at his sides, his face crestfallen. You turn around and can't help but notice the fat lump swelling beneath his trousers.

"Oh, Tab, are you hard for me? Again?"

"Don't mock me, please. It's that gold plated pussy of yours!"

"Awwww, you know I love you poppa. Now let's go. Later, I'll let you do whatever you want."

"I'm gonna hold you to that, Daisy," Tab says miserably, slouching forward.

"We need to bring over the pasta and the salad, so help me carry it, please?"

When Torch opens the door, her face brightens and her eyes widen as she takes in Tab. He's straightened up and looks as eager and pleasant as an eighth grade Boy Scout leader. You told Tab not to change after getting off work, so he's still wearing his custodian work pants discolored with grease and grime and a clean but perspired in tee shirt with pit stains. He looks pleasingly working class and the sexy musk of his sweat drifts around him nicely, mingling with his *Old Spice* aftershave. As you stand next to him, Torch's eyes wander from Tab, to you.

"Damn Daisy, you look hot tonight!"

"Where the party's at, Torch! That's why we're here. We wanna par-tay!"

"Hey, do you mind if Blaze comes over? He's got kinda a crush on me. He's turning eighteen soon, which will be nice cause I won't have to worry about the cops coming around to arrest me for statutory!"

"What? You crazy girl!"

"We've been getting busy for the past few months. And dang, that boy sure knows how to swing his ass between the sheets!"

"You and Blaze? I love it. Torch and Blaze settin' the world on fire!"

"He's real sweet; I could get stuck on a boy like that."

"And he really likes you, I know cause he told me!"

"Did he really? Oh my God! Look at me! Come on in. I'm sorry, you just both present such a pretty picture here, I got totally distracted lookin' at you."

"I also brought some Gallo over, Torch!"

"Wow, thanks! I know it's cheap and stuff, but it's actually my favorite."

"I bet it is, you party animal. And truth be told, it's *my* favorite, too!"

"Really?! Cool!"

"Yep!"

"And you brought dinner, just like you said you would!"

"That I did!"

For the next three hours you and Tab slum with Torch. After you all slowly eat dinner, Tab teaches Torch how to do the Hustle step by step and she pretends she doesn't understand just so he'll show her again, touching her hips and going through the motions one more time. You sit and watch, laughing and cat calling from the stained overstuffed chair next to the kitchenette.

"You better not steal my man, Torch, or I'll have to kill ya!"

"You're my sister; I'd never steal Tab, though if I wanted to, I could!"

"Bitch! I'll kill you!"

You and Torch bust out cackling, your laughter wild and uncontrollable as you notice Tab looking over at you and trying to disguise the concerned look in his eyes. You're drinking the cheap Gallo Torch likes to swill and after another forty five minutes you notice Tab becomes giddy and starts laughing, too. You know why—because he hates every minute of it and having to pretend he likes Torch is practically killing him. He's bent over with tears coming to his eyes. She leans into him and he gently pushes her away, for the third time, pretending to be clumsy, and drunker than he is. He's about ready to lose it and you realize you may have to leave earlier than you'd thought.

"Gimme some more of that garbage SWILL!" Tab yells from where he's standing, startling Torch, who stumbles and then starts laughing hysterically.

"Poppa-Daddy-Big Boy! Your wish is my command!" you squeal back.

After you carry over the bottle, Tab takes a big gulp, burps loudly, and then sets the bottle on the floor beside the couch. You stumble with him over to the couch and sit down, noticing for the first time the fine beads of perspiration on his peach colored forehead. Torch changes tactics and begins regaling you with stories of her time as a punk rock singer and bass player. She stands in the middle of the living room and acts out the parts. She talks about "the Fuck House" on NE Stark Street and how one cold December they got a girl named Darcy to bleed onto a Tampax pad and then decorated their Charlie Brown Christmas tree with it, taking photos and laughing uproariously at the bled-on Tampax pad, swilling beer and yelling: "Merry fuckin' Christmas!" Torch tells you how she stole multiple boys from their fiancée's and pregnant girlfriends all during the 1980s, explaining that *all* the girls did that and it was expected if you were in the punk scene. The love triangles were endless and the scene completely incestuous as everyone had slept with everyone else, she explained nonchalantly, nodding her head up and down affirmatively.

Torch shows you both how to dance punk style, a frenetic jerky dancing that looks painful to watch, let alone mimic. You and Tab watch, dismayed, your faces confused and bewildered by the frenetic movements. After Torch starts coming down from her frenzied dancing and energetic storytelling, she slumps over to the old plastic record player, out of breath, and puts on the B-52's, apologizing that she listens to them because she doesn't really like puck rock music anymore. She finally came to a point in her life when she realized it was just "so much stupid noise."

As Torch starts another story of a wild party at the Fuck House, with over 100 people, including a drunk girl with a video camera, the door bursts open and Blaze storms in making a beeline for Torch with an angry look on his face. He notices you and Tab sitting next to each other on the sofa and mumbles a surprised greeting, then strolls up to Torch and starts pulling on her loose pullover shirt and kissing her as they stand in the middle of the living room.

"I'm fuckin' horny!" he announces petulantly.

He looks over at you and Tab, tangled up on the sofa and becomes excited by the sight of you—your limbs intertwined and the suggestion of some kind of graphic impending intimacy looming heavily in the air.

"Are you guys makin' out er what?"

"Could be young man!" Tab slurs drunkenly.

You're both drunk, but reach the same telepathic conclusion simultaneously.

You turn to each other, open your mouths and start nosily sucking face, your tongues flicking at each other like hot pink serpents. Blaze continues to watch, his smooth grey face fascinated and expectant, his eyes wide. "Fuckin' awesome! Just like in middle school! Group fucks, man! I loved those group fucks—watchin' your best buddies porkin' some girl." Blaze turns to Torch and tries to kiss her. She pulls away and walks to the overstuffed chair and plops down, opening her arms. He walks over and falls into her lap and they commence making out for the next two minutes. You and Tab watch, smiling. The record player replays the B-52's vinyl over and over—the *Summer of Love* album from 86' until Blaze turns and angrily demands some wine.

"Gimme some of that wine!"

"Are you sure you're old enough to drink, young man?" Tab slurs. "I heard you're not even... not even twenty one yet!"

"I'm a man, old timer—turnin' eighteen soon! I can do anything any *other* man can do. I lost my cherry when I was ten! I been bein' a man ever since. And I *love* me some women! Especially old ladies like Torch here. She's game and she'll do most anything, won't ya Mama?"

"Whatever you want, baby," Torch mumbles.

Tab stands, picks up the Gallo bottle, walks over and hands it to Blaze who grabs it without saying thank you, and drinks deeply. He promptly burps and then laughs at his own burp. Blaze turns back to Torch, as she's lying back on the overstuffed chair. She has a drugged smile on her face, her red lipstick smeared all around her mouth, and her eyes are almost closed. Blaze presses the spout to her mouth and lifts up the bottle, forcing her to drink. Torch arches her back, opens her mouth and drinks, her eyes closed tight while Blaze holds the back of her head firmly and she gulps mouthfuls of the cheap wine. It spills out the sides of her mouth and drifts down, onto her neck and over her heavy breasts packed into a tight black bra. Blaze reaches down and sucks the spilt wine from her neck and breasts and then starts kissing her again as he sets the bottle clumsily on the end table next to the chair. After a moment, Blaze turns back to Tab, who's still standing there, looking around the room, but not really seeing anything. Blaze explains to Tab, as if he's addressing a child, that he's going to take Torch to her bedroom and "fuck her until she comes."

"You guys can stay if'n you wanna watch?" Blaze offers.

"A man hasa do what a man hasa do!" Tab drunkenly slurs, smiling stupidly.

"So, you wanna watch old timer?"

"I'll pass young feller, I'll pass." Blaze smirks and turns to Torch, hauling himself off her lap and then looking down at her authoritatively.

"You get up and get yer fat ass in that bedroom!"

Torch smiles, gets up and walks into the hallway without a word, swinging her hips. Blaze follows behind and reaches out and smacks her plump butt soundly. She squeals at the hard slap and is silent. He shoves her in the back to walk forward more quickly as she whimpers for him not to be so rough this time. Blaze slams the door and you hear them as they stumble into the room and fall on the futon. You hear Blaze laugh, telling Torch he likes it rough and she'd better start getting used to it.

Tab is still standing in the middle of the room. After a moment, he walks over, reaches down with his hands and pulls you up by your wrists, lifting you off the sofa and into his arms. He's kissing you and gripping your hair in his right fist. His tongue is in your mouth and the taste of cheap red wine is intoxicating as you go limp and open your mouth wide, your knees buckling, falling into him. He pulls away slightly, yet as his tongue slides over your teeth and flicks across your swollen lips; you open your eyes and see he's watching you, the expression on his face brazen and calculating.

"Tab? Are you okay?"

"I wanna fuck you so bad right now, but not here. Let's go to your place. I'm gonna fuck you on the kitchen floor. I want you on your hands and knees, with your ass high in the air so I can spank it!"

"I told you, I'll do whatever you want. I told you, that."

"Yes, you did. Let's get going!"

CHAPTER SEVENTEEN

Stuck on Sex!

*Y*OU AND TAB WAKE UP the next morning both hung over. You're lying in his big bed with the charcoal sheets, and the comforting dark shadows undulating like the ocean on the black walls. The smell of Patchouli incense is heavy in the air as you think back to the night before. You remember your pathetic performance at Torch's apartment, trying to act working class and common, yelling, using bad language, catcalling. You think back to how much you enjoyed it, and how much Tab seemed to enjoy it too, and you start to wonder about yourself. Are you losing control over your impulses—over your own proclivities? It was such a blatant act, so forced at first but then you found yourself relaxing and enjoying the shamelessness of it, knowing that your mother would have been horrified, and your sisters, too. Knowing that Gayle would have been mortified—looking at you in shock, as if she'd never really known you.

The brazenness of Blaze and Torch fucking in the other room comes back to you, the noisy echoes of her whimpers and moans and his grunts and barks. The naturalness of the act, of wanting it for yourselves but as a private experience in the cool dimness of your spotlessly clean kitchen, with you on all fours and Tab behind you, pumping hard. It all comes back and you fight the feeling of repulsion and shame and the undeniable arousal that it brings. You fight the secret feeling that you want to take it further—that you want to go back to Torch's again some night, with Blaze there and Tab, drink, get drunk and yell even more. "Bitch, I'll kill you!" It felt so satisfying to say that. Who are you? Have you *ever* known?

Tab stretches in bed, reaches for your waist and cuddles, spooning you. His erect penis presses against your buttocks and you start getting turned on again. Do either of you ever get enough? Will you *ever* be satisfied? He sucks on your neck and whispers in your ear.

"Jeez, Daisy, I thought I was stuck on sex, but you're the most driven woman I've ever known, even more than Verona. I mean, you never say no. What happened to *you* Daisy? What happened to make you so stuck on sex?"

"Whaddaya mean what happened to me?" you ask, annoyed.

"Were you molested too? Is that why you get so angry when you talk about Blanche and what she did to me? Is it some kinda misplaced anger over something that happened to you?"

"It not important, I just like sex a lot but it wasn't always this easy, you know."

"Is that right?" You turn around to face Tab, yawning lightly with your hand over your mouth and curling your legs to your chest, scooting away from him, establishing a physical and measurable distance.

"Yes, Tab, it is. My ex-husband was terrible in the sex department and I never knew how to break the ice either. I was actually kinda repressed if you wanna know the truth."

"Repressed? How can that even be possible? I don't believe it."

"Would you shut up? It's only been since I've been with you that I want it this much."

"Isn't that a line from that movie *Body Heat* with Kathleen Turner?"

"What movie? I don't know *what* you're talking about, Tab!"

"I don't believe you. Somehow I *know* there's more to it."

"Oh, really?"

"Tell me about your *first* sexual experience. Not the PC version of when you lost your virginity with your high school boyfriend, but your *first* sexual experience. I've told you most of *my* secrets, and now you can tell me summa yours."

You make Tab wait as you think about whether or not to tell him, but in the end you know that Tab is the only person you *could* tell. He's the one person who would understand and not judge you for it. He waits patiently, watching your eyes as you come to a decision and finally start speaking, slowly at first.

"I've never told anyone before. It was… it was kinda like what happened to you, but even more looked down upon. It was completely illegal what happened to *me*."

"How long did the relationship last? I'm presuming it was a relationship?"

"Yes, I guess you could call it that. I always thought of it more like a love affair."

"How old were you and how long did it last?!"

"Three years. I was thirteen when it started and sixteen when it… ended."

"Thirteen? Tell me about it. Tell me what happened."

"His name was Raymond. He worked at the Stadium Fred Myer in the produce department. He was thirty eight, half Italian, half French and he looked like a movie star. He lived in NW just off 23rd avenue. There was a doorway fronting the sidewalk which led to his house down this long, narrow alley that had once been open to the public. The door was unmarked and locked and right in the middle of this long strip of shops. It was like a secret locked door and no one ever noticed it. It was like it was invisible. It was a weird spot for a house and he'd gotten it cheap for that reason, years before."

"And?"

"My friend Danielle told me about him. He knew the neighborhood kids from MLC?"

"MLC, what's that?"

"It was one of the neighborhood schools. The Metropolitan Learning Center."

"Oh. Did you go there?"

"No, I never went there. I went… to a different school. I met Danielle at the Couch pool in summer one year. It was where the neighborhood kids would go to cool off in the summer, built in like 1917 or something. It was inside MLC, which used to be called the Couch School. Anyway, she's the one who told me about Raymond and invited me to his place one day."

"What was his line? I mean who invites neighbor kids to their house unless they're up to no good?"

"Well, I lived nearby, in NW. He'd feed us, and let us hang out at his house. A lot of the kids thought he was a child molester but he seemed to just like to help kids, both boys *and* girls. At least that's what I first thought. Some of the other kids were from really poor families so they relied on his help, on his charity I guess you could call it. He'd give them money sometimes, to take home to their parents if they were having a hard time in winter, as long as they swore they'd never tell who gave it to them. He told them to say they'd found it in the park, in an empty brown paper bag."

"And they never told their parents, or anyone else?"

"No, we never told anyone about Raymond. At one time, there were seven of us. Four girls and three boys."

"What was the catch? What did he expect in return?"

"I don't think he expected *anything* in return… from the other kids. I think he was looking for something special, out of the ordinary and for the most part, I think he was just being kind. He said he felt sorry for the kids from poor families because that's how *he'd* grown up."

"Of course that's what he said. That's what they *always* say, Daisy."

"Well, it's what he said."

"And?"

"His house was always unlocked, the basement part anyway. He lived in the basement. The first and second floors were locked and decorated like a museum with old fashioned furniture and closed draperies on all the windows. All those rooms were really dark. He let me see them once and it was so creepy, like the place was filled with ghosts or something. I got really scared and he laughed at me."

"Ghosts, huh?"

"That's how it felt."

"Go on?"

"The basement had been totally renovated, with a big room and pool tables, a bar, and a kitchen—but the alcohol was always locked up, he never gave any of us alcohol. The kitchen had a window that let in some sunny light, and a dark old bathroom, painted pink and grey for his dead wife when she lived with him for the three years they were married. I never did figure out when she died, but he said it was some sort of cancer. He had a huge bedroom with no windows, which was right next to the bathroom. He always kept that room locked, though, like the top floors of the house."

"Did he ever let you in his bedroom?"

"A few times. Mostly we hung out in the party room and in the kitchen."

"Interesting, go on."

"Once I looked in the cupboards of the bathroom and found this huge box of *Tampax* pads that had belonged to his wife but that he'd never thrown out? They just stayed there, year after year collecting dust in the back of that cabinet. It was so weird. One day I asked him if he wanted to throw them out, and he got really angry. Told me no, that he liked having them there, that they reminded him of his beautiful wife who died."

"Tell me how it *started*."

"I'm getting to that. So, well… I was prettier than the other girls. I think he took a special interest in me for that reason. The other girls in our group were chubby and plain-looking with dirty blonde hair although Danielle had red hair. I always had good skin, big eyes and a nice body and he loved my ringlets because, they're so *rare* you know? I'd come over about five times when he made that clear to me—that he liked me in a different way. I'd been thrilled to eat with the other kids. Lunch meat, sliced cheese, Wonder Bread, cookies, potato chips, bananas, apples, sour cream, and candy bars! My mother was strict about never overeating, but a lot of the time I was hungry. It was a kid's dream and his refrigerator was always full. We'd just walk down the stairs into the basement in the back of the house and walk right in and start eating. He'd usually come home an hour later."

"You guys never trashed his place, never made a mess?"

"No way. Why would we do that, and ruin such a great thing?"

"What would he do when he came home to a house full of kids?"

"He'd sit around, tell us about his day. Ask us if we were still hungry, or did we wanna play pool in the other room, or watch TV. He never seemed smarmy or weird, just cool. And he was so good looking. Even though he was kinda like an old man to us? He was still really desirable looking."

"How did it *start?*"

"It was the sixth time I showed up, we always came right after school let out at 3:15 and there were only four of us—me, Tiffany, Bret and Mike, Danielle was sick that day. He asked them to go upstairs and hose down the driveway and start washing his new Volvo and he'd give them some money. I'd help sort through the dishes in the sink because we'd just eaten a whole mess of really good homemade Lasagna he made the night before that he warmed up in the microwave for us. They didn't wanna wash dirty dishes so they ran upstairs to spray off the driveway and wash his car and we were left alone. We were by ourselves for about forty five minutes. After they'd been gone about five minutes, he came up right behind me and hugged me from behind as I was getting the dishes sorted."

"Were you scared? Did you try to leave?"

"Of course I was. Scared and thrilled at the same time. I knew he liked me. I could tell. Did I try to run? Not even. Everything Raymond ever did to me, I wanted him to do."

"What happened then?"

"I leaned into him, pushed my butt into his crotch, arched my back, turned my head, looked up at him, and smiled. He whispered that I was different and he could tell I was trustworthy. I remember he used that word—*trustworthy*. He turned me around and put his hands on my shoulders like he was telling me a grand secret, like he was really relying on me. He looked me right in the eyes and it almost felt like he was scolding me, like if I didn't do what he wanted, I'd be in trouble."

"That's how they do it, the fear factor, intimidation."

"He told me he wanted me to come back in two hours but that it had to be our secret. I just looked up at him and nodded my head. But the truth is I couldn't wait to come back. He asked me if I liked him and I told him I liked him so much. That made him smile. He had a blinding smile. Perfectly straight white teeth in a tan golden face, with Easter blue eyes and salt and pepper dark hair. And he was tall and muscular, kinda like the silent film actor John Gilbert?"

"Yeah, I know who John Gilbert is, go on."

"I went home, told my mother I'd gotten a new job babysitting for a young couple in NW, and timed it so I came back at exactly seven, two hours later. My mother was so distracted earning a living and taking care of my siblings and me, she didn't even ask to meet this new family. When I got back to his place, I tiptoed down the flight of stairs into the basement, walked in the door and there he was sitting at the kitchen table. He was wearing a pair of jean cutoffs, no shirt and no shoes, and I could tell he'd just had a shower because his hair was still wet. My heart jumped into my throat the minute I saw him. I knew

I'd be naked soon and he'd be doing whatever he wanted to me."

"He looked that good?"

"Like a movie star. He stood up, took me by the hand and led me into the pool room without saying a word. He put a tape into the VCR player, a porno of a man fucking a teenage girl. I was mesmerized by it. I couldn't take my eyes off the screen. He turned the volume way up and whispered to me that no one could hear anything, that his basement was sound proof."

"Sound proof?'

"My heart started to pound. He walked over to a recliner and sat on it leaning back. Then he motioned for me to sit on his lap, so I crawled up on his lap, sitting there, kinda awkwardly and watching the porno. I could feel his hard dick beneath me."

"You weren't scared?"

"Not really. I mean it was exciting. I knew it was wrong, but I wanted it to happen, if that makes sense?"

"Yeah, it makes sense."

"He pulled at my shoulders and made me lay back on him, with my back over his front, telling me to lay flat like that and relax. I did what he said because he was… well he was kind of authoritative. Then he told me he was going to teach me how to kiss. I didn't say anything, I just nodded my head. We lay like that for about an hour, and he taught me to French kiss, telling me to open my mouth and let him stick his tongue in."

"Did he make you come?"

"He reached across my pants and unzipped them and slipped his hand down inside. He pushed his fingers in and started rubbing my clitoris. I couldn't believe how pleasurable it was. I reached up and started kissing him again, opening my mouth. He massaged like that with his hand for about ten minutes slow and deliberate and then I came. I'd never felt anything like it before."

"It felt that good?"

"What do you think, Tab? Did the first time with Blanche feel good?"

"Good point."

"Yeah, it felt good. But after I came, I got upset, it was so confusing. He comforted me and told me everything was going to be okay. Then he told me to lay back again. He started to pull my jeans down, but I protested. I didn't want him to see it. I felt self-conscious. He scolded me and told me I must not appreciate everything he'd done for me and my friends, how he'd fed us and helped their parents with the electric bills when it got cold in winter. He kind of yelled at me when he said it."

"What a bastard."

"Do you want me to continue, or not?"

"Go ahead."

"So, I whispered I was sorry and then he told me he should spank me for being ungrateful, that he could tell I was the kind of girl who deserved lots of long, hard, bare bottom spankings. He continued pulling down my jeans, to about my knees. I lay there, limp and compliant, my arms hanging loose at my sides, my legs falling open. He liked that, how passive I was, limp and passive. He cupped his big tan hand over it and started massaging it, slipping his finger in and out. He ordered me to watch while he did it, so I did."

"Did he make you come again?"

"He made me come two more times. I was so exhausted after that last climax, I could barely move. Then he told me that I belonged to him now, that no other man would want me. That I wasn't a virgin anymore."

"Wow!"

"He lifted me off him and pulled my pants all the way off and made me take off my shirt and bra. I stood naked in front of him as he took out his penis. It was so big and covered in all these ugly looking swollen veins. He sat back on the recliner, spread his knees open and told me to suck. I got on my knees and sucked for about fifteen minutes as best I could. When he started to come, he sat up and masturbated all over my naked chest. He barked and made all this noise when he came. I thought he was dying or something the way he carried on. Then he collapsed back into the chair."

"Did he throw you out after that?"

"No, he didn't throw me out; we continued to make out and fondle each other for another two hours. But he never fucked me. He said that wouldn't happen for a while and when it did it would be really special. All I knew was that it felt really good being naked with him and kissing him and it felt incredible when he made me come. I knew it was wrong, though. Don't think for one minute I didn't know it was wrong, but I was so lonely, so starved for affection, and the sex felt like exactly what I needed."

"How often did you see him"

"I came by every Monday, and Friday at six sharp, for about two to three hours. After, he'd hand me cash, to give to my mother. The babysitting part of it had to be believable. She never once asked to meet the family that had hired me. She was just glad I was making a little money and handing it over to her. My father left when I was eight, so we struggled. I'd get thirty dollars for three hours, at twice a week that's $60 a week. But there was no mistaking it— I always felt like I was his prostitute and I think he enjoyed the process of handing me dirty cash after making me get naked and making me come. I think there was some kind of weird thrill in it for him."

"And you never got pregnant?"

"No, we used the *rhythm method* when he was sure I couldn't get pregnant.

He loved to come in me, and the rest of the time, he used condoms."

"What happened to the other kids? How did they react?"

"The week after he first made me come, he told them they couldn't come by anymore, because someone had stolen a watch. It was a lie but it worked. He cut them all off, just like that. They stopped coming by and then it was just us. They were mad of course, but he told them his father would be coming to live with him soon and was dying of cancer so Raymond was gonna go broke caring for his father—another lie but it worked. So for a little over three years it was just us. All we did was suck and fuck and kiss and suck and fuck. That was *my* introduction to sex. It shaped the person I am today, I guess?"

"I knew something happened to you. I *knew* it!"

"How could you tell?"

"It was just something in your eyes, a kind of overall resignation."

"Resignation?"

"Yeah, a kind of resignation—in your eyes. It's still there. I recognized it."

"I'll have to take your word for that."

"When did he fuck you for the first time?"

"You wanna know that, too?"

"I wanna know it all. *Tell* me."

"It was three months later. It was the night we celebrated our three month "anniversary" as he called it. We spent the evening together and he sat me down and told me he was going to have to take my "cherry" and that it would hurt but he would be as gentle as he could. He made me a special dinner and gave me presents—jewelry, colored pencils and stickers, things a girl would like, *and* a new nightgown and matching panties. I couldn't take those with me though. The nightie and panties had to stay at his place. He said they had belonged to his wife and she was really skinny like me. He made it so special I was able to forget that a 38-year-old man would soon be fucking a 13-year-old girl—me! The reality was that it was rape; only to me it didn't *feel* like rape. To me it felt like love. Love and the best kind of sex, the best kind of fucking you could hope for."

"I know the feeling, Daisy."

"But it got really hard to concentrate in school. I'd think about him and need to go to the bathroom and masturbate in the stalls. I'd never masturbated before but he showed me how and told me to do it whenever I needed to, or when I thought of him, or missed him."

"I remember feeling that way too, after me and Blanche, that first time? I couldn't concentrate in school either. It was like once that door was opened, there was no going back."

"That's exactly how it felt, just like that, Tab. Like the opening of a door."

"Did it hurt, when he fucked you?"

"That first time? Not really. He'd been fingering me for the three months previous to the night he fucked me. Pushing his fingers in, trying to loosen up my pussy for when he'd push his big cock in for the first time. He wasn't really gentle though. He fucked me hard that first time. He said it was going to hurt and that he'd *try* to be gentle but he fucked me really hard, too. It was like he couldn't help himself."

"But you said you liked it."

"I loved everything Raymond did to me. He was like a drug. I couldn't get enough."

"Did he come in you?"

"Of course. And he wept afterwards—just cried and cried, tears just streaming down his face. I felt terrible for him. Tried to comfort him, patted his shoulders, and told him I loved him. He choked that he was sorry he'd taken my cherry but he couldn't help himself—that he was so lonely after his wife died and I was so pretty and young and fresh. He said we were meant to be together. That I was his wife now, that he was going to marry me, make me pregnant, start a life with me. I'd be his child bride. I'd swell up with his baby and we'd have six children together, but it would take a while and I'd have to be patient. I'd always be pregnant he said. Filled with his growing love, swollen forever with all his babies."

"Six children? He told you that?"

"I know. It sounded stupid, even to me."

"Yep, pretty stupid, alright."

"After he fucked me and came inside me, and got over his tears and all the sobbing, he took out this camera and snapped shots of me naked. His eyelashes were still wet with tears as he snapped all those photos. For the three years we were involved, he snapped hundreds of photos of me, but only from the neck down. I felt like a movie star. I felt so loved when I heard his camera clicking and felt the warm flash."

"What a dirty bastard. I'd like to kill him, Daisy."

"We both had our Svengali lovers didn't we? Yours was Blanche and mine was Raymond. I was thirteen and you were fourteen."

"Somehow what he did to you seems worse. He *violated* you!"

"You just don't know how beautiful Raymond was. His face was just… it's hard to put into words how handsome he was. I'd have forgiven him anything; let him do anything to me. I mean, I really did, didn't I? For over three years he did whatever he wanted. Came inside every orifice, fucked me hard, fucked me soft, fucked me fast, slow. He spanked me—whipped me with his leather belt until my butt was covered in welts."

"You never told him to stop?"

"No. He loved to spank and whip me. He'd think up all kinds of reasons why he needed to. And when he was done, he'd say: "We need to make love now, now that you've been properly punished." And we would. We'd make love, but only after I apologized for being "a bad girl" and forcing him to whip me in the first place."

"That's so sick."

"Yeah, it probably was. But it was also fun. I *loved* the sting of his warm hand on me."

"Was he better looking than me?"

"Not better looking, but equivalent—just different coloring. He was swarthy and tan, really dark skinned with dark hair and blue eyes. You're more honey colored. You're just different."

"And it lasted till you were sixteen?"

"Last time I saw Raymond I was eighteen."

"I thought you said you were sixteen when it ended? What happened?"

"Boredom—he found another little girl, and his interest was diverted. I was devastated of course. Had to keep it all to myself, and while that was hard, I never did tell anyone. Learning to keep secrets began when I first started seeing Raymond. It became a sort of survival. I spent the next two years of high school masturbating constantly in the restrooms before school and even after school let out. It took over two years to finally get him out of my system."

"That's terrible, baby. I'm sorry."

"It was hard but I learned I could survive, so I think that made it worth the pain, the self-loathing, the compulsive need to masturbate. It taught me to rely only on myself."

"Are you okay... talking like this? I don't wanna upset you."

"I'm fine Tab. I've never felt comfortable talking about it before, but with you? With you I feel like I could talk about anything, literally anything and you'd understand. Funny, huh?"

"We do have that quality together."

"It's nice to tell someone, finally, after all these years."

"And you never wanted to get even with him?"

"I felt *sorry* for Raymond. He was so compelled to be sexual. It was like an addiction for him. I knew in time his luck would run out and I was right."

"He got found out?"

"The girl he took up with after me ended up getting pregnant and she told her father."

"Pregnancy *will* complicate things."

"The family called the police and they came and raided his home, and found all these photos. It made the newspapers and caused a huge scandal. With me he'd taken all these photos of my body but never any of my face. I was described as "the unknown brunette" when they found his photos of me, and the photos were never released, so the public never saw them. With her he'd taken full on shots of her face and body and photos of them together, using a tripod. He was arrested and looking at a lot of prison time. The girl was from a middle class family that lived near Wallace Park and somehow he'd met her—at a summer picnic, I think."

"So, how much time did he get?"

"Something like seven years as I recall."

"And you visited him?"

"How did you know?"

"I didn't. Just guessed. But you did?"

"I did."

"But why, Daisy, after he threw you away—why would you go and visit him?"

"For one very good reason, of course!"

"To show him what he was missing?"

"Exactly."

"How many times did you see him in the jail?"

"Only the one time—that's all it took. I wore this dress he'd bought for me. It had white, pink and blue flowers on it and he really liked it on me. Told me it reminded him of baby clothes, the colors ya know? I wore my makeup how he liked with bright pink lip gloss, pale *Coty* face powder and lots of black mascara to bring out the blue in my eyes. I hadn't seen Raymond in two years, since I was sixteen, so I was eighteen then, and looked even better than I did at sixteen. I was still thin but my breasts were larger. Although I *didn't* look like a prepubescent child anymore, which I guess was what he wanted."

"I bet you looked beautiful, Daisy."

"I looked pretty good that day. I pushed my chest out and did the whole pout and the wide blank eyes just to torment him. He was *destroyed* when he saw me. Told me it was a mistake to take on the little blonde girl—that she couldn't compare to me. *She* didn't know how to suck like me. *She* didn't know how to stick her ass in the air and arch her back like I did. *She* didn't know how to take a dick in the ass, or a hard spanking, or a whipping with a thick leather belt. As he whispered I could tell he was getting turned on. I looked down and saw he had a huge erection. He was forty three by then, and he *still* couldn't get enough."

"And?"

"He begged me to come see him again and write him, *and* send him photos. Told me we could finally get married now, since I was eighteen and we wouldn't be breaking any laws. I told him I loved him—told him I couldn't wait to be his wife. It amused me how he thought I'd ever really marry him—a convicted sex offender who'd been on the news? Are you kidding?"

"You got your revenge, didn't you, baby?"

"What Raymond did to me was reprehensible!"

"Yes, baby, it was."

"He stole my innocence, warped it, and twisted it all up. He put his disease in me. It's never gone away. I carry it with me every day inside my mind, inside my brain. And I still love him to this day. To this day I still love him and sometimes even miss him. It's sick what he did to me. What I *allowed* him to do."

"You couldn't have stopped it, honey!"

"Of course I could have stopped it. I didn't *want* to stop it. I wanted it. I was as much to blame as Raymond was. Remember when I told you I was no good? This is why."

"You can't blame yourself. You were a child, Daisy."

"Anyway, as I sat there across from him in the jail, I touched myself lightly over my dress, pressing my hand in, making sure he could see. The look on his face was so tragic, so full of that desperate melancholy, that lust he'd always been so afflicted with, that he'd been born with and cursed with. He wanted to fuck me so bad at that moment."

"And?"

"I whispered to him how I'd masturbate that night thinking of the first time he fucked me, remembering how much it had hurt, how big his cock was, and how good it felt later on. I told him I'd remember how I begged him to fuck me again and again, and how he had."

"What this guy did to you was so wrong, Daisy!"

"After we stood up, we pressed our hands to the glass like star struck lovers in a TV drama, and I looked him right in the face, with so much love and forgiveness in my eyes. And he fell for it. He fell for it hook, line and sinker. It was funny. I had to stop myself from laughing. He was so stupid to fall for it. Such a chump, just like I'd been a chump when he dumped me for the blond girl."

"And you never saw him again?"

"No, I never did. But I wrote to him once. I told him I'd met someone and would be getting married soon. I asked him to give me his blessing and told him I knew he could be happy for us. I told him the young man was my age but looked just like him. I worded the letter carefully, not giving anything away about our past in the event it was read by staff."

"But there was no future husband."

"Of course not. I was *only* eighteen. I'd just barely managed to graduate from high school as it was. I was getting ready to go to college. I'd gone from a straight A student to a distracted girl beating off in the bathroom and getting low B's and C's. My mother was so disappointed in the change, so disappointed in the way my grades plummeted. But she never had a clue. No one did. We hid the secret so well."

"That might have been for the best, Daisy. Can you imagine how hard it would have been if your family found out?"

"I thought of that, believe me. I didn't envy that blonde girl, not for one minute. And my god, she was only twelve when he started in on her. He really was a… a pedophile I guess. Isn't that what they call them now?"

"At least you were able to avoid that. That girl's life was probably destroyed, having everyone know about it and hearing it on the news? Her father probably had to arrange an abortion."

"The rumor was that her parents sent her to the White Shield Home for unwed mothers up on the hill. Then after the baby was born they put it up for adoption and moved out of state where they started over and changed their last name. They were rich you see? They had to completely start over."

"Probably for the best."

"If it had been me, I would have hanged myself. I could never have faced *that*. It was a bullet I dodged. Believe me I was always conscious of that."

"It's a good thing no one found out. No one found out about me and Blanche either. I never told anyone… except you that is."

"I never told anyone about Raymond except you, Tab. It feels kinda good to get some of it out of my mind, at least a little."

"You never told your ex-husband?"

"No way! He would have *blamed* me for it. He would have told everyone we knew. He would have delighted in telling his whole family and all our mutual friends about how I'd been sexually abused by a pervert and how I'd probably brought it all on myself."

"It's funny how easy it is for us to talk about these things, cause I could never talk to anyone else about Blanche, not even with Ruby or Verona. I wonder why that is?"

"Because we understand each other, Tab, because we trust each other with our secrets."

"Secrets, all our little secrets."

"Secrets are what we do sometimes, huh? Especially when we're young. The human race and all our endless little secrets, like pennies in our pockets."

"Like pennies in our pockets, Daisy girl, like pennies in our pockets."

Talionic Night in Portland: A Love Story

CHAPTER EIGHTEEN

Ways to Punish Yourself

A FEW DAYS AFTER YOUR unexpected confession to Tab you're lying in bed pushing the Snooze button for the third time on your outdated Sony alarm clock. Tab called an hour before to say he loves you and will be thinking of you all day—that he's never loved a woman with quite this intensity before. You whispered into the phone that you love him too, and the smile on your face was genuine when you said the words and the lightness in your heart real.

Once again you can't believe your luck, to be with the kind of man you've always wanted—a man in full possession of all the qualities and attributes that will ever be important. To finally be with the most uncomplicated, loving and accepting man you've ever known, but a person, like you, who discretely carries within him the Bottomless Sadness. It's always there with its infinite complexities, lingering within the periphery of his awareness. And you know no matter how you smile, no matter how you embrace moments of genuine happiness, that inner core you both carry will follow you to all destinations. Learning to accept the Bottomless Sadness, learning to deal with it, that's the talent, that's the *real* gift.

As you lay on your bed, you see Tab's face flutter within your mind's eye, the humble quality of his demeanor and his tentative topaz eyes. His incredible handsomeness, the sleek perfection of his body once again astounds you, and you begin feeling a physical manifestation of the synergy of his rapport. It seems to descend upon you like golden droplets that absorb into the thirsty skin of your body, baptizing you with their presence. Stretching your legs like a cat, you decide you won't go in. You decide you're sick, not feeling well; at least *that's* what you'll tell them, because lying to people who don't matter has never been a problem for you.

You feel a wonderful lightness, as if a mountain of weight has been lifted. And you know why. The fact that you felt comfortable enough to tell Tab about your twisted childhood, your biggest ever secret, lets you know he's the *single* person you will ever trust as an adult. And that he is the only person who could possibly understand. He knows what it's like to think fondly of your abuser—

to think back to the crimes of an adult predator and to question your own culpability in those crimes, to hate yourself for the pleasure you derived, to condemn yourself for that reason, looking for ways to punish yourself, or ways for others to punish you, instead.

Tab knows what it's like to look back on the times you were seduced by a pedophile and to miss them. He knows what it's like to wish you could bump into that person just one more time—to relive some of it all over again in some dark secret place, away from everyone else. If only one more time when the fear and the pleasure combine to create that feeling of total sublimity in the body. Rejecting the amorality of the experience but rather embracing only the physical, anatomical pleasure, your pink button once again buzzing under the soft pressure of Raymond's beautiful, calloused fingers.

Tab is the only person you know who could understand. You know you can't tell anyone else, because your secret wouldn't be secret if anyone *other* than Tab knew. He's the single person who will never repeat what he heard you say. Like you, he knows how to keep secrets and why keeping secrets is so important. As you lay in bed, you consider the inevitability of what must happen with Gayle, what you must make manifest in order to go forward with your plan, because you're *still* going to do it. You're still going to bust into Gayle's office and teach her a lesson with sulfuric acid, spray paint and pancake batter, carried under your arm in an unassuming, tan all-leather *Kenneth Cole* overnight bag.

The feeling of being freed from that previous weight gives you the courage to not call in, to just not show up. You know when Helen calls your cell to see if you're alright, you'll just casually mention you overslept. You won't apologize and you won't say you'll be right in. She'll have to tell Gayle what you said and what your attitude was. Confused and disconcerted at your mysterious and inexplicable apathy, you know Helen will be upset at the smile in your voice. How you seemed smug, almost challenging as you sweetly trilled goodbye before hanging up on her as she spoke, mid-stammer, about to ask when you'd be coming in.

Helen will eventually get your position. She'll go from what she currently does as an executive assistant and sometime film editor to a first rate promotion. She'll be Gayle's new assignment editor and she'll be glad of it, though clearly she won't be making any more money. Assignment editors don't generally make money, especially if they're women. Helen and Gayle won't miss you when you're gone either; not really, particularly when they find out you ran off to Seattle with a grade school custodian. And that is *all* Tab will be to them, merely a grade school custodian and nothing more. You can hear them as they gossip in the silence of your mind:

"Did you hear, Gayle?" Helen will begin: "Daisy fell for some *grade school custodian* named Tab Hunter, after that dumb actor! Can you believe it? They ran off to Seattle together! I hear they're getting married! He's never even been to college, can you just *imagine* it? I bet he can't even read!"

And you hear Gayle respond: "I always *knew* there was something wrong with that girl, something dark and bizarre and twisted. I could just never put my finger on it. Tiffy says she heard from a friend, of a friend of a friend, that they're both into S and M and they go to those clubs on a regular basis? The one in Portland, I think it's called *Club Sassoon,* or something? Who woulda thought that girl who always seemed so sweet, refined and above it all would turn out to be a sex pervert!"

"I know Gayle, but that's exactly what Daisy is—a pervert! She fooled us all! I even heard someone from her apartment over on Clinton Street called the police on a Saturday morning because they were making so much noise...ya know, when they were doin' it?"

"Well, I don't know about that, but she was a damn good assignment editor. I'm gonna miss the self-important, tortured little shit."

"Hey, Gayle, you wanna hire that private investigator I told you about—to see what she's up to? Where she's working? Whether they got married? Where they're living? What church they go to? Where they shop for groceries?"

As Helen and Gayle's voices trail off in your mind, you realize you don't care what anyone thinks anymore. The fear of what others might think has been slowly evaporating since you and Tab first started up and you saw what was important in him, and what was *not* important in others. Now, all that matters is Tab and your life with him, creating that life, and trying to preserve your well-known cool head in the process. Trying to preserve that needed distance you've always maintained with all those other people who will simply never matter.

As you rest in bed, you find yourself looking up at the ceiling, bug-eyed and suddenly preoccupied. You've been thinking of the *Seattle Post Intelligencer* the past few days and wondering how you'll be able to reinvent yourself there. You need to call them and fax copies of your resume and the significant stories you helped with or wrote yourself back when you were still a street reporter. But around noon, your house phone begins to ring, and lazily you answer it. You're pleased to hear Tab's voice and want to share the good news. You're not going in today, you'll be free, and you're pretty sure Gayle will soon fire you, but you keep *that* part to yourself.

He had a *feeling* you were still at home and took a chance. But how does Tab know these things? His intuition is uncannily accurate and sometimes even spooky when he's looking at you in bed, and telling you he doesn't believe something you've just said. It's never been anything important, usually just little white lies but Tab always seems to know. He looks right at you and quietly says: "I don't believe you. I don't believe you, Daisy girl." You're learning you simply can't lie. To others yes, but not to Tab.

"Hi Tab! I thought I should tell you, I'm not going in today. I'm taking the day off. Did you wanna leave the school early and come pick me up? We could spend the day together—only if you *want* to of course."

"I still have to complete my sixty days notice, baby. You know, before I can leave and get a good reference for the Washington Ferry Company? But I'll be by after clock out, okay?"

"Okay, then. Do you want me to make something special for dinner? Anything you want. I'm actually a good cook when I apply myself."

"I'm sure you are. Are you gonna be slaving away in the kitchen like a good little kitchen wench?"

"Yes, Papa, and for you I'll do anything. What shall it be, cheesy spaghetti and meatballs or perhaps a steak and a baked potato?"

"Hmmm, I think I'd like cheesy spaghetti *and* a steak, medium rare, no meatballs. Can you do that?"

"I'm on it. And bring us a bottle of good red wine, nothing cheap, your appetite and your complete and functional basket. It will be needed later on."

"Why, you shameless little hussy—my basket is always ready, willing and able, you know that."

After you shower and spray your new *Mitsouko* perfume on your neck and shoulders, you slip on the new lilac colored empire-line dress Tab bought for you only a few days before. It's covered in tiny pink rosebuds, and shows off your thin arms and delicate collarbone. As you look at yourself in the mirror, pleased, you consider the logistics of going to the store for food. That means leaving the apartment, and leaving the apartment when you're alone means sprinting to the car with the keys held out like a dagger and jumping in to avoid the potential danger of Ruby and Verona lurking nearby. When you're not with Tab, the sensation of felt jeopardy is visceral, tugging at your middle, grasping hold of your guts with determined claws. It's easier in the morning, just after dawn and still dark, knowing that Ruby and Verona don't generally rise till noon. But in the late morning or early afternoon there's always the off chance you may run into them.

They could be on another unexpected errand of vengeance, having decided to trash your rose bush with a pair of rusty shears, or break a window with a crumbling brick, or leave a burning paper bag filled with dog shit on your front stoop. You imagine them planning it, laughing and thinking they're *so* original. You visualize them hiding in the bushes somewhere, hoping you'll fall for the con, getting your shoes all poopy as you try to put out the fire, stomping frantically, only to realize you'd been had. But *you* won't fall for the Burning-Bag-O-Poop trick—not since you were a teenager. It was actually meant for your mother, but she wasn't at home when you answered the door. She'd driven to the store to buy some readymade macaroni salad, Pepsi, and frozen pizza for dinner—getting ready for another dismal silent dinner where the wordless absence of your father droned on incessantly, and you were left to hold down the fort until she got back.

It happened the year she had the affair with her married boss and his distraught young wife found out. For those crazy three months that the woman harassed your mother, you and your confused and frightened siblings saw a kind of humiliated hesitancy in her that you'd never seen before, and it pleased *you* particularly, being the eldest. Your mother was finally anything but perfect. But the choked sobs you heard when she wept in her room, late at night, your younger siblings fast asleep, and only you able to hear, made you see how alone and unhappy she was. She transferred to a different secretary job and after the requisite few months of silent unspoken grief, your mother became even more exacting and inscrutable, swallowing her toxic emotions entirely and showing you by her example how to do the same.

As you consider the dinner you've agreed to make, you realize you'll have to be exceptionally careful, because you know full well that until you and Tab finally split town, neither one of you will be safe and you want everything to be perfect for Tab's dinner. You notice for the first time in ages how you're falling back into the slippery pleasures of domesticity, except that this time it's with Tab and not your neurotic ex-husband. Again you're thinking that perhaps Seattle is more than a pipe dream—maybe a life with Tab *is* something that could work.

You grab your leather bag, step into your red satin flats, and pull on your black leather jacket. Standing at the door you take a deep breath, open it and look to the left to see if the coast is clear. No one is about, not even Blaze loitering in front of his apartment harassing passersby for beer money. You tiptoe out, pull the door closed and silently jog to your car, slipping in, stuffing the key in the ignition and punching down the locks. As you glance in the rearview mirror you see Torch walking in the opposite direction, dragging her pull-cart along to do some shopping at the New Seasons down on Division. She seems forlorn and bent over, an older punk rock chick that never quite made it, can barely pay her rent, and doesn't have a car or even any friends to speak of anymore. The sight of Torch's dark figure slouching down the street tugs at your heart and you swallow hard to make the feeling go away. What is it about Torch that makes you sad for her? What is it about her that makes you care, knowing she's a two-bit tramp who would bed down with Tab in a hot second if she could?

How much pity have you given to other people, only to have it backfire in your face? How many times has your kindness been mistaken for weakness? Too many times. There will be no more wasted pity on others. No more being mistaken for weak because you were stupid enough to feel sorry for some three time loser with nothing to offer the world other than 'the poor mouth' and a lot of sad stories of better days, lost dreams and denied short term loans.

As you sit in your car, safe within its locked confines, you decide to drive all the way across town to Strohecker's up on SW Patton Road. You want to make sure the steak is good quality and the pasta sauce is something fancy and imported. Maybe you'll even buy some of their overpriced Greek olives and saltwater taffy while you're there.

As you walk in the door of Strohecker's and notice the aisles of food and the exotic, colorful labels on the various canned and bottled goods, you glance over to the produce section. It's known for being nicely stocked with fresh vegetables, and gleaming fruit and as you walk over, you see a tall emaciated woman with dyed blonde hair. She's wearing tight Calvin Klein jeans, a Columbia Sportswear jacket and tattered grey Espadrille flats, the casual Preppie uniform. As you pass, she looks over disdainfully and sticks her nose in the air at a comically high angle just as she turns away, and sashays down the adjacent aisle, swinging her flat bony butt.

You've just been snubbed.

Instantly, you think of the 1953 Bugs Bunny cartoon where Bugs announces to the bull: *"Of course you realize, THIS means war!"* You stifle the urge to laugh, remembering your favorite cartoon, but also because the woman is old and wrinkled and way past her prime. She's with an old man who looks exhausted and disgusted. He's listening to her ramble on about how hard it is to find a good housekeeper and you're not certain if he's her husband or her brother. Instantly, you feel sorry for him as she drones on, looking at him and exploding: "I just don't know *what* I shall do about this, Walter! It's so hard to find good help these days. I want someone *other* than a Mexican housekeeper!" The man rolls his eyes and looks away in embarrassment pushing the cart in front of him.

As you stand near the peaches, fingering them and bringing one to your nose to inhale its peachy sweetness, you continue watching the couple. They pay for and collect their groceries and push them out to the parking lot. You walk closer to the door and watch as they load two small bags into the back of a beat up older model Volvo with numerous dents and scuffs on the worn pale gold exterior. As you look through the glass door, the woman turns and sees you watching. She notices your calm gaze and the expression on her face changes to a look of surprise, then embarrassment and then resentment. She looks down, takes a deep breath, raises her chin and glares at you defiantly. You smile brightly and silently mouth, while pointing over: "Love your car!" The woman grimaces a smile and barks in the nearly empty parking area "Thanks! Our *other* car is at the estate!"

You widen your eyes in delighted disbelief, and laugh heartily, then flip your ringlets over your shoulder and happily turn your back, dismissing her as she continues to glower at you with abject hatred. It felt good. If anyone deserved to be taught a lesson that old hag did. But why are some people like that? Why do they invite ridicule by behaving in the most supercilious, and sanctimonious ways? Why is it so important to keep up appearances in Portland in just *that* way—when so often all that happens is they succeed in making themselves look like a fool?

You wander through the store, collect your items and then walk to the checkout line and purchase them with cash. You have cards but when you shop at Stroheckers you always buy your items with cash, just to see the reaction of the employees and today you're not disappointed. The girl at the cash register looks at your cash with a look of mild disgust and takes it from you without a word. She pinches the legal tender between her fingers as if it's contaminated with the Black Plague. She looks to be about twenty, with a shock of thick shoulder length wheat-blond hair and is probably a college student working for extra money and a local SW Portland girl. As you collect your bag you glance over at her, flip your hair over your shoulder and then pointedly say: "Thank you *Ma'am*." A look of shock and dismay spread instantly across her face after you called her "Ma'am." Your adventure in Strohecker's was just as you imagined it would be, and you feel intensely satisfied with your visit. You stroll out the front door, head high and a placid smile on your face, with your bag of groceries in hand, and you can't help but think how some aspects to Portland culture will just never change.

****

When Tab walks in the door, using his key, he looks over at the table as he peels off his work jacket and sets down his heavy toolbox. His eyes are wide and there's a happy grin on his face. The table is set with a deceased aunt's fine antique *Holmes and Tuttle* silver and there's a two set placement of Desert Rose china. You're naked beneath a black and white frilly *Frederick's of Hollywood* apron you purchased online. You gracefully wave your arm toward the steaming food on the table like a proud magician who's just performed a complex trick. *Voilà!*

"I'll be damned Daisy, this is just perfect. Desert Rose china, too? Oh, baby, I could eat you up."

"Dinner first, Tab!" you trill as you pull out his chair and then sashay around the table to the opposite side.

"I hope you like it; it's what you asked for. My famous cheesy pasta and a nice fat New York steak, extra lean, just like you."

"Extra lean, huh? Lemme wash ma mitts first."

"Then wash your mitts, we don't want the food to get cold!"

"You're like the most perfect girl in the world, you know that?"

"I'm starting to think maybe you're right."

Sitting down and settling your naked butt onto the hard chair, you twist the rich pasta onto your spoon with your fork, carefully swooping it into your mouth and chewing deliberately as you slowly contemplate the pleasure of the food. Tab returns to the table, slides into the chair and digs in, eating in that graceful yet expedient way that you love—his table manners are perfect as he cuts into the steak and mops the chunks in the rich roux-like substance beneath, chewing the meat and smiling at the same time, his eyes on you all the while.

"Nice and bloody, just how I like it!"

"That's not blood. It's called myoglobin. It comes from the muscle tissue."

"Huh! You know, you've been kinda gettin' domestic lately—have you noticed that?"

"I have not; I'm just more comfortable with you, that's all."

"Whatever it is, it's perfect. I *missed* you. I couldn't think of anything else but being with you right now."

"Did you really?"

"God, I can't wait to open you up like a Christmas present!"

"Would you stop? You're gonna get me all excited."

"That's my plan, baby."

"You know, I drove all the way up to Strohecker's for all this stuff? I wanted to make sure your dinner was made with only the best."

"I've never gone there. Isn't that where the rich folks shop? Up on the hill?"

"Pretty much. You can get nearly the same items in any other store but there's so much glamour in being able to say: "You like it? Oh, I got it at Strohecker's!"

"I seem to remember someone telling me the same thing years ago. That it really wasn't much better than the other stores, just the *fashionable* place to go."

"That's exactly it, Tab. But the other truth is that they *do* have some nice exotic imported canned and bottled goods that you can't easily find anywhere else, unless you special order them."

"It's perfect. This is really sticking to my ribs, baby."

You're still laughing lightly at your joke about Strohecker's when there's a sudden and familiar knock at the door. Not that you've ever heard that particular knock on *this* apartment door but you know the knock instantly. It could only belong to one person. She got word that you didn't come in and didn't even call. She's furious and this is it! Gayle's going to can your ass and better that Tab be there to see it and experience for himself how hideous she can be, then to not experience the impressive rush of Gayle's rage, aggression and infamous hostility.

Tab had just finished his third bite of steak and second bite of pasta when he glanced at you, alarmed; thinking no doubt that it was Ruby or Verona at the door with a butcher knife or hacksaw and simple murder on their minds. The question mark in his eyes made you smile and you raised your hand silently to calm him.

"It's okay, Tab, it's only my boss. Gayle," you whisper.

"Isn't she the woman you hate?"

"Well, yes, I guess you could say that."

"Are you gonna get it or... should I?"

"Well, I'm not really dressed for it am I? Besides, I want her to see us like this. Hey, take off your shirt! Come on, do it Tab!"

"Okay, that's enough, Daisy. I'll answer the door but I'm not taking my shirt off to torment some lonely old barfly."

"Okay, fine just answer it!"

"Daisy?"

" Please?"

"That's better. Jesus, you know, all I wanted was to eat my fuckin' dinner in peace!"

"It will be over soon, don't worry."

Tab's work boots sound heavily on the floor as he slowly walks over. He opens the door reluctantly and stands in the doorway, slouching. His face is expressionless, his tone distant as he asks the large woman in the overly tight hot-pink ensemble: "May I help you with something?" Gayle is trying to look past him into the apartment, moving from right to left, shifting her considerable gelatinous bulk from one foot to the other, uncomfortable in her mustard yellow, nail-sharp stiletto heels. She's angry and heavily made up, having mopped on the Mary Kay slop for just this occasion. You can see she's gone overboard, piling on the war paint, with rouge and lip gloss and all for the thrill of firing you personally.

"I'm looking for a *Miss Daisy Rose Butterfield!*" Gayle spits with quivering hostility.

You shift in the chair, cross your legs and swing your right foot encased in a glossy black pump up and down, just as Tab steps aside and the door falls open. Gayle peers in and sees you sitting smug at the dinner table, adjacent to the kitchenette. You lick your lips, gather up your long ringlets in your right hand, and flip them over your shoulder with elegant contempt. You tilt your head and smile at Gayle as she steps awkwardly into the living room. Her gelatinous body shivers with each step while Tab tentatively closes the door. Her three double chins look markedly pronounced as she scowls disapprovingly and her weak chin sinks into the flesh of what is commonly referred to as a "no neck" neck. You struggle not to laugh.

"What a dump! This place looks like a movie set... from a porno!"

"I'll have to take your word for that. What is it you want, Gayle? I'm busy. Can't you see we're eating?"

Gayle storms toward you, stopping just short of an invisible threshold fifteen feet away. She stands glowering as you adjust the black and white frilly apron, making sure it covers your pert breasts and lap, but your bare thighs and hips reveal perfectly the extent of your gorgeous nakedness.

"You! You—irresponsible child! How dare you not call in today? How dare you talk to Helen the way you did! Look at you, dressed like a slut! Who do you think you are? And who's *this* moron?" Tab sighs heavily as he trudges back to the table, sits down and resumes eating, his head down, his shoulders hunched forward in fatigue and resignation, cutting into the steak with elegant deliberation.

"Gayle, this man is my fiancée. I would appreciate it if you didn't talk about the love of my life in such a demeaning and inaccurate fashion." Tab raises his head, his eyebrows lift in that way that means he's overcome with sentimentality and may cry at any moment.

"But Daisy, you never once said that I was the love of ..." Tab begins, and then falls silent. He's smiling distractedly and trying to eat, looking from you to Gayle stupidly like a grateful father at the wedding of his ugly duckling daughter.

"My sources tell me he works as a grade school custodian, is that right? You're willing to give up your life and your future in television for a... CUSTODIAN?"

"What's wrong with being a custodian? I... I actually enjoy my work. Besides I'll be moving onto better things once we..."

"It's okay, Tab. Don't bother. She's just jealous that we're happy and *she* still has to *pay* for it. Isn't that right Gayle? You still have to pay for the poor men who service you. I can only imagine they probably feel so humiliated afterwards. I mean, aren't you close to sixty now and well over 260 pounds? Tab and I are actually in love and *he's* not a pompous stuffed shirt like you and all your loser friends!"

"Pompous stuffed shirt? Are you crazy? And yes, I am fat! I've been fat my whole life, but you know, I gave you a chance when no one else would. Do you remember how awkward and shy you were, Daisy? How no one could even touch you without you jumping? How you were always washing your hands all the time and going to the bathroom, doing God only knows what in there? That's why they let you go from your first position, because you couldn't fit in. And that god awful NAME?! I told you to change it years ago. But—noooooo!

You *had* to be true to who you were. Or *something* like that!"

"My mother named me. I won't apologize for it. She also named my two sisters Rose and Pansy and my brother Leaf, so I guess you could say it runs in the family. As to being shy, yes I was, but time and life experience changes that. When you realize you don't care anymore, that's when you realize you've achieved real freedom. That's the best feeling of all—realizing you just don't care what anyone thinks anymore!"

"Well, my father named *me*. And it was awful. Gayle is not the name I was born with. Not in North Carolina. My father burdened me with the delightful name of… Bertha! Bertha Mabel Grimes, until I finally got out of that stinking one horse town and came all the way to… Portland, Oregon! To go to college, of course."

"Ah, yes, Portland, Oregon. It's *such* a paradise here."

"You only say that because you were born and raised here. You'll never really know how wonderful Portland is Daisy, because you have nothing to *compare* it to!"

"Don't you tell ME about the town I've lived in my whole damn life. I know every inch of this fucking town in ways you *never* will!"

"Yeah, well, coming to Portland was the best thing that ever happened to me. That's when I became someone else. You can always reinvent yourself, Daisy! That's the American way! Haven't you ever read *The Great Gatsby?*"

"*The Great Gatsby.* Yes, I have read it—in college. But the reality is, I'm Daisy and that's all I'm ever going to be! But I'm NOT Daisy Buchanan. I am NOT a victim. Not anymore!"

"There's nothing wrong with being someone else. When I came to Portland, that's when I decided for myself that I'd be Gayle! Miss Gayle Anne Gabriel! And I'd leave all the memories of high school and all that bullying behind me once and for all."

"I don't like your initials Gayle."

"What?!"

"GAG. Your initials spell G. A. G. No thanks!"

"Oh, Daisy, the point is, I made something of myself and so can you but… I can't make excuses for you anymore. You're done. You can come to the office tomorrow and clean out your desk. And even though I'm terminating you, I hope you understand you can still make something of yourself… If… if you'd only change that name of yours! Just like I did!"

"I'm happy for you, Gayle. And I am sorry you were bullied, but I'm protecting what is left of the rest of *my* life, and no, I won't change my name. Furthermore, I don't care *what* you think of Tab. I don't care what you think of *any* aspect of my life. You're certainly no better than I am. And I don't care *what* you think about Portland. My life is not for *you* to live, Gayle."

"What are you talking about?"

"And as to Tab? He's a better man than you'll ever find. The kindest most uncomplicated man I've ever known. Well, you've fired me and now you can just get the hell out. So? Get out! Get out of my home! My fiancée and I have to finish our dinner so we can go into the back bedroom and fuck. As you can see, I'm dressed for it. I'm dressed for my life Gayle, and I'm dressed for fucking."

"You ungrateful little shit!"

"Just get out. Get out Gayle."

Tab stands up and looks directly at Gayle as he wipes his mouth delicately with a white linen table napkin. His demeanor is firm as he stands to his full height, his mere presence and size an unspoken threat. He opens his right arm, extending it in a gentlemanly manner and says: "I'll walk you to the door Miss Gayle," just as Gayle turns and stomps in the opposite direction, the brown asbestos tile floor squeaking under the weight of her obese quivering body.

"I have no idea *what* she sees in you!" Gayle mutters as Tab opens the door.

"I wouldn't expect you to, Ma'am."

"Well, don't screw it up Mister Universe. Don't run her off. She's a rare bird that one!"

"I have no intention of running Daisy off, and… thank you for the advice."

"Is it true you have a doctorate in mythology from some university in Illinois?"

"Uh, yes, that's actually true. In my home you'll even find 329 books all on Greek mythology. Yes, I'm afraid it's true. It's my burden to bear. The only thing I was ever interested in reading or studying—good old Greek mythology."

"But you work as a custodian. I'll never get over that. She left it all for a grade school custodian, moonlighting as an underpaid college professor. Good grief!"

"Well, nobody's perfect, Miss Gayle."

"Apparently, not! And stop calling me MISS!"

"Whatever you say, Miss Gayle."

As Tab closes the door and locks the deadbolt, you kick off your black pumps and quickly tiptoe over, silently in your bare feet. He turns around to face you. His shoulders are hunched and there's that defeated look about him, the sadness you instantly recognize. You know Tab has been put down before in just this way and it breaks your heart. You look up beseechingly, because once again Tab *is* the drug you need. But it's not just his face and body and what that face and body can do for you, it's his soul, too. Tab smiles with the magnanimous understanding of a humble king, that attitude of his that you know so well. Because he knows his body, and the soul he carries around in it, is what you need more than anything. More than money. More than property.

More than wisdom or a drink.

"I'm sorry. I'm so sorry she said those awful things. Please? Let me comfort you?"

Tab reaches down and scoops you up. He's tired, hurt and even angry. Gayle was not what he was expecting, but you won't let her ruin the night. Tab carries you through the darkened hallway to your bedroom and the small double bed with the profusion of violet crazy quilts made of second hand scraps of silk and velvet. He sets you down carefully on the bed, as the purple shadows collect, casting their macabre impressions on the walls, and pulls off the little apron you're wearing, casually with a dim smile, tossing it to the floor. He murmurs he's going to go and get the wine bottle. You hadn't even had time to open it before Gayle burst in on the scene. Tab slumps back into the bedroom, holding the wine bottle and stands over the bed looking at you darkly. His face is inscrutable and expressionless as you stretch and reach out, your arm extended in a gesture of supplication.

"You said I was your fiancée, Daisy. Don't mess with me like that just to get back at some woman you hate. Don't mess with my *heart* like that!"

"But Tab, I only wanted to…"

But he raises his hand wordlessly, and you stop speaking. He returns his attention to the opened wine bottle. He offers the bottle but you shake your head no. Tab lifts the bottle, chugging one third of the dark red liquid in long easy swallows. He offers the bottle again but it's not a request, it's a demand. You take it and swallow a long drink, looking up for approval.

"No, drink more. I want you to drink more," Tab whispers thickly, his tall lean body swaying like a tree in mild wind. You gulp down several more swallows of wine and a single dark purple droplet drifts down your chin. Tab reaches out and wipes it away with a finger and puts the finger in his mouth. He nods his head in silent approval, and motions to the night stand. You place the bottle gingerly on the nightstand as Tab begins to strip and loosen his boot laces. After kicking off his boots, he stands over you and you open your arms.

He steps forward, maneuvers onto the bed, and pushes the quilts out of the way. He lies on his side, draping one long heavy leg across your thighs, pinning you down as he sinks his hands in your glossy hair. After several minutes of deep kissing, with the wine emanating warmly from both your mouths, he grips the fleshy underside of your knees. He's holding you down, and with slow deep strokes, it doesn't take long to start coming. It begins just as you feel the sadness rise up, with the pleasure, creating the sublimity. It travels through the length of your entire body until your mouth opens, and the silent sob begins forming at the very moment Tab closes his eyes and let's go. His fat cock is pulsing, gold cells firing simultaneously in both your bodies and the Bottomless Sadness kept at bay for another day, another hour, another moment.

Talionic Night in Portland: A Love Story

CHAPTER NINETEEN

Wednesday Plans

ONE WEEK AFTER GAYLE STOMPED into your home, disrupting your dinner with Tab, covered in war paint and stinking of *Scoundrel* perfume, you realize you're going to have to go through with your promise and break into her office like you've been planning. It's the one thing that will give you some self-respect back, at least you think it will—to finally be able to say *you* had the last word. That *you* committed the last deed—that last gesture of control in your sick relationship with Gayle, and yet were able to walk away, utterly unscathed. That's your fondest hope—that it will end just like that.

When Tab arrives to collect you, you quarrel mildly on the drive to his apartment. He's waxing sentimental about the California King he says he *must* sleep on in order to feel truly rested and relaxed. You begin to resent his blatant disaffection for your apartment, insisting more and more that you both stay over at *his* place because your bed is just too small and the heating system unreliable. You don't want to bicker and so for several minutes you say nothing as he drives the truck north heading to Peninsula Park, and speeding through the dark, slick Portland streets. His gold colored calloused hands glide easily over the steering wheel, and as you gaze out the window sullenly, Tab says: "You can't go through with that plan, Daisy. Daisy?" That's when you lunge forward, holding your purse in your lap like a drowning person clutches a life jacket in deep water, and firmly remind him that *nothing* has changed.

"It doesn't matter if you come with me or not! I'm *going* to do this thing. I already told you Torch agreed to help me, at least with a little of it. If you wanna stay home, that's fine, but I am *going* to do this with or without you."

"Daisy, can't you listen to reas…"

"And by the way I looked up that word you like to use all the time—Talionic? Doesn't it mean an eye for an eye or something? I see why you like it. It's a cool word. Just look at this like the Talionic Night? The Talionic Night in Portland!—cause that's what it's gonna be!"

"Can't you just let it go, Daisy? This scheme is only going to get us both in trouble. Neither one of us has a criminal record. Do you wanna take that kinda risk? Baby, it's not worth it. It's just *not* worth it."

"Why are you always trying to *control* me? This is *my* choice, not yours!"

"I'm not a controlling type, Daisy. If anything, I'm too easygoing."

"This is something I *have* to do. I don't expect you to understand that. In fact, I don't want you with me. I'll do it alone."

"When are you planning to do it? Just so I know." After a long silence you answer.

"Okay, it has to be this Friday. We have to have an alibi and we can't have any kind of paper trail that could incriminate us on our trip to Seattle, so we won't be taking a train, or a bus, or using any of our credit cards. Also, when we do it, we're going to have to leave both our cell phones at your apartment, or somewhere else, like hidden in bush or something… or we could ship them over, to Seattle, maybe? You know, law enforcement could triangulate our cell phone locations through the satellite pings!"

"If it was to *come* to that and the cops generally only do that in cases of murder, Daisy."

"Right. Well anyway, we'll be driving down in *your* truck, and we won't stop for gas. If we have to stop for gas, we'll pay with cash, but if we fill up the tank first on that… that land yacht of yours, we probably won't have to stop for gas on the drive over."

"Did you *ever* think we'd be going down any other way? Daisy, I'm not going to just abandon my Ford truck. I've put a fortune into rebuilding that old beauty. I mean seriously, what kind of man do you think I am?!"

"The kind of man who would never be without a vehicle?"

"Thank you!"

"I'm *only* going over the details, Tab."

"And whaddaya mean *land yacht*?"

"No offense but seriously Tab, your truck *is* a gas guzzler."

"Christ, whatever! Were you able to sell your Lexus?"

"Yes! Because God forbid *I* should have a car!"

"Baby, we already discussed this. You said you were fine with it and that you actually wanted to get new wheels once we get settled in Seattle."

"Yeah, I know."

"When did you sell it?"

"Two days ago, don't you remember? I got six thousand for it. It was used, but still in fairly good condition."

"Good and you have all your things packed, and your little cast iron bed's ready to go?"

"Yeah, it only takes five minutes to take it apart. I don't have much stuff. Everything else I'm giving to Torch and Blaze and his juice-head mother, Penny. The only things I want are my boxes of odds and ends, my clothes, and the antique bed and the oak antique nightstand. They belonged to Mother you know?"

"Yes, I do remember you telling me that. That's good of you, though, giving your old furniture to the juice-head and her kid."

"I try to be kind and do my part for the community."

"Do you, now?"

"Yes, I do. It's important to give back, Tab!" you trill sarcastically.

"How are we gonna get into her office? Isn't it at a TV station? How on earth is *that* shit gonna work?"

"She's actually got *two* offices, the one we're going to is not at the station. Obviously! Its downtown and I have keys. I had them made a couple years ago when she went on a trip to Romania, and I had to use her office for various projects. Since the building is not the actual TV station, there's no real security, just a new guy, who doesn't even know me and there are *no* cameras."

"Well, thank God for that."

"Exactly."

"Is there a sign-in sheet for after hours?"

"Yes, but we'll print fake names, followed by the name of the janitor company. And they never ask for ID. Also, we'll be wearing gloves, so no fingerprints."

"The janitor company?"

"Yes. I'm going to get all dolled up as the janitor. I know exactly when they come every evening. I'm going to call the actual company though, tell them I'm Helen, my coworker, and inform them that Friday's duties will have to be cancelled due to a late evening meeting of producers, assignment editors and street reporters, and that the office will have to be cleaned no sooner than Monday morning."

"You think that'll work?"

"Sure, they don't care. It's less work for them."

"Okay."

"That way, Friday will be clear for us. The real janitors won't show up. I even found an old torn uniform they threw out a few months ago. I nabbed it and mended it. It's as good as new with the official logo from the company and everything—*Portland Janitorial & Cleaning Company!* I knew I'd find a use for it one day. I've got it *all* planned, Tab!"

"Are you going as yourself, or what?"

"No! I'm going to wear the *uniform*! I'm going to be the janitor and… you're going to wear your custodian uniform and walk in *with* me."

"What?!"

"I'm gonna tell the new security guard that *you're* there to unclog a sink."

"Okay, but why?"

"Because, I'll need a reason for you to be there *with* me. I'm gonna tell him that it has to be done before the Saturday morning meeting in the main office on five, so that's why you'll be with me. There is no meeting on Saturday but *he* won't know that. Does that make sense?"

"I suppose… and then?"

"I'm gonna wear a blond wig under a stupid NIKE cap. And I'll get to use those brown contact lenses I bought. Also, I have some bright orange lipstick and dark shading for my cheekbones, to lower the actual line of the cheekbones! See? I've thought it all through!"

"Good Lord, Daisy."

"If the kid even sees me, he'll never be able to connect the *false* image of me with any photos of the *real* me. And you're going to wear a stocking cap to hide your beautiful hair, every golden strand of it. You're also going to wear a special theatrical bite I bought at a gag store that will make it seem like you have no front teeth. It means you're going to have to smile big at the guy and have him see the bite, so he'll think you're missing a bunch of teeth. And you're going to slouch too, so you seem shorter. Got it?"

"Sure. My beautiful hair, huh?"

"Yes, Tab, your beautiful hair, like every other inch of you."

"Take it easy with the flattery. It's not like I haven't heard these things before."

"Oh really? An attitude have we?"

"Will Torch be with us?"

"No, she will have dropped me off in SE at my ex-husband's mother's house several hours earlier. The old woman's a dedicated hippie from the sixties and a total space cadet who smokes grass all the time. *She's* going to be part of my alibi."

"Who is?"

"Sally! My ex-mother-law!"

"Does Torch know any of the truth of it?"

"No way. I haven't told her anything—you know that."

"Yeah, you don't wanna confide in that one, that's for sure."

"Listen, don't bad mouth Torch. She can't help it is she's an idiot. She's only done the best she could. I'd be living *her* life if I hadn't had a little luck and education."

"Does she know why you're doing it?"

"I told her it's so I can get a photo album back from my ex-husband. Naked photos of me. She ate it up—she loved it. She's the hero see—helping out her best friend… her *only* friend, really. I even made a fake photo album, just to convince her, from some black market instamatic's I got from this guy who used to work at Cindy's porn shop downtown."

"*You* know a guy who worked at Cindy's?"

"Tab, I used to be a reporter. I know lots of people in low places."

"Okay. Then what?"

"I'll be showing her that later and only a glimpse after I come out of the house and tell her she's not needed anymore. Though I may give it to her, tell her it's for safe keeping."

"Oh, Daisy."

"Stop complaining. Listen, she *has* to think that's why I'm going there. I'd never tell her the *real* reason—that its part of the false alibi I might need, just in case."

"Of course not."

"So, how are things with the new place?"

"You mean *our* new place?"

"Yeah, our new place?"

"I finalized the sale of the townhouse. I've had all my things shipped over already. My king I'm leaving with Stan, so he'll have a nice big bed to fuck my soon to be ex Ruby on… that miserable wench. We can buy a new bed the day after we get to Seattle. Stan was thrilled when I called to tell him he could pick it up."

"Did you tell him you know? That he's been screwing Ruby?"

"Yeah, I told him *and* that there are no hard feelings. I wished him luck with her, but he's a total drunk too, so I reckon they're perfect for each other. They'll both be in jail by the end of the month I suspect."

"God, this fucking town is so incestuous. I'll be so glad to start over in Seattle where no one knows us. It's gotta be better than P-Town!"

"Me too baby, me too."

Friday morning, you meet Torch at her place and hand over several hundred dollars in cash. You sit with her in her dusty, mildewy apartment, identical to the apartment you're leaving, and cry actual tears recounting the days your ex-husband used to beat you and take x-rated photos of your young bruised body. You tell her you have no real friends—that *she's* the only one you can trust, or count on. She looks over at you with a pained expression on her face, her eyes bleeding empathy like a wound bleeds blood.

As you sniffle, and wipe your eyes, Torch grabs your wrist and strokes the back of your hand like a first grade teacher comforting a child with a skinned knee. She promises she'll drive you to the house to get the album of "nudies" back. And when you tell her you might not *have* to break into the house, but you want her there anyway, that you think your ex-husband's mother might give you the photo album without a fuss, you notice that her eyes actually start to tear up. She tells you she's willing to beat up anyone who threatens you, steal *anything*, or commit any crime. She'll do anything for you, her only friend.

"I just want you to know how much your friendship has meant to me. Are you sure you want me tuh have all this money, Daisy? I mean, heck, you've given me so much already. I'd just *do* this for ya, just cause! You know, like on the house? You don't hafta pay me."

"But I *want* to Torch. Because you've made these last few months so much more... well, not as lonely as they'd be otherwise. Remember that night we all got drunk and Tab and I made out on the couch while you and Blaze were... in your bedroom?"

"That was great. I wish there could be more nights like that, Daisy."

"There will be Torch. I promise. I promise we'll come back and party."

"Would you? We could have so much fun together, Daisy. Just you, me and... the boys!"

"Yeah! Us and the boys!"

Later, when you talk with Tab, he says it's a crazy and unnecessary addition to your already complicated plans. But you know how important it is for Torch to think you're going to be occupied with something else that night. If anyone interviews Torch about that particular Friday night, you want her to tell them adamantly that you were nowhere near Gayle's office but rather were deep in SE at the home of your ex-husband's mother's house. The pothead hippie from the sixties, Sally, and that Torch dropped you off there, and waited outside for an hour and then left after you came out, showed her the phony photo album, and told her you'd be spending the night. You've planned everything so carefully, now all you and Tab have to do is get from Portland to Seattle without being pulled over for speeding or have any other mishap occur on the drive over.

Thursday morning you have Torch, Blaze and Penny come to your apartment to go through all your furniture and other disposable possessions. The atmosphere is slightly competitive as you try to decide which items to give to each of them. You realize you may have to break up a fistfight when they start arguing over an overstuffed chair. You suggest flipping a coin and they agree, standing around with Torch and Blaze glaring at each other and Penny looking lost and haphazard as usual.

"Listen Blaze! Daisy told *me* I could take that overstuffed chair. I don't give a shit about the other stuff, but I want that damn chair."

"Hey, you don't have to yell, Torch! You'll upset Mama! She can feel the vibrations of yelling and it makes her scared so shut yer trap already!"

"You know what punk? You know what?"

"Yeah, what?"

"Don't you talk to *me* like that! You still want me to share my beer with you and give you my ass every Saturday night; you better start talking to me NICE with some respect!"

"Okay you guys, why don't we flip a coin for the bigger pieces, okay?"

"Sure, Daisy but I get to flip the coin. Is that cool Torch?"

"Yeah sure baby, flip the damn coin and get it the fuck over with."

Blaze calls heads; Torch calls tails as Blaze tosses the coin high in the air. He catches the silver quarter and slaps it on the back of his left hand dramatically, stone faced. He uncovers his hand slowly, ceremoniously, his eyes wide and expectant. Torch peeks over and sees that she's won, while Blaze slumps, his face losing all emotion and expression as he realizes Torch will be getting the nice new overstuffed chair covered in fabric blazing with purple and pink peonies.

"Don't worry baby, we can try it out later if you still wanna come over? I got me some wine and I'll make ya a burrito, from scratch, the ones ya like?"

"Yeah, okay. I'll be by, but I wanna go through the rest of this stuff. And WE need the dinette set! WE need that, for me and Mama!" Penny nods her head empathically standing next to the kitchen, grunting an affirmation, and pointing to the dinette set with wide eager eyes.

"No problem Blaze, you and Penny can have my old breakfast table. I'm sure you can get lots of good use out of it." Blaze is quiet a moment, and his face softens.

"You know Daisy, you're cool for bein' a stuck up—well, anyway, you're kinda cool."

"Thanks Blaze. No one's perfect but I try to be nice when I can."

"Ya ain't got much stuff though, do ya? Like only the bare mina-mums. Like if you wanted to split you could, real fast. Like now, huh?"

"I suppose, yes."

"So, what's going on with you and that custodian dude? You guys still fuckin?"

"Blaze, don't be rude. That's Daisy's business."

"Tab and I are still fucking, every night and I've never been happier. We're leaving for Seattle Friday, where we'll continue our fucking. That's tomorrow, but we'll be back, just like I promised Torch. We'll come back for a special visit. I'll take ya all out to dinner at the Spaghetti Factory, you know, over on Macadam? And later we'll party back at Torch's place. You're not gonna lose your place, are ya Torch?"

"Not anymore, thanks to you, Daisy!"

"Yeah, I know where that place is. I been there before, what you think I'm a peasant er somethin? I've eaten at fancy restaurants!"

"Not at all, Blaze! You little shit!" you laugh good naturedly.

"That's tellin' him Daisy!"

"I like how you... you know, cuss like how *we* do. Deep down you don't think yer better-n-us do ya?"

"I don't Blaze. That's because I'm *not* better than you."

"I told you Blaze, Daisy's the real deal. Just think, with that brand new sofa-bed of hers, your mom will be able to sleep right for a change and not hafta sleep on that little old beer stained loveseat you guys got!"

"I know. I appreciate that. Thanks, Daisy."

"Okay, let's start hauling this stuff out. I have to get this apartment emptied out soon, and I still have a lot of work to do."

"I'll help Blaze and Penny... Penny shouldn't do no heavy liftin' huh Blaze?"

"No way. Hey, MOM?! No helping okay? It's just gone be me and Torch, and you gotta get outa the way okay, Ma?"

As Torch and Blaze begin pulling out the sofa bed, you direct Penny to the dinette set and smile at her. She sits down, looking worried and uncertain as they stumble out with the sofa and she folds her hands in her lap. After a few moments, she scratches her head and twists her short grey curls. Blaze yells from the front stoop for a neighbor to come and help. The man strolls over. He's a slender Asian man, and he slaps Blaze on the back, agreeing to help, and mentioning something about a bottle of red wine Blaze still owes him. They each grab a corner of the heavy sofa bed and start pulling it across the street, joking about the last time they got drunk together.

"This is great, man! Mama's gonna have a real bed instead of that cramped old love seat! This is awesome Daisy!"

"I'm glad someone can use it, Blaze."

"And dang if it ain't like brand new, too."

CHAPTER TWENTY

Getting the Show on the Road

I KNEW IT WAS THE correct move to go to Seattle; Tab had always been right about that. But I still had to come to terms with Gayle and all her destruction. Someone had to teach her a lesson and it might as well be me. And someone *had* to warn her daughter, Mary Jennifer, about how toxic her mother would always be, and that Gayle would essentially ruin her life. Getting everything to work together cohesively so we could leave Portland behind was the hard part. Preparing for and executing the perfect Talionic Night would be the biggest challenge of my life. But I knew I had it in me. I *knew* I could orchestrate it. It would just require some planning and proper execution of those plans, combined of course with that illusive thing called luck.

I woke up early—to the smell of Tab making a breakfast of hot Lipton Tea, sautéed mushrooms, poached eggs and buttered toast with lemon curd. After a hot shower together and a quickie against the bedroom wall, we drove over to my old place on Clinton. I walked into the apartment and strolled around feeling better than I'd felt in a long time, as Tab stood reluctantly by the door, rubber necking. He could never get used to being at my place, not after that notorious Saturday when Ruby and Verona came by and all Hell broke loose. But, I had to say goodbye to my haunted little apartment, now empty—as I said goodbye to all the places I had lived in and left. I didn't feel sad though, leaving this place, I felt relieved. Ruby and Verona would be left squarely in the past and Tab and I would carry on a life filled with fulfillment, companionship and pleasure. And wasn't *that* the American dream after all? Happiness at any cost?

I placed the key on the tiled kitchen counter for the manager to pick up and turned to go. As I was leaving the kitchen, I looked over and saw a scrap of dappled sunlight filtering through the backdoor window. It was a place where I would often linger in the morning in my fuzzy pink slippers, letting what little sun there was warm my face as I sipped hot coffee. I looked over, and noticed yet another brownish purple slug had slimed in under the doorjamb and onto the cheap linoleum floor. I left it there, knowing it would slime back out in a few hours, as they always did.

Tab and I were just closing the door when we saw Torch and Blaze across the street. We slowly ambled over, interlacing our fingers as we held hands and stopped at the end of the walkway. Blaze turned eighteen a couple of days before and was no longer jail bait. I could sense Torch felt relieved and quite happy, no doubt because his age was no longer a liability to her freedom. Their enormous age difference didn't seem to matter to either of them, but I knew it wouldn't last. Blaze was still only a child and Torch was looking at fifty one day.

Penny stood in front of her unit, a wide smile on her face, clapping her hands, delighted, her grey curls springy and recently washed, while Torch and Blaze pretended to waltz on the sidewalk next to the grass. I could see that Penny's unit was now furnished with my dinette set and sofa sleeper. Someone had placed two decorative pillows on either side of the sofa in an attempt to make it look homier, and it added an effortless showroom-floor quality to the picture. Blaze and Torch pranced around, dancing on the grass still wet with morning dew. Then Blaze dipped Torch, but her heavy hips were too much for him, and he lost his grip. They fell onto the soft grass laughing, their limbs akimbo as they rolled around, finally getting back up and falling into each other playfully, poking each other in the short ribs.

Penny and Blaze's old loveseat had been hauled out and left on the sidewalk below the bay window of the unit, and a wino was draped across it fast asleep with an empty bottle of *Muscatel* gripped loosely in his hand. He had a tattered olive green Fedora resting over his face and a dog eared copy of *Tender is the Night* face down on his chest as he snored softly. As I looked closer I realized it was the drunk, Darrell, who had tried to grab my breast and Tab had knocked out cold—Blaze's uncle, and I was reminded once again how incredibly small Portland is.

Penny had finally finished a set of new curtains she'd made out of pink floral fabric, an inexpensive top sheet she'd bought years before from the downtown *Newberry's* and then cut out and sewn together. The curtains hung half open over the large living room window and gave the apartment a quaint feel it had never had before. I could see the dim outline of a milk-glass vase on the dinette set filled with several pretty orange Tropicana roses from a neighbors rose garden. The entire scene touched me, making me glad I'd given them the furniture instead of donating it to a local charity. As they looked over and saw us, they waved and smiled. I knew they were happy because of the furniture, making their lives perhaps just a little more comfortable. But I also knew I'd never see them again once the night was over, yet strangely I was missing them, already.

"Don't forget us!" Blaze yelled, laughing as he smacked Torch's ample rump.

"I'll call you on your cell later, Daisy!" Torch said, with a wink and a nod.

"I'll be waitin' on that call girl!" I called back.

"Take care of Daisy, Tab! And you *know* what *I'm* talking about!" Blaze ordered.

"You know it!" Tab called back glumly, his face expressionless, his shoulders slumped. When Tab and I got into the truck, laden down with a few boxes in the back and my cast iron bed and antique night stand, I realized I didn't know how all our things were going to get from Portland to Seattle, but figured Tab did know. He sat motionless at the wheel, and I knew he was tired and disgusted.

"Where is all our stuff? I mean, you have a lot of stuff, even more than I do?"

"I told you already. I shipped it yesterday. It's all good, don't worry. All we have to do now is drive you downtown. I mean that was part of your burglary plan, right?"

"Burglary? Yeah, right. She's gonna call my cell here in a few minutes. She'll be picking me up from the Plaid on Division and then she's gonna drive me to Sally's."

"And then?"

"Then, I'm going to make her wait outside and after about an hour, I'm going to go out and show her the fake photo album, then tell her that I'm gonna spend the night. I might have Sally come out on the porch and wave over at her, to make it believable. That's also when I'll give Torch some more money—for helping. Then, after that's done, you'll meet me nearby and we'll drive down to the office and... you know."

"Yes, I do know. Once again Daisy, I'm going to ask you to please *not* do this thing."

"Right, okay, Tab!"

"Daisy? Please?"

"I'll call you and give you the address of Sally's house once Torch drops me off. You can wait outside on the street a half block away for me to be done. It might be a three hour wait, can you handle that?"

"Looks like I'll have to, huh?"

"Let's go have lunch, I'm starved. And I *don't* want to be hungry when Torch picks me up in Penny's old sky blue Duster. God, I just hope no one sees me driving around in that heap. It's amazing anyone can still turn it over."

"I thought she didn't have a car?"

"Penny?"

"Yeah, what happened?"

"Torch told me her younger brother's a mechanic and he gave it to her last week or something. Trying to make up for when he used to beat her up all the time when they were kids."

"Well, that was generous."

"It's a heap. It barely runs."

"Where you wanna go?"

"I was thinking *Dottie's Café* off Clinton, just down the street?"

"Dot's? Yeah, they're good. Good chicken garlic sandwiches *and* good booze."

"We won't be having any booze tonight, Tab. We need our faculties. Only lemonade."

"Only lemonade!" Tab mimicked sullenly.

After we had lunch Tab dropped me off at the Plaid on Division, and parked across the street, deep in the shadows of a large maple tree while I waited for Torch to pick me up and take me to Sally's. After waiting ten minutes, Torch stormed into the parking lot in Penny's beater, waving and cheering, and pounding the steering wheel excitedly. *Fooled around and Fell in Love* by Elvin Bishop was blaring from the speakers as she pulled into the handicapped parking space. She was completely oblivious to Tab glowering darkly in the driver seat of his old Ford pickup across the street, like a serial killer waiting to pounce.

"Come onnnn Daisy! Let's go get that fuckin' photo album! Let's get this fuckin' show on the road!"

"You know how to get to Sally's right? I gave you her address last week."

"I got it—don't worry. And if you need me to strong arm that old lady; I can do *that*, too!"

"No, she's actually really nice. An old hippie who raised her son on a commune."

"A commune? Now *that* is hysterical!"

"Tell me about it. But apparently, too much freedom and too much goodness made him the opposite of what she'd hoped. He grew up and became an unlucky businessman and a narrow minded Republican."

"A Republican? Sheeeit!"

"I still can't understand how I *ever* got tangled up with him."

"Well, I'm here to help, Daisy. And *that's* all in the past, anyway!"

"I can't thank you enough, Torch. You really are one in a million."

"Hop in! Let's go do this thing!"

It was almost dusk as Torch drove south toward Stark Street. She parked in the dim shade of an old fourplex which sat right next to Sally's restored 1906 Victorian painted lady. Torch waited, sitting in the driver's seat as I got out carrying a tattered duffel bag and my pink Coach purse slung over my shoulder. I glanced back at Torch and winked playfully. She nodded in response, her eyes steely, the blood red lipstick applied perfectly on her full rosebud mouth, the pock marks on her cheeks on prominent display with too much ivory colored foundation and too much *Coty* face powder.

Sally's front porch was littered with potted plants and various sad looking gnomes with chipped paint and forlorn dark eyes. But the photo album was exactly where I'd left it the night before, sitting behind a large ceramic pot filled with bright green *Tongue of Mother-in-law,* reaching up in narrow stalks as if to escape. Sally had probably walked right by it and hadn't even noticed it on her way to work that morning. I discreetly bent over as I stepped onto the front porch and quickly tucked the album under my arm in front of my waist, and then walked to the front door. As I stood in front of her door, gathering my thoughts for a moment, I lightly tapped on the stained glass window. Sally came to the door almost at once and she was a hippie vision in beads, feather earrings and an assortment of seedpod necklaces and antique silver rings. Her gold and silver hair floated about her shoulders, and her petite Gidget figure was perfect. Even at sixty one Sally still had men chasing after her.

"Oh Daisy! My sweet lost darling. How have you been? It's been forever since I've seen you. *You* never answered my letters."

"I know, I just…"

"It's okay, honey. You know I rarely if ever see him anymore. He just turned out to be so different from how I expected. Even his father doesn't much like him these days."

"I just came by to chat before I move. Yes, I'm not surprised about *him* either. Funny, he had every opportunity to turn into a loving human being and… he became a failed Mad Max of the real estate market in Omaha, instead. Is he still living there? I shudder to think what *that* must be like."

"He's still there. He met a nice girl from the Omaha Ballet Company and he's officially destroying her life now, too. She called last week to tell me she was leaving. He called the next afternoon and asked if she'd called me to tell me anything and I told him no, of course. I don't know the girl very well, but I wouldn't want *any* woman to be burdened with *him,* much as I love him, ya know?"

"I know, Sally."

"I think she moves out tomorrow. I try not to get involved. Otherwise, he asks me for more of his *loans.* Well, *you* remember."

"Yes, I remember."

"So, you're moving? Good lord, where to?"

"Uh, Delaware—there's a good paper there, the *Wilmington Morning News,* and they need a new associate editor. Thought I'd give TV news a break for awhile."

"Oh, my God, Daisy, I'm so sorry. Please come in. I just made Scottish Short bread and I can make us a hot mug of tea, or coffee if you'd prefer?"

"Thank you Sally," I murmured as I walked inside. Sally's home was as spacious and beautifully decorated with fine antiques as I remembered it. It had the intoxicating scent of patchouli incense drifting through the air, as if it had been burned in the house since the day it was built. We stood in the foyer and she approached me, embracing me tenderly, patting my back and touching my hair.

"Oh, those ringlets! I *have* missed you. I've told that boy time and again that he'll never, find a girl as great as you. He sure hates it when I say that."

"I've missed you too, Sally."

"Here, let's go in here, it's more comfortable than the drawing room! Would you like coffee or tea?"

"Do you still drink that wonderful Earl Grey?"

"Oh yes, absolutely. I special order it from *Harney & Sons*. There's just nothing like it."

"You had multiple kinds as I recall?"

"Yes, let's see, I have Viennese Earl Grey, Winter White Earl Grey and Earl Grey Supreme. There's just something about having the best when it comes to tea."

"And you have all those?"

"Yes, which one would you like?"

"I think the Earl Grey Supreme."

"That was always your favorite! Remember?"

"Oh yeah, I guess I'd forgotten."

We walked past the kitchen and into the refurbished solarium and I fell into one of her cozy overstuffed loveseats. I kicked off my flats, curled my legs under me and hugged my purse. It had been years since I'd been in her home and I had to admit, I missed it. Then, as soon as I opened my mouth, I began lying, as I knew I would. Sally was one of those people who loves a good story, whether it was true or not and I couldn't let her down. She'd never actually come out and accused me of lying in all the years I knew her, but sometimes I wondered if she really *was* as naïve as she came across to people. How could anyone be that trusting?

I casually told her a story of how I'd met a red-haired architect named Troy Spurlock and would be starting life over in Delaware, explaining that the photo album I had in my arms was something I'd rescued from the desk of the boyfriend of an old girlfriend from my work. It was the same old story, I told her, of a couple who had fallen madly in love and then after getting drunk on bottles of cheap white wine taken loads of cheesy instamatic photos of them having sex and using sex toys with names like Black Bomb Dildo and Red Rider Vibrator. We giggled and I asked her if she wanted to see and pretended to open the photo album, but she just laughed and said she'd have nightmares if she saw anything as ugly as any "up close" photographic depictions of sex organs. I laughed and tossed the photo album next to my purse, as she walked to the kitchen to make the tea. I considered for a moment that I'd given her a conflicting story about the origins of the photo album than what I'd told Torch, but decided a conflicting story might be useful in the long run, as witnesses are notoriously unreliable in what they can remember or recount accurately.

Looking out the window to the backyard area, I remembered all the dinner parties we had had together, back when I was still married to her son, and thinking we would be married forever. Back when we had all those mutual friends that we thought would be our friends forever, only to later realize I couldn't remember half their names. Even then, shortly after I'd married her son, I knew it had been a mistake. I knew one day I would leave him just as I did—with an apartment filled with the fine antique furniture we'd bought together, a short careless scribble of a note and his life to himself—to begin living all alone, starting as soon as he read the note and ran to my empty closet with tears in his eyes, and his unquenchable rage and clenched fists springing to life.

After we talked for almost an hour, I told Sally I had to make a phone call and would walk around the block. I stood up, grabbing my purse and tossing it over my shoulder, as I bent down and discreetly slipped the photo album under my arm. I left the duffel bag on the floor, while Sally busied herself cleaning the dishes and tidying up the kitchen, and strolled out the front door, walking directly to Torch's car. She was expecting me to go back to her place and "party" with her and Blaze, but I told her there'd been a change in plans. I could tell she was disappointed but when I handed her the photo album, her eyes brightened. It was something I'd traded from an old informant of mine, who had gotten it from a pervert collector. I knew her mood would improve once she opened it up. The photo album was nothing but lots of headless porn shots of a young dark haired woman from a few years ago. I knew she and Blaze would be thrilled with it, thinking the shots were actually me. Then, as soon as I handed Torch a fat envelope filled with crisp new cash, any remaining disappointment faded completely, and she transformed. In the span of two seconds Torch became utterly delighted that she'd be getting more money than I'd promised *and* a kinky photo album into the bargain.

"Sally's just really sad about her son—my ex-husband? He turned out to be such a loser but as you can see I got the photo album back! Now, as to that photo album you're holding... will you... will you keep it safe for me, Torch?"

"You want *me* to keep the photo album *for* you? Sure, no problem. You know you can count on me, Daisy!"

"You won't look at the pictures will you?" I camped, smiling flirtatiously.

"Me? Never!" Torch camped back.

"Perfect. Well, I better get back to Sally. She was literally crying her eyes out in there."

"Okay. Thanks for the money and I'll keep your photo album safe, I promise. Will you come back and party with me and Blaze, like you promised?"

"Absolutely, we will, Torch. Would I lie to you?"

****

After I'd spent another hour with Sally, I asked if I could stay over, telling her I was exhausted and wished to spend the night one last time in her glorious old home like in the old days. She accepted immediately and told me I could take the bedroom next to the kitchen. I shyly asked if she might burn some more Patchouli incense and she agreed, getting up and fetching a small black cone and a clear glass dispenser, handing them to me with a smile. We stood across from each other awkwardly and she leaned in and hugged me. We held each other silently for a long moment. The grief in our embrace was felt by both of us. I could tell by the way her breathing shuddered and she steeled herself against the emotion that was passing through her. She pulled away and told me she would always feel like a mother to me and I could stay with her no matter what, that I would *always* be family to her. I quietly thanked her, and looked down, trying to quell the tears that were dangerously close.

"Oh Daisy. I'm so sorry. I'm so sorry he did those things..."

"It's okay. I forgave him years ago."

"If he wasn't my son...well, I'd have *nothing* to do with him, you know?"

"It's okay Sally. I understand." I whispered.

I turned away and walked toward the old room I'd slept in so many times before as she gathered fresh bedding for her bed from the kitchen pantry and then slowly walked toward the dining room. I turned around and looked after her, not quite understanding the feeling of instant loss and nostalgia that I associated with her beautiful face and her adorable tiny body and kind Minnie Mouse voice. I wanted to linger in conversation with her, but felt the futility of it. What could it possibly accomplish? She would never be my mother. As much as I would have loved that, Sally would never be that woman.

"Do you still keep your bedding in the pantry instead of the linen closet upstairs?"

"It's just easier that way. You know me, the path of least resistance."

"It makes sense, though. I'd to it, too!"

"Well, I spend most of my time in the kitchen as it is."

"Goodnight Sally and... thank you."

"Say no more, angel. Enjoy the incense."

"Yes, thank you."

I slowly closed the door to the bedroom, walked over to the bed and pulled the sheet and quilts down. I sat on the bed, and carefully lit the cone, setting it on its glass dish on the nightstand. I sat and watched the lavender-blue smoke drift up, and the haunting scent fill the room. I fell onto the bed and kicked my legs around, messed up the bedding and hit the pillows a few times, which were brand new. Then, I reached up and pulled out a single strand of glossy dark hair and laid it across the white pillow, smiling as it coiled into the shape of a curl, again. I sat up, scooted to the edge of the bed and listened to the funny sounds of the old house. The squeaks and whistles of the wind drifted through the fireplace flue, producing a sinister and mournful sound. And the creaking of the floor as Sally's ancient deaf dog Tobias walked across the upstairs hallway reminded me of a lifetime ago, when she would proudly introduce me to all her friends as her "brand new" daughter-in-law, smiling from ear to ear, her hand on my back, Tobias scampering at my feet.

I stood up and walked to the oak secretary and found pens, decorative stamps and stationary inside, knowing instantly what I would do. The stationary was cream colored with an elegant navy trim and I could see Sally had special ordered it from *Nieman Marcus* in case a guest might find themselves in need of letter writing materials. Sally always thought of things like that, to give her home that special touch. I sat on the bed and wrote a short letter, using a nearby book to write the letter on. I thanked her for the tea and shortbread and wrote down a bogus time—of 5:25 am. I apologized for not making the bed, or having breakfast with her, and told her we would need to get together for dinner soon, perhaps in the next three months. Then I kissed the bottom of the letter, and the red imprint from my Lancôme lipstick looked perfect. I knew she'd love it. Poor Sally. She had never really known me at all, and probably never would. Like many people, she would never know what I was truly capable of.

After Sally had taken her bath and gone to bed, closing the door to the master bedroom, I waited another hour, and read the book on the nightstand; a book called *Theft* by Peter Carey, knowing after the first chapter that I would take it with me. I picked up my purse, stuffed the book under my arm, and slipped out the back door as silently as a Ninja, making certain it locked behind me. I walked barefoot from the back door, and out onto the large back porch area, tiptoed gingerly by a small barrel of fragrant Cortland apples Sally would undoubtedly use for baking pies, and stepped down the three concrete steps onto the soft dry earth below. I continued through the side walkway and out onto the street and headed north, stepping onto the cold sidewalk.

As I was walking, I stopped abruptly, pulled on my flats, and tugged my purse and the book closer to me. I made a mental note that I had left the duffel bag in the bedroom, but it was only filled with some of my embroidery—a set of pillowcases I was working on. I knew Sally would set it aside and keep it safe, telling me later how much she loved the purple and yellow pansies I was making. And I knew she wouldn't miss the book. She knew I'd long had a problem with stealing books from cafes and doctors offices, and she used to tease me about it. She was always giving me books as gifts and loaning me books I never returned. Sally would see the book missing and she would smile, knowing I had taken it. She would find the strand of my hair on the pillow case, and tape it to a piece of paper, light a red candle and say a prayer for me. I would *always* love Sally and I promised myself I would stay in touch with her. If she ever got old and helpless, I would be there for her. Sally would *always* be someone in my life, no matter how many years or months might go by before we saw each other again.

I saw no one on the street and felt intensely grateful I'd made a silent escape with not one person seeing me. The shadows deepened and I felt the chill of the midnight air as the heat from my cheeks and neck began to dissipate in the breeze. The scent of moss and rain lingered in the Portland atmosphere and began drifting in my open mouth and deep into my throat. I walked the three blocks to where I knew Tab would be waiting for me on SE Belmont Street, with my change of clothes and all our gear packed into the Ford. When I approached, and he saw me, I could tell how tired and apprehensive he was. By contrast, I felt jaunty that everything was going as planned. If the police ever questioned Torch or Sally, they would both have rock solid alibis for me, plus evidence in the form of the phony photo album and the letter, with my finger-prints all over both objects. Now, all we had to do was get to Gayle's office and settle those old scores. As I walked to the truck, Tab reached over and unlocked the door. He was silent and resentful I could tell, as I slipped inside.

"Where to?" he asked quietly. I told him the address, in the heart of downtown Portland.

"I see you're in your uniform. Do you have the bite too, Tab?"

"In my pocket, and I'll put the cap on as soon as we get there. Do you wanna do your makeup here and change or what?"

"Let's pull onto a side street, maybe somewhere over on PSU campus next to the Broadway Lab. There should be some parking spaces available now. It's nice and isolated over there after hours. I don't want to be around any unseen cameras or areas where there might be a lot of people. It's probably deserted up there at his time of night."

"Okay. Let's get going, then."

Several minutes later, after crossing the Hawthorne Bridge, Tab pulled the Ford into a particularly dark street north of PSU's Native American Center on Broadway. The area was perfectly deserted as I began to take off my jeans and light pink sweater, pulling on the oversize Janitor uniform over my bra and panties and zipping it up. I looked over at Tab as he watched me, and knew he pitied me, but there was something else in his gaze—was it fear?

"You match," he said sullenly, nodding his head to my set of bright red undergarments as I finished dressing.

"I'm dressed like a whore tonight because *that's* how this character would play it!"

"This character?"

I said nothing as I slipped on the blonde wig and began applying the makeup, glowering darkly at Tab for a short moment. I inserted the dark contact lenses, applied the orange lipstick and then the dark shading to my cheekbones. I pulled on the cap, knowing the kid working security would *never* be able to place my new fake face with my real face. When I was done, I turned to Tab.

"How do I look? Is *this* the kind of woman you wanna spend time with?"

"Stop it!" Tab hissed, looking away, embarrassed.

"What's wrong? Don't you like the new me?!"

"Baby, I don't even *recognize* you. Come on; let's just get this over with. I want this night to be over!"

"It's show time, bubba!" I camped sarcastically as I smeared on more orange lipstick.

Tab sighed heavily, then pulled on the cap, and pushed his hair inside. He took the bite from his pocket and stuffed it in his mouth, forcefully biting down on it and then aggressively turning to me smiling goofily like Gomer Pyle. I was unimpressed and laughed dismissively.

"Your new nickname is The Toothless Wonder! He gets the job done cuz he ain't got no teef!"

"Gee, thanks, Daisy!"

We got out of the truck, and walked with military purpose several blocks north, heading down Broadway not speaking, before finally turning east and walked directly to Gayle's office building. As we approached the front door, we simultaneously reached into our pockets and pulled on the thin black leather gloves I had purchased only that morning from *Meier & Frank*—with cash of course.

After walking in the glass doors, I shambled over to the night watchman's desk, swinging my hips seductively, and casually showed the bored security guard my phony ID. Tab lazily reached into his pocket and showed the guard his ID, too. They were ID's I'd managed to squirrel away a couple of years before—ID's I had discreetly promised to hold for a certain drug dealer informant in the process of being arrested on fifth and Alder and would be looking at hard time. I knew they would come in handy one day and so there we were showing the fake ID's which the kid barely even glanced at. I laughed, snorting loudly as I scribbled a phony signature on the sign-in sheet. Tab took the pen-on-a-chain and signed too, with a dramatic flourish that was not a signature at all, but just a couple of long ink swipes.

"Never was good at that dag-blam cursive writin' everyone hadta learn in scoo!"

"Me neether tootsie!" Tab said. He laughed in a forced way, and smiled broadly as I'd instructed him, turning his head to the security guard, so the man could see the bite in his mouth and that apparently Tab had *no* front teeth. He energetically gave the security guard the thumbs up for no apparent reason.

"How ya doin' mister?" Tab asked, faking the accent of a region-less, generic city hick from Portland. The young man didn't answer. He just rolled his eyes, looked at both of us in disgust and went back to reading the graphic novel in his hands, with the words *Queen Bee* emblazoned across the front in bright yellow.

"Yer set to go and clean now," he mumbled sullenly, "have fun."

"Thank ya love! You know, yer cute!"

"Yeah, well, I'm *not* into older women," he sneered, not bothering to look back at us.

"Well, s'cuse me, then!"

"Come on, Connie!" Tab said sighing in disgust but still perfectly in character.

As Tab and I stepped into the elevator, I could feel my pulse quicken. I was getting the first of several adrenalin jolts I knew would make me jittery but able to do what needed to be done. The old Otis Elevator doors closed and we slowly rose to the fifth floor.

"Connie?"

"It was all I could think of."

"Did you *know* a girl named Connie?"

"I've known *three* girls named Connie."

"And you slept with all of them, haven't you?"

"Baby, you want me to lie?"

"Just forget it. I don't even wanna know the details."

"Okay, then."

"This is incredible, though. Everything is going so smoothly."

"The night's not over yet. Don't start celebratin' just yet. There's still a whole world of wrong that can happen, trust me."

"A whole world of wrong? God, I love your euphemisms. They're so original!"

"Is that a putdown?"

"No, Tab, it's not! By the way, do you have that bag with all the stuff in it, including my change of clothes?"

"Yeah, I got it. Its right here. I'm holdin' it."

As the elevator ascended, I reached into my bra and removed the cheap metal key. It was the coveted key to Gayle's office and as I looked at it, it sparkled with something like seductiveness, like a secret wink only I could comprehend. I had polished it the night before with Ivory Soap and steel wool, and it shone like sterling silver. When the door to the elevator opened, Tab stepped out first, then stopped and waited for me to take the lead, unsure where to go.

"It's over here Tab, to the right," I whispered, stepping forward.

"Do you hear that Daisy? I think there's someone here."

"What? Wait… yeah I hear it, too."

"Daisy is that… is that fucking?"

We skulked down to the end of the hall and there on the left in Gayle's hideously pink office, with the door wide open was Helen partially clothed and bent over Gayle's desk. Her back was arched, her ass high in the air, her head thrown back and her boyfriend behind her fucking her hard. The lights were off and the room was illuminated nicely by the bluish ambient light from the city outside. Tab and I turned to each other dumbfounded, our eyes big and incredulous at the sight before us. Helen's white ass glowed in the dim light like one of Jupiter's pale yellow moons as we watched silently for a long moment. Helen, the social climbing goody two shoes was getting a high hard one from the egghead boyfriend she regularly liked to brag about. He was better looking than I'd imagined he would be, and also nearly bald, but the dynamic of the relationship was displayed for their audience of two. Though Tab might not have seen it, I certainly did. Helen whimpered and whined as her boyfriend told her she was a dirty little slut who deserved to be punished. He was definitely the one in charge.

"Uh, excuse me but *we're* the janitors!" I announced loudly with what I hoped was a southern accent.

"Oh my God!" Helen gasped. She turned sharply, her eyes sleepy, unseeing and terrified.

"Awwww sheeeit! You told me this would be okay. Damn it Helen!"

"I thought it would be? I did! Please don't be angry? Oh God, where are my glasses?!"

"Get the fuck out, you fuckers, before I call the po-lice!" I camped, snickering meanly.

"Yeah, okay lady, jus give us a minute."

"No, you get out NOW you fuckin' degenerate!"

"Okay, okay!"

Watching Helen and her egghead boyfriend stumble around and grab their things, adjusting their clothes, and run out of the dim office was hysterical and a total guilty pleasure but I couldn't help but wonder how she had gotten a key, too. In their haste, they didn't even look at us. Helen would never know it was *me* who had walked in on her getting slammed from behind, as she was draped over Gayle's desk with her ass in the air. I knew the unexpected incident was a good omen. It meant that nothing bad might happen from that point on, and that I would be able to finish with Gayle once and for all and wouldn't even have to use my key to get in. Everything would go perfectly. I just *knew* it.

"Get out, before we call the cops!" I yelled after them as they ran down the hall, and scrambled into the elevator.

"If that don't beat all!" Tab said laughing. He pulled the bite out of his mouth and stuffed it into his pants pocket.

"Helen! That hypocritical little slut! Always acting like such a prim and proper lady!"

"I guess everyone fucks. Ain't that right? Even dorks like them."

"Tab, you know that's *not* proper grammar. I really hate it when you talk like trash."

"I thought you *liked* how I talk?"

"You know that *ain't* is slang. You're better than that."

"Yeah, okay. Hey, you know technically we aren't even breakin' and enterin' so I guess we don't have to worry so much."

"Don't stress about it, Tab. The cops will just think it's another kick-in when they get the call. Just another hopped up middle-aged doper trying to steal office computers and sell 'em for cocaine money so he can get a hard-on. You know how it is."

"Well, not that *I'd* know about that exactly, but yeah..."

We walked into the office, and I ceremoniously took the large Pepsi bottle of pancake batter I had lovingly prepared the night before from the bag Tab was carrying. I twisted open the top, looked up at Tab to my right, and smiled wanly, batting my eyelashes with theatrical innocence. Tab looked down at me with that familiar expression of troubled concern, as I began to toss splatters of it everywhere. Long glittering ribbons of creamy pancake batter sailed across the room, hanging in the air with exquisite beauty before landing with a pronounced *splat*. As I tossed pancake batter everywhere, I quietly sang the song, *Whistle While You Work*, from the 1937 Disney cartoon *Snow White and the Seven Dwarfs* and giggled meanly.

"I'm a MEAN girl!" I announced in a sultry whisper to the silent room.

Tab watched, saying nothing. His eyebrows were knit together suspiciously and his long gorilla arms hung at his sides impotently as he held the bag of supplies. Under his gaze, I felt powerful, superior and absolutely turned on. I suddenly remembered the old bum on the street corner as he screamed to an uncaring world: "The more evil ya get, the more ya enjoy it!" and I marveled at the brilliant simplicity of his ebullient statement and how no matter how I tried, I'd *never* be able to forget his words, and their inherent truth.

Gayle's cheap fiber board bookcase was hit, with her collection of tedious romance novels, and cheesy true crime stories. I made sure to soil each book meticulously. After the bottle of pancake batter had been extinguished, I took out a can of spray paint and sprayed WHORE in big black letters across the pink wall next to her desk. I walked to the adjacent wall and sprayed METALLICA and GUNS-N-ROSES across the wall in messy capital letters, watching with satisfaction as the paint from each letter dripped down the wall ominously like a black magic curse. With my tennis shoes on, I lifted my right foot and then leaned back and propelled myself forward. With all my strength I kicked the wall with my right foot, feeling the sheetrock give a little under the force of each blow.

"Why are you doin' that, Daisy?"

"Some cop I talked to once. He told me it's what teenage boys do when they burgle places. Spray paint the names of stupid rock bands everywhere and then kick in the walls. They say it's how they know if it was a real kick-in. There's a pattern that they look for."

"Ya learn somethin' new every day."

"We want the police to just think its teenage boys out *wilding* or something."

"Wilding?"

"Never mind, Tab."

On Gayle's "wall of respect" I sprayed over all the framed articles and awards and framed photos of important people that she had prominently displayed. There was an old photograph of Gayle with disgraced police Chief Penny Harrington, both smiling frantically as if they'd just won at Senior Citizen Bingo that I gave special attention to. After each framed something or other was befouled with spray paint, I took the edge of the can and slammed it sideways into the center. The edge of the can shattered the glass of each framed accolade with a satisfying crunch that gave me the goose bumps and a corresponding tickle in my crotch.

"Awww, look at that. Isn't that just so pretty, Tab? Tab?"

But Tab didn't answer. He just stood there looking over at me with resigned golden eyes. He held the bag in his hands in front of him, almost protectively, dreading I knew, the introduction of the sulpheric acid. Spray paint and pancake batter was one thing, but sulpheric acid was quite another. I knew he would try to dissuade me from using it and I was prepared for a fight.

"WHERE is the sulpheric acid, Tab?" I asked calmly.

"Baby, I have it in here but I'm going to ask you to reconsider using it. It would become more than just barging in here if you use sulpheric acid to destroy anything. It would be… it would be another felony."

"Damn it Tab, I *knew* you'd try to talk me out of it. Just hand it over!"

"Daisy girl, you don't know how to use it. If you get even a little on anything organic, it will eat right through. I *don't* want you to use it!"

"So what! I wanna destroy her desk! That one right there. I wanna ruin it!"

"I can't allow you to destroy a defenseless antique desk, Daisy! I *won't* allow it."

"Give it to me, Tab!"

"Do you realize that is a 1940s English Chippendale mahogany writing desk?! I won't allow you to destroy it, it's an absolute gem! It would be a crime!"

"You're personifying a desk?! Lemme splash it across the carpet, then!"

"Daisy, you can't splash it! If even a little gets on your skin, if will eat right through it!"

"But I thought you said?…"

"Anything organic baby—like your SKIN!"

"Listen, *you* don't need to yell at me. I'm stressed out enough already! You think I'm stupid just because I'm a girl!"

"Daisy, that's not what I…"

"Yes, it is, that's what you think. I *know* it! That's what *everyone* always thinks!"

"No, it isn't! Oh, for crying out loud, Daisy!"

I charged at Tab with my hands outstretched ready to grab the bottle from the black bag he was carrying, but I stepped on a slick of pancake batter that had landed on the floor and sailed in his direction. I careened forward on my left heel sliding on the carpet just as my right leg rose in the air like an off-center, unskilled ice skater practicing at the Lloyd Center Rink. Tab dropped the bag, bent his knees, and tried to catch me like a baseball umpire catches a ball, but as I was moving forward my body shifted and veered to the left. I skidded low into the bottom portion of Gayle's wood desk like a little leaguer sliding into first base. Upon impact the side of my head smacked into the edge of the left front leg, and I felt the hot blood instantly as it began to trickle down my forehead. I scrambled to a sitting position and looked up at Tab, my voice trembling with emotion and tears pricking behind my eyes.

"I can't believe it. Look what you did? I'm injured and it's YOUR fault!"

"Yes it is my fault, isn't it? Because I shouldn't have allowed you to do this. I shoulda just tied you up to my bed like I wanted, and force-fed you sleeping pills and whiskey!"

"Force fed me what?"

"I'm being sarcastic, Daisy, but you're right. It *is* my fault. I shoulda put my foot down and *never* let you talk me into this! Oh Daisy, can't you see why we're here? Can't you see *why* you're doing this?"

"All I know is I'm bleeding and it's… oh, *where* is it coming from? It's not my forehead is it?" Tab stepped closer, bent down, extended his hands and yanked me to my feet. He reached into his pocket and pulled out a clean handkerchief and patted at the blood gently as I stood there fidgeting, moving my weight from one foot to another, breathing heavily and fighting back tears.

"Okay, hold still. No, it's on your scalp. That's good. We can hide it. I don't want people thinkin' I'm beatin' you or some damn thing!"

As I stood there, Tab suddenly let go of me. He stepped away, lifted up his hands as if to indicate he was done with me, and turned his back. I watched, bewildered, as he violently threw the bloody hanky across the room. He took several deep breaths, and began running his hands through his hair. He walked over, and with deliberate delicacy bent down and picked up the hanky and stuffed it into his front pocket. I felt cast aside and the sensation was new and frightening. Tab had never done that before and what was worse, he refused to look at me and stood with his back turned, his shoulders still raised in anger.

"Tab? I… I just want you to know how much I appreciate that you support me. I just want you to know that…"

"Daisy? Just save it, okay? You know I thought I was gettin' away from this kind of thing… this kind of… insanity! I thought you were *different* from Ruby and Verona, but I guess…"

"No, Tab, I am different! I promise, I promise, I *am* different!"

As I took a step forward, I walked into another slick of oily pancake batter and my feet went out from under me. I landed on my back, my head thudding the carpeted floor as I sucked air from the painful impact. Tab turned around sharply just as I landed, his eyes huge. He strode over and reached down for me, pulling me up roughly by my wrists. Before I knew it, he had reached under my armpits and was hoisting me up, and turning me sideways midair, maneuvering me onto Gayle's wooden desk just behind him. I landed with a soft thump and sat there stunned as Tab stood over me breathing heavily. I sat breathless for a moment, looking up. Time seemed to stand still as he gazed down at me, his face filled with disgust, consternation and love. I reached out for him with both arms, my eyes wide and pleading, but he took a step back, and raised his arms with his palms out, silently telling me no. Tab gazed down at me hard, and as I sat there, it suddenly came to me that the idea of breaking into Gayle's office was the stupidest idea in the world. I was filled with instant and furious remorse. I sat there and in only the span of a few seconds my face began to screw up and I burst into silent tears. My shoulders shook as I slowly dropped my head, the shame consuming me all at once.

"Here we go…" Tab said, quietly and without judgment. Then more authoritatively: "Daisy, you're gonna listen to me. You're gonna listen to me, God Damn it. I think I know *why* you hate Gayle so much."

"I don't wanna talk about it. You don't know me well enough to…"

"No! You're gonna listen!"

"What if I don't wanna listen?!"

"Daisy, I'd be angry too. If I'd been born a girl and *my* mother didn't care enough to protect me. If *my* mother didn't ask who I was babysitting for? If she just let me walk into the lion's den, the way your mother did? I'd be angry, too!"

"That's not IT! My mother was practically a saint!"

"No she wasn't. Far from it, Daisy. You told me about that affair she had!"

"Now, you're going to insult my dead mother?!"

"What she did was wrong. She didn't *protect* you, baby. She left you to your own devices and Raymond preyed on you. That's the truth of it. If I could find him and kill him, I fuckin' would!"

"I made the choice. I wanted Raymond. I wanted him! I *wanted* him!"

"You were thirteen, Daisy, with a father who left years before. It was a choice you should never have had the *freedom* to make. It was wrong. Even if it felt good, baby, it was wrong."

"It *did* feel good, though! It *did* feel good!"

"I know how that is."

"Yeah, but you don't know me well enough to…"

"Daisy, you're *projecting* your anger at your mother onto Gayle. It's *not* Gayle's fault your mother didn't protect you. Gayle is *not* your mother."

"I KNOW that!"

"But do you know it *emotionally*? Do you know it on the inside?"

"You think you can psychoanalyze *me*?"

"What did you say to me about what Raymond did to you? Do you remember?"

"I'm a journalist and a writer. I have a photographic memory! I remember everything!"

"Okay, then what did you say?"

"I said… I said: *"What he did to me was reprehensible, Tab!"* THAT is what I said."

"Yes, that *is* what you said. And it's true. What he did to you *was* reprehensible, Daisy! He stole your innocence. He let you partake of the poison apple and you've never been the same. You ate the poison apple, baby, just like I ate the poison apple. And that's what makes us how we are. That's what makes us *who* we are. Always hungry, always in search of more, always looking for that next best thing we're after—trying to solve the mystery, trying to put the puzzle pieces together but… never, ever succeeding."

"Always hungry?"

"It comes clear doesn't it? It just takes a little time."

"God, I'm tired. I'm so fuckin' tired."

"Baby? Are you ready to go home now? So, we can start over and be done with all this… insanity?" I didn't answer. I just looked up at Tab, my eyes big and owlish, and nodded my head. My face was slick with tears, and my mouth screwed up in shame, and grief.

"We need to get out of here and back to the truck. We need to get started on the road to Seattle, okay?"

"Can I change clothes later, at a rest stop or something along the way?"

"Yes, that's fine. But we need to get outa here. We're already seven minutes behind schedule." As Tab helped me off the table, I looked around at the mess and felt the fabric of the uniform sticking to my hot flesh as I began to take off the black leather gloves.

"Don't you take those off! Not yet anyway."

"Right. Sorry. And I'm sorry about... I guess I just never thought of it the way you..."

"Sometimes the most obvious answer is right in front of us, and we rarely see it."

"What are you gonna do with the sulpheric acid?"

"I'll just put it next to the door here. The container's only half full, anyway. They'll think the custodian used it to clear the drains or something."

"You didn't touch it with your bare hands, did you?"

"Of course not."

We walked to the door and I stopped and turned to look over the room and survey the damage. It was enough. Though Tab had put a stop to my projectile rage, I was still strangely satisfied with the messy destruction. The only thing untouched and pristine in the entire room was the warm-hued antique desk Tab had heroically defended. Looking at it as it shone like a diamond in the dim light, I felt glad Tab had insisted it not be harmed. I knew one day Gayle would lose it, she would sell it or give it away, and it would end up in better hands. It was beautiful, a lonely and lost thing from another century, an ancient emerald amidst the rough hewn pebbles of the postmodern world, something exquisite and untouched—something *worthy* of protection.

Something like what I had been and like what Tab had also once been.

I'd at least done some of what I'd wanted, but now I had to think about the sliver of an idea that Tab had planted in my brain. Was it true I projected the anger I felt for my mother onto Gayle? Could it really be that simple and straightforward? That garden variety? Tab took the bottle of acid from the bag he was holding and tossed it into the waste basket by the door, took my hand, and began pulling me with him out of the room, as an impatient father pulls a misbehaving child.

"Wait, the key! I don't want it anymore."

"What are you gonna do with it?"

"I'll just drop it in her desk."

I pulled away, carefully walked back to the desk, stepping around the pancake slicks already hardening on the carpet and pulled open the top drawer, which Gayle always left unlocked. I dropped the key among the paper clips and push tacks and that's when I saw the letter from Mary Jennifer. While Tab watched, I grabbed the letter before he could object and shoved it into my pants pocket. I tiptoed back to him and we walked quickly to the elevator going down to the first floor in silence as he gripped my elbow in his gloved hand. I felt like a child as Tab steered me past the security guard who didn't bother to look up. Tab opened the front door, and I stopped suddenly, sneezed a fake sneeze and loudly squealed: "That lady and her boyfriend sure made a mess! We're not obligated to clean up a mess like that! God, some people!" I saw the young security guard look up curiously.

"Hey! Aren't you guys gonna sign out?"

"I don't think so! I slipped up there. Jeez, what do those people do, have orgies up there? That's not what *we* signed on for. We're not obligated to clean up a mess like that!" We turned and disappeared out the door as the security guard shrugged and went back to reading his book. Once out on the sidewalk Tab sighed heavily.

"You know, sometimes I really wonder about you. What was *that* all about?"

"I had to give him something to think about—something he'll *remember*. In case the cops question him later, see?"

"But what if he goes upstairs? What then?"

"Trust me, he couldn't care less. He's not gonna do anything."

"Let's get going, we need to get outa here!"

We hustled down the sidewalk, and I found myself dogging Tab's steps like a frightened child. He looked down at me annoyed, wrapped his beefy arm around my shoulder, and roughly pulled me to him, still angry.

"Got damn Daisy, what am I gonna *do* with you?"

I didn't answer, just leaned into him, looking down, and clutched my arm around his broad waist as I struggled to walk at his pace. As the streets were bare, we saw no one, not even an old bum out collecting cans for a bottle of wine. My makeup was smeared and the tears were still slick on my wet face. I knew I looked like some kind of horrible tragic nightmare. And more than anything, I knew in *no* way was I better than Ruby, Verona, Gayle, Helen, Penny or Torch! I was no better than the wino who was Blaze's uncle who Tab punched out the night we went for a Taco Bell run. I was myself one of the walking wounded people laugh about.

I was that damaged, and that lost.

We made it to the Ford in silence and got in, tossing the bag of supplies in the back. Tab revved up the engine, loudly gunning it. He tore off his gloves and threw them in my lap without a word. I took his gloves and pulled mine off, stuffing them into my purse. As we headed out, driving north and bound straight for Seattle, I rolled down the window, looked out and tried to catch my breath. The streets were empty and slick from a recent light rain and the air had that wonderful Portland smell—moss and lilacs and fragrant chlorophyll drifting down from the SW hills. Tab reached under his seat and retrieved a plastic bag, pulling something out.

"Here's a wet washrag. Clean up your face, and take *out* those contact lenses!"

"Thank you."

"Uh huh."

I leaned forward and took out the contact lenses, tossing them out the window, where they flew lightly in the air behind us, before landing in the street. I was scrubbing my face with the washcloth, and getting off most of the makeup, when I thought back to the way my mother had always told me I was better than other people. It was never better in a good way, but always in a cold and superior way, as if all other people were beneath us. Now, I knew different. I was definitely no better. I never had been. But why had my mother raised me to believe I was? Was she hoping it would give me an added bit of confidence in dealing with this messed up world? Though I knew Tab would disagree, I was no better than anyone.

I also knew the sexual abuse I'd endured had transformed me fully. I would never be the same girl I *could* have been had I not been exploited. I would always be damaged, no matter what happened or how enlightened I became. I would *always* be damaged goods—sexually driven, suspicious, fearful, and angry—and emotionally cut-off in ways I could never readily explain. And Tab would be damaged too, though his damage would manifest itself differently, he too would be damaged.

We would be damaged together.

The realization hit me hard as Tab continued to drive, and I dropped my head in shame and wept quietly. He looked over at me only once. As he drove he reached over with his right hand and gripped my arm, stroking the flesh of my forearm back and forth but not saying a word. Several minutes passed before he returned his hand to the steering wheel and still he said nothing. I relished the kindness of his silence and wept a little more. Finally, I unbuckled the seatbelt, pushed off my Converse sneakers and curled up, laying my head on his right thigh. He began to stroke my head, the way one pets a cat, his big hand stroking my hair and caressing my forehead. I closed my eyes as another realization hit me, yet again.

"Tab?"

"Yes, baby?"

"I really… I really love you, you know?"

"I know you do, sweetheart."

"Thank you."

"For what?"

"For saving me tonight."

****

On the drive to Seattle, Tab and I were mostly silent. I sat up after an hour and stared out the window. The confusion I felt was still monumental. What was driving me? Had I ever known? Were my motivations really as simplistic as Tab had suggested? Projection? Was it true I'd fallen for the oldest trick in the book—blaming someone else for something they weren't guilty of—because they reminded me of someone I resented? It couldn't be. Or could it? And what was it about Gayle that reminded me of my mother? My mother had been reserved, cold, and thin to the point of almost being anorexic. She had been an eerie lookalike for the 1950s model, the haunted and exquisite Anne St. Marie. So, what was it about Gayle that could possibly have reminded me of my mother? Would I ever know?

We pulled into the Scatter Creek Rest Area, with Seattle still in front of us, and got out and stretched. My skin felt cold and I remembered I'd sweated profusely during our little stint in Gayle's office. My hair felt lank and hung down heavily, and I could taste salt on my upper lip. The perspiration had dried on my skin and I felt chilled and exposed in the overly large, zip-up janitor uniform.

"I think I should get into a change of clothes before too long. I don't want anyone to see me dressed like this."

"That would be a good idea. You need to get a coat on, too. It's getting chilly."

I walked into the restroom in only my socks and the janitor uniform, locked the door behind me and stripped, as Tab stood outside nearby. After I took off the uniform and socks and stuffed them into the garbage can, far below the used paper towels, Pepsi cans and fast food containers, I took off my bra and panties and bunched them up in my purse. I stepped away from the sink and found what I was looking for—an empty Evian water bottle on the floor. I filled it with water and poured it over my head again and again, until I began to tremble from the cold. I swiped at my slick skin back and forth, and poured more water over my head, finally drying off with paper towels.

I stood there, leaning over the garbage can, naked and cold, and saw the janitor uniform hidden under the trash and paper towels and remembered the letter from Mary Jennifer. I reached in and pulled the letter out of the pocket, quickly folded it and shoved it into my purse. Looking back down at the uniform, I hated it. It seemed to be a physical representation of all my colossal dysfunction, and I hated the sight of it. Without thinking, I put my finger down my throat and proceeded to vomit all over the janitor uniform sandwiched between the other refuse. My lunch from earlier that afternoon came up in waves and the pink sludge spilled over the fabric of the uniform, soaking the paper towels and dripping to the bottom of the container, a steaming foul mess. I knew later, the uniform would end up in a landfill someplace. No other person would try to salvage it, to be used later in a crime, the way I had. I turned and stumbled to the sink and rinsed my mouth out. I swallowed handfuls of cold clear water, gasping and sobbing quietly as the stench of the hot vomit drifted up to my right.

After a moment of just standing there, bent over the sink, I glanced at my purse and saw the red shimmer of the bra and panties. I might throw them away later, as unwanted witnesses to my momentary madness, but then I might not. Perhaps I would keep them as a souvenir, to wear for Tab later. I pulled on the oversize pink V neck sweater, and tight red stretch Capri's I had carried in with me, and stepped into my new suede flats. After I peed in the toilet, wincing at the cold metal of the toilet seat on my tender skin, I washed my hands and put on a thick layer of shimmering peach frost lipstick. I combed my wet hair, trying to liven up my lank and depressed looking ringlets, but was unable to. I looked at myself in the reflection, and still I loved the image I saw—of a thin, attractive woman staring back at me. But I was confused by her. I whispered to my mirror image, stern and forceful:

"Don't mess this up, Daisy. He's the best you'll ever do. No man can light a candle to Tab. Go back to being the cool girl, the girl who likes to get off and have fun, the girl who likes to laugh. You're pushing forty. *Don't* fuck this up!"

I walked out of the restroom a new person, my head high and though my legs felt rubbery and weak, as if I'd just run a twenty mile marathon, I felt hopeful in a way I hadn't only five minutes before. I stood outside the door motionless for a moment and looked across to the parking lot. Tab stood against the Ford truck, leaning into it, his head down, looking at the asphalt vacantly, a vision of masculine beauty, and unassuming humility and gentleness. I loved him fiercely in that moment and felt the growing possessiveness and irrational passion that he was mine; all mine and God help *anyone* who ever tried to change that. His yellow hair was on fire under the artificial glow of the streetlight. As he looked up, his eyes softened and he smiled, hopeful and almost shy as he appraised me. I could tell he was looking me over from head to toe as I walked toward him, with my chin high. I flipped my hair over my shoulder and put my hands on my hips.

"Well, hello there, Mister!"

"Daisy? You look like yourself again?!"

"I *am* myself, again!"

"Good."

"I washed my face and got most of the mascara off, too."

I walked up to him and stood directly under him, my head tilted, looking up, leaning into him, and my hands touching his lean belly.

"You really are gorgeous, do you know that, Tab?"

"I have been told that upon occasion. I try to keep that to myself, though," he said mildly.

"When will we be at the new place—in Seattle I mean?"

"Soon. Why?"

"I don't know if I can wait much longer. I *need* you. Can we go park somewhere?"

"Sure baby, you can sit on my lap. It'll be good for both of us, then later… "

"Yes, even more. I love it when it's like that. When we're exhausted but we do it still?"

"Yeah, cause we got to. You and I… we got to."

"Can we go park now? I'm really worked up."

"I know a place, baby, just behind those Douglas Firs over there."

****

After Tab and I spent twenty minutes in the front seat of the Ford truck and after we both came together, and I draped myself over him, my arms hanging limply down his back, my cheek resting on the hard bones of his right shoulder, we cleaned up in silence, passing each other paper towels, with dumb smiles on our faces. We sat in the truck, and leaned against each other, numbly eating cold cheese, rosemary and onion sandwiches Tab had gotten special order from the Greek Deli on Burnside. We washed them down with bottles of cold lemonade, and there was no need for words. There never was, as Tab understood my tears and why they sometimes happened after I came, and I understood his need for silence after he came.

Tab started up the truck and once again we were off, finally knocking off the last miles to Seattle and our new condo. I felt dazed, content and depleted but totally safe as I began to fall asleep, my head lolling against his shoulder, the seat belt straining against my middle. He looked over at me and smiled as we stopped at a long light. The colored aura of the traffic light drifted into the truck and bathed us in a filmy red glow. He leaned over and pulled my face to his, kissing me, his tongue in my mouth. His mouth was sweet like fruit, and his lips slick like the finest raw meat.

I woke up a little after one in the morning and saw the exquisite image of the high rise buildings of downtown Seattle stacked together blackly. At a distance the structures looked as mysterious and unknowable as the first image of the Land of OZ, with Dorothy standing hypnotized, looking over from the Yellow Brick Road.

The Columbia Center stood to full effect, clad in dark layers of Rosa Carnelian granite. With its three geometric facades, the result was a multi-dimensional image as seductive as any mirage in an isolated desert, and I looked at it in awe once again.

"Look Tab, it's the Columbia Center. God, it's so beautiful."

"It always looks like three towers, but it's only the one."

"They sure know how to make high rises in Seattle!"

"That they do!"

I sat up, excited and continued to watch, feeling hopeful. It had been a couple of years since I'd been to Seattle for a story I was investigating, and as we drove farther, I was glad to see the Publix Hotel, run down as it always was in the heart of Seattle's Chinatown, unchanged and still there on fifth Avenue. A new beginning, that's what Seattle represented for us. Finally leaving the cluster fuck of Portland and its incestuous closeness behind, Tab and I could start over. Moving to where no one would know us, we could create a new future unhindered by the tentacles of Portland's social webs and the relentless, mean-spirited competitiveness of its various subcultures.

"God, I can't believe you did this all on your own."

"I have business experience, Daisy. I've owned two houses and one duplex in my many years of life—other than this new Condo, I'll have you know."

"I never knew that about you! Somehow, I'm not surprised, though."

"Why is that?"

"Because… you're *always* full of surprises!"

"Oh, baby, you'll like it! It's light and airy, with a view of Pike Place Market. The kitchen is large, with yellow walls. It's sunny and cheerful—a little utopia. I know you're gonna love it. And it's spacious, too. We'll both have lots of space for our projects *and* all our books!"

"The photos of it were perfect. I guess we'll still have to buy a bed, huh?"

"Nope, I already got us one!"

"You did?"

"You bet."

"Do we still have to put it together?"

"Not at all, that was part of the job. I asked the movers to do that—so we wouldn't have to. If you pay extra, they'll do just about anything."

"Did you really?"

"Sure did, babe. And I told them to use the new bedding I bought."

"You bought new bedding?"

"I got you some pretty mauve sheets and a matching duvet, because I knew you'd like that color, mauve with little sunflowers. Chose it just for that reason."

"You don't mind the bedding being pink? That won't offend your manly sensibilities?"

"I can handle flowers and mauve sheets. I'm man enough, baby."

We pulled into the parking lot of the *13 Coins Diner* on Boren Avenue, and Tab produced his Visa credit card with a dramatic flourish as he unbuckled his seatbelt, turning to me suddenly with a grin. He opened the door, threw his legs out and pulled off his custodian uniform, tossing it in back to reveal tight black jeans and the white v-neck tee shirt he was wearing underneath. He motioned for me to stay put, swept out of the truck, strolled around and opened the passenger door.

"My lady?" he asked, extending his hand in mock formality.

"Yes, you may!" I said, taking it and giggling.

We walked to the diner in silence and I could feel Tab's exhilaration. We had made it. We'd gotten away and would likely not be connected to the damage in Gayle's nightmarishly pink office. Even if Gayle suspected it was me, no one would believe her, and if the police ever investigated, there would be utterly no paper trail connecting us to the Talionic night, nor any physical evidence of any kind. Even the sullen security guard would likely not support the idea that a pale blue-eyed brunette in her thirties ever went up to the fifth floor with intent to commit criminal mischief, or destruction to property. He would look at any possible photographs of me, and shake his head firmly, insisting it could *never* have been that slight, delicate blue-eyed woman. He *would* remember Helen and her boyfriend and the two trashy looking janitors—the woman a loud, cheap looking tart wearing too much makeup with bushy blonde hair, dark eyes and orange lipstick. But he would *never* connect the woman with the orange lipstick and prominent cheekbones to me.

As we walked in we could see the diner had a vintage interior with high backed, swivel chairs, and an open kitchen where you could watch as they prepared your food. They had an eclectic menu one wouldn't expect from an all-night diner, and the room smelled like delicious smoky cooked meats. After we were led to a table in the back, and handed menus, I realized how absolutely ravenous I was. I ordered the beer battered cod with cole slaw, and Tab ordered the prime rib dinner.

"Oh my God, Tab, I'm *so* hungry!"

"Yeah, me too. Can't wait to cut into some meat!"

"And then what happens, after we eat?"

"Then we go home, baby, to our new place."

"I feel really lucky. I feel lucky to be with you."

"You are lucky, and I'm lucky. We're *both* lucky!"

"And Ruby and Verona won't come after us?"

"They better not, but I don't think so. Those two girls are generally always broke anyway. They're not gonna come after us if they have no way to get here, and they generally don't. I wouldn't worry, baby. Besides, I told Ruby's new guy—my old brother-in-law—that I was moving to Missouri... alone."

"Missouri?"

"Yep!"

"That's hysterical Tab!"

"I know, pretty clever, huh?"

When our food came, Tab and I ate in luxurious silence, eating slowly, savoring each bite and treating ourselves to a single glass of wine. Despite the comic confusion in Gayle's office, and my reluctant epiphany, and subsequent meltdown, I felt powerful and capable in a new way. I had done it, what I'd originally wanted to do, and had come away with a deeper understanding of my past. I also knew Tab would remain a rock of stability. His good nature would not be altered by the unusual episode I had long termed *The Talionic Night,* a night which I had dreaded and looked forward to simultaneously for months.

"What will we tell people? About the timing?"

"What I told you before, baby. That we left yesterday, in the early afternoon, and spent the day in the new place, sleeping. There's no way anyone can prove otherwise. The difference would only be a matter of a few short hours."

"But what if they tracked our cell phones?"

"That only happens in cases of murder and it requires a court order. It's just not gonna happen."

"I should *know* that."

"I heard about it on a cop show I saw years ago."

When Tab and I got to the new place, slipping in after parking in his designated parking spot in the basement, we went up in the elevator to the top floor. I could barely believe it was real. We walked down the long hall and he handed me the key to the unit. I looked at him unsure but he nodded to the door, smiling, encouraging me.

"Go ahead Daisy, this is our new home. I want you to be the one to open the door."

"You're too good to me, Tab. You're just too good ..."

"Stop it and open the damn door. Go on!"

I inserted the key in the lock, turned it and felt the door release. We walked into a large condominium, smelling the sharp sweet smell of new paint. With the huge windows directly in front of us, the bathroom was to the left and the kitchen, with enough space for a table. I walked into the living room and saw the balcony and the windows and realized how much space there was. We'd have more than enough room for two sofas, tables, and bookcases. All around us were boxes and smaller items of furniture.

"How many bedrooms again?"

"Three, baby. The master bedroom, for us. A guest bedroom and a room for your office, for your writing. I can do my furniture refinishing on the balcony, its easily big enough."

"God, Tab, its perfect. Its... just fucking perfect!"

"Let's go to the bedroom."

I felt a tickle of apprehension flash through my guts and knew I would love this new room I hadn't seen before. Tab guided me into the hallway, his hand on my back. We walked to the right of the living room, walked past the two bedrooms on the left, to the back bedroom, on the right, the place where we would sleep and fuck, forevermore. There in the bedroom was a new bed. Tab bought it secretly as a surprise. It looked like an art deco metal bed from the 1920s with the rounded headboard and footboard and the gilded accents, but it was much larger, a queen, indicating that it was indeed an expensive reproduction. I walked over to it and grasped the footboard in both hands, shaking it to see how strong it was. It was rock solid and didn't budge an inch. It would survive Tab and me, and our daily onslaughts.

The bed was made perfectly with the mauve sheets. The yellow sunflowers splashed across, and as I stood there looking at it, I began absently kicking off my flats and then quickly stripping. Tab followed suit and before we knew it, we were on the bed, tangled up and naked once again.

****

The next morning the sun drifted in through the long draperies that Tab had closed during the night. It was 11:38 a.m. and I was exhausted. I was sore from sex and my skin felt hot and tender. Tab was watching me, lying on his side, naked, and up on one elbow. I felt content and empty. There was nothing I could want for, other than a shower and breakfast with some good strong coffee.

"Hello baby girl. How you feel?"

"Hmm, I feel wonderful. I slept like a log."

"After you came that third time, you just passed out. I guess I'm doing my job right."

"Oh, stop it!"

"You wanna go for breakfast, I'm thinking Starbucks somewhere."

"Yes! I want Starbucks! But first a shower. Have you showered?"

"An hour ago."

"What have you been doing?"

"Unpacking my books, your books, hanging up clothes, putting together our book cases, unloading the rest of the truck. Your antique bed and night stand are in the living room. They'll be perfect for either the guest room or your office, whichever you choose."

"You did all that while I was asleep?"

"Sure did, baby."

"What did I *ever* do to deserve you?"

"Just you being you. You don't have to be anything other than the hot mess you are."

"I am a hot mess, aren't I? Which reminds me, I need to get into that shower."

"The shower and bathtub are great. You'll see."

"And there's that extra toilet—the one I used last night, huh?"

"Yep, a bath and a half as they say!"

"Tab, I want to make your morning special. To say thank you for everything you've done. Do you want a blow job? It's been a while."

"I love it when you talk like a tramp. The thing is, I'm gonna need a bit of a break. After we get back from breakfast and coffee we can get naked again, how's that?"

"Your wish is my command."

"I like how that sounds!"

After the shower, I dressed in a light pink calico dress, with a rounded low-cut front and gathered sleeves and waist. I slipped on my new suede flats and put on a layer of pink lip gloss. I got out my bottle of perfume, spraying the *Mitsouko* Tab had bought for me all over my neck and shoulders. As we walked out the door, Tab took my hand, swinging it in his like a teenager.

"We're gonna have a great day, Daisy. Just hanging out and bein' domestic!"

"I can't wait to decorate! I've never actually lived in a place that someone owned, before. My ex and I never got to that point."

"Well, I own the place and we can add your name later, once we make it official. No more having to answer to the landlord. We can have pets, cats, dogs, birds. We can do whatever we want."

"Where are we gonna go for coffee and food?"

"Let's go to the original Starbucks, on Pike Place."

"Isn't that the one that opened in 1971?"

"That's the one, baby."

We walked to the Starbucks at 1912 Pike Place and wandered in, looking around. As we walked in the door, I noticed once again that the exterior of the building looked like an old storefront but seemed smaller than I remembered. There was a long line wrapping around the narrow interior near the bar and I stepped forward, presuming I was stepping at the back of the line. As Tab stepped in behind me, an older woman with bleached blond hair snarled at him that he had cut in line. I looked behind me and saw her—an emaciated woman with skin the color of a roast turkey and hair the texture of a Brillo pad. The neon pink lipstick she wore seemed to radiate with an energy all its own and her green frost eye shadow was momentarily blinding.

"Hey! Dumbo! You just cut in line. Didn't you learn any manners when you flunked Kindergarten?!" Tab looked behind him confused and began to apologize.

"Take it easy lady; we didn't see you in line." The woman ignored me, and continued to focus on Tab.

"Hey! You stupid meathead. Who do ya think you are? Some kinda male model the world's just supposed to cater to?" Tab looked over at me, smiling with his eyebrows raised, which I knew meant he was *not* going to argue with an old scrap of a California divorcée with a chip on her shoulder. He was going to leave it to me. I was glad of it and found myself growing more furious by the second as I took a step forward.

"How dare you talk to my husband like that? Who do you think you are— bitch? You're lucky I don't just slap you!"

"Aww fuck yourself, twat! And your moron boyfriend in that brand new *Ferry* jacket can go screw himself, too!"

"Don't you have that backwards? Clearly, you're the twat. And an *old* twat at that."

"Daisy?! It's okay, honey, it's not worth it."

"Do you know this man is a doctor of mythology—that he holds a doctorate?"

"What do I care what he is? I was in line first, and *I'm* from out of town!"

"I don't give a damn where you're from. And so what if he's wearing a uniform jacket. He works for the *Washington State Ferry!* He does that to earn a *living* because he's a working man, something you're obviously not familiar with."

"I know all about work!"

"Oh really?" Well, in case you don't know, WORK is what you do these days, unless you're a hateful old divorcée with a chip on her shoulder the size of the state of Montana!"

"I'm not divorced, I'm married!"

"I don't believe you. No man in his right mind would marry someone like you. And if you didn't want to be cut in line, maybe you shouldn't be standing over by the coffee mugs, acting like you're browsing for Christmas gifts you… miserable old bitch!"

"How dare you talk to me like that! What's your name? I want to know your name!"

"My name? That's easy; it's Mrs. Ruby Blaine, resident of Portland, Oregon! Bitch!"

Tab suddenly doubled over, turning around, trying desperately not to laugh. He spun back around and reached over, grasping my forearm protectively and began to pull me away, his face cutting up into a huge grin as he tried to hold it together. One of the barista's rushed over and intervened, pressing her hand on the back of the woman and nodding towards the door.

"I've told you before Jenny, not to treat our customers like they're your hired help. I'm sorry but you're going to be 86ed again, for the next ten days. Understood?"

The woman, Jenny, seemed to lose all the wind in her sails and began apologizing profusely as the disgusted barista continued to lead her out the door. The Barista walked back and apologized, telling us she would buy both our drinks *and* sandwiches as well, with two complimentary matching cobalt blue decorative Starbuck's mugs thrown in for good measure. Several minutes later, after we got our coffee, and food with the two mugs wrapped nicely with tissue paper, we walked outside and stood in front of the old brick building, sipping our hot coffee and beaming at each other as we peeked into the paper bag. It had been fun to tell off an awful old woman and then be rewarded for it. The wind was gusting outside the Starbucks and once again I was reminded of the beautiful condominium waiting for us only a few short blocks away. There we would be starting over, safe and sound and all to ourselves, no solicitors and no visitors allowed. Tab looked down at me and smiled.

"Daisy, I don't hold a doctorate. You don't hafta tell stories just to build me up."

"I was going to talk to you about that. There's a test, an exam, it takes a few hours. I'm going to arrange it at Washington State University. It's an overall knowledge exam, like a competency based exam for various majors. If you pass it with a high enough score, you can earn a bachelors degree.

"Really? But why? I've never taken a college class in my life."

"You wouldn't need to, Tab. The fact is you know more about mythology than some people I know who majored in mythology and graduated with degrees, some of them advanced degrees. It's worth a try, and frankly, I *know* you can do it. You'll ace it and then you'll have a bona fide college degree. Free of charge."

"If that don't beat all. Really? Without even earning it?"

"But you *have* earned it. You have, with all those books you've studied and read over the years. You *have* earned it. You know the subject inside and out."

"Are you sure? I've probably only read and studied seven or eight hundred books on mythology in my life, so I don't see why they'd think I was..."

"Yes, I'm absolutely sure. And you're the only person I know who knows the difference between August and *Augooste*."

"That's nothin' though. *Everyone* should know that."

"Tab, let's go home now. We need to get back into bed and snuggle."

"Yeah, I'm ready for that special reward you were gonna give me. Remember?"

"I remember."

"Baby! I'm crazy about you, do you know that?"

Tab took the bag from me, smiling down at me with that magnanimous warmth of his, like an appreciative king with a merciful, understanding heart. His yellow hair was on fire in the morning sunlight as he gripped my hand in his and we turned, and walked in the direction of home, saying nothing the entire way. Instead we just looked around us, and listened to the howling wind from the chilly sound, and the muted music of the nearby traffic. We stepped over the broken glass, drifting newspapers and cracked concrete of downtown Seattle, and felt perfectly at ease in The Emerald City—our new home. As we continued walking, we passed one of the countless ancient cobblestone alleys with all their grief, unspoken secrets and circling ghosts, and stopped. We looked into the alley for a long moment as if we were gazing into another century, and into another time.

After a moment, we faced each other, saying nothing. When I looked up at Tab, my face was expressionless, and my eyes were filled with the blank acquiescence that told Tab I would always be his, and I would follow him anywhere. He bent down, and pulled me up, lifting me to the tops of his steel toed work boots. With his hands on my waist, my arms rose and I gripped his shoulders, balancing there. A passing car full of laughing teenagers honked at us as Tab looked down at me. He glanced over for a moment, distracted, by the car, and then back at me. His large topaz eyes were filled with the Bottomless Sadness, the resignation and the relentless desire I knew so well. Our mouths met, teeth clicking briefly and we kissed. With Tab's tongue, bubble gum pink, and deep in my mouth, I knew I was exactly where I wanted to be.

Chapter Twenty: Getting the Show on the Road